BUGSY'S GHOST TERRORIZES VEGAS
and other tabloid tales

Gary Alexander

BUGSY'S GHOST TERRORIZES VEGAS

and other tabloid tales

**The New
Atlantian Library**

NEW ATLANTIAN LIBRARY
is an imprint of
Absolutely Amazing Ebooks

Published by Whiz Bang LLC, 926 Truman Avenue, Key West, Florida 33040, USA.

For information contact:
Publisher@AbsolutelyAmazingEbooks.com

ISBN-13: 978-1949504019 (The New Atlantian Library)
ISBN-10: 1949504018

BY THE SAME WRITER

Pigeon Blood
Unfunny Money
Deadly Drought
Kiet and the Opium War
Kiet and the Golden Peacock
Kiet Goes West
Blood Sacrifice
Dead Dinosaurs
Dragon Lady
Disappeared
Zillionaire
Interlock
Loot
Gold
*A Book of Facts a novel
*Father's Day
*Damn Near Broke
*Bad Elements
*Humpty Dumpty Goes Kersplat
Harry Saves The World

...and numerous short stories

*Published by New Atlantian Library

BUGSY'S GHOST TERRORIZES VEGAS

and other tabloid tales

CONTENTS

ROSWELL WOMAN IS AN ALIEN LOVE CHILD

"You make me sick, you make me wanna toss my cookies," said Bucky Washburn.

"I —," said Sean from Springfield.

"First you say the NBA's soft in the paint, then you say the refs oughta crack down on rough stuff under the bucket. Which is it?" Bucky Washburn demanded.

"Uh —," said Sean from Springfield.

"Hey, bozo, you can't have it both ways. We overpay these guys to bang bodies and when the ball comes off the iron they better pound the boards or I wanna know why I'm shelling out a hundred clams a ticket to watch some seven-foot prima donna who's drawing ten mil per year. If him and his rich pals are pussyfooting like you say they are, which is a crock, and you're meanwhile bitching that the refs ain't blowing their whistles till they're blue in the face, you'll have to pardon me all to hell if I dunno where you're coming from."

"I, uh —"

"We're outta time," Bucky said, disconnecting Sean. "Saved by the bell is what it is. Sean and these other turkeys the last three hours, they must live in the same home for retards. But I got hopes that tomorrow we'll find intelligible life on the planet. This is Big Bad Bucky Washburn for Bucky's Jock Talk on KJK, K-Jock, the world's finest all-sports station, so till then, boys and girls, remember Bucky's motto, a good loser *is* a loser."

Bucky threw off his headset and killed switches with an angry slap. Today's call-ins had been a steady stream of wimps, morons and fairies. He'd gone ballistic when some homo wanted to ban fighting in hockey. That brought them out of the woodwork, the worst being a weenie who'd argued before Bucky shouted him down that boxing should be banned.

Must be something they're putting in the water, Bucky thought as he stood and stretched his 5'6" 280-pound frame. Jimbo was doing scores and sports update. Moose, the midday host, wasn't in yet.

It was just as well, considering Bucky's mood. Moose was a pussy in his own right. He'd reason with every yo-yo who knew how to dial a phone, for Chrissake. Bucky Washburn was paid to talk, not listen.

He barged out of the studio. Station employees read his foul humor and gave him plenty of space. Shaved pate, permanent five o'clock shadow, neckless head tapering into rounded shoulders, bulging eyes, square jaw grimly set, the Buckmeister lumbered through, discharging a contrail of testosterone. This was a galoot not to trifle with.

Bucky grabbed his mail, squeezed into his plaid logger's coat, and went out to the biggest, tallest, widest, most bechromed sport utility vehicle that money could buy. Bucky was the highest-rated and highest-paid sports talk jock in town, and KJK's ratings numbers were consistently in the top five. He was a local celebrity who regularly guested sports bars and golf tournaments. He deserved to drive the best, a *man's* rig, not some faggoty yupmobile made in the Black Forest.

Bucky drove home to a district near downtown that was undergoing spasms of gentrification. Transients and financial planners coexisted. Union halls and boutiques too. Futon stores beside taverns where anything could happen.

Sociologic schizophobia, Bucky reflected, driving by an auto body shop. Up the block, a restaurant with a cutesy name in neon and candles on the tables was opening up for the expense account lunch crowd.

Diversication is what he thought they called it. Everything from zillionaires to folks down on their luck to kids with weird hair and earrings all over their zit faces, boys you couldn't tell from girls and vice versa and proud of it. Live and let live, Bucky thought, although he'd take a wino over a queer any day of the week.

Bucky lived at the top of a high-rise condo. He'd paid a bundle for the joint, which looked out at the city skyline and if he lowered his eyes, at the old brick buildings across the street converted into low-income housing. That was okay with Bucky too. Mostly geezers in there and they didn't bother nobody.

He parked in the basement garage and rode up to the twentieth floor. A forty-year-old in a transient profession, the talk jock traveled light and furnished sparely. His decorating themes were genuine leather and imitation leopard skin.

An HDTV, the screen of which had never been illuminated by other than a sporting event, highlighted the living room. Hanging above it was a painting on black velvet of a fullback barreling for a first down in a crucial third-and-short situation, his lowered helmet a functioning clock.

Bucky stripped out of jeans, sneakers and sweatshirt. He showered in water as hot as he could stand, singing discordant bars of college fight songs. He emerged pink and steamy, toweled down, wiped off the mirror, took an outfit from the closet, and held it in front of him.

No.

He tried another.

Then another.

Then another.

He settled on a burgundy velour number that snugged gently at the waist and swept into a full skirt that ended at the ankles. One shoulder was bared and coarse tufts of hair poked over the top of the dress. Provocative, he decided, without being slutty.

He pirouetted and the pleats flared, exposing stumpy, hirsute calves. He was in a size-26, the maximum available in the catalogs, and it clung in the midsection. Bucky Washburn looked like he had swallowed a bowling ball.

"Pretty," he trilled at the image in the mirror. "Oh so pretty."

This was Bucky's quality time, when he kicked back and read his fan mail. He poured light beer into a brandy snifter, swooshed into a recliner and propped his feet on an ottoman.

There were three letters, his daily average. His was an electronic audience, listeners energized by what they'd seen on the tube. The writers were too bashful to phone in. Bless their pointy heads, the majority couldn't write worth a damn, couldn't spell or punctuate or nothing.

The first wondered if O.J. would ever play again. He'd seen the Juice on CNN and thought he looked in shape. Jesus H. Fucking Christ. Bucky lobbed the wadded letter at a wastebasket.

The second was a thick sheaf of computer paper. The writer took Bucky to task for once saying that southpaws didn't hit to the opposite field as well as right-handers. He was proving the contrary with statistics dating to 1959. Get a life, Bucky thought, slinging the printout.

The last had no return address. Not unusual. Probably some pipsqueak without the stones to identify himself before unloading on Big Bad Bucky. He tore open the envelope, prepared to skim a few lines before flinging it against a wall.

The text was brief, a photocopy of words and letters clipped out of supermarket tabloids and pasted on plain paper: WE KNOW WHAT YOU ARE, YOU CROSS-DRESSING PERVERT. WE KNOW WHAT YOU DO. HAVE $2000 IN SMALL UNMARKED BILLS READY. YOU WILL BE CONTACTED.

The letter fell from Bucky's trembling fingers. How could this happen? He'd been so careful.

His eyes flooded and tears ran down puffy cheeks. His career was finished. His career and his life, which were one and the same.

~ ~ ~

Mrs. Orville (Alma) Spangler squinted through bifocals at the luxury condominiums on the other side of the street. Her view was partially obscured by snowfall and the planter box outside her daylight-basement window, even though winter and urine had shriveled the vegetation. Dirty slush was accumulating in the street, the wet snow they'd predicted. It seemed to her that forecasts were correct only when they promised foul weather.

Her sight line was adequate, however. The lights had gone out in the condominium unit long ago. The occupant had not departed by lobby or garage.

Mrs. Spangler checked her watch, a Timex given her by Orville on their 20th anniversary. She'd wait 15 more minutes, when her surveillance subject would be exactly two hours late.

Mrs. Spangler was neither young, nor aging gracefully. She had been petite in her youth, her features a bit too bunched to be considered pretty. Now she was bordering on shrunken.

She had been abandoned as an infant, left in a basket on the porch of a childless New Mexico farm couple, who raised her as their niece. In adolescence, Alma realized there was something different about her, as did her classmates. Something different, but nothing anybody could put her finger on. A little strange, a little aloof, a funny look in her eyes at times.

She came to realize that her arrival in the summer of 1947 at a farmhouse 3 miles from Roswell was no coincidence. She realized this despite her adoptive parents laughing and saying she was being silly. A child with a disturbingly vivid imagination.

A coincidence? Bosh. Did they think they had raised a fool! How could anybody who'd ever gone through a supermarket checkout line and knew how to read not know the truth?

Mrs. Spangler's adoptive parents, long deceased, and her late husband comprised her family. Children were a genetic impossibility. Orville hadn't known her true origin. She'd convinced him her barrenness was a "female problem." So tragic. She knew she was the sole survivor of that awful crash the government tried to cover up, *she just knew*.

She received a steady stream of junk mail from funeral homes and cremation companies. She wished she could afford cremation so she wouldn't be cut apart for an autopsy or embalmed, so her secret could die with her.

The old steam radiators clanged, as if a lunatic was smashing the boiler with a sledgehammer. Only in the summer was the heating system adequate. To settle her stomach, she brewed a cup of tea. Shivering inside a knit shawl, she sipped. It tasted weak and bitter.

She checked the time. Very close to two hours late. She sighed, steeling her courage. She bundled up in scarf, galoshes and overcoat, and trudged out into the cold slop. The condominium lobby was marble flooring, potted palms and prints of English hunts on the walls. La-di-da. Naturally the entrance was locked, to keep out the riffraff.

Mrs. Orville (Alma) Spangler took a deep breath and buzzed 2003.

No answer.

She buzzed again.

"Yeah, yeah, yeah, hold your fucking horses. Who is it?"

Mrs. Spangler flinched. Words would not escape her lips. Mr. Washburn used the same tone in the intercom as he did to the beer-soaked louts who called his program to rehash sporting events they had already seen. Sports mania had claimed her Orville in the prime of his life, yet another reason why she loathed the man in 2003.

In the kitchen cooking, Mrs. Spangler had discovered Orville when he failed to respond to her call to dinner. He was bolt upright in his recliner, can of beer impaled between porky thighs, bag of chips spilled on the end table, tub of clam-garlic dip overturned on the carpet. Orville's face was the color of cranberry sauce and a football game still blared on the TV. The medics who came for him said that he'd possibly become overexcited, the game a contributing factor in his seizure. The lead had changed a dozen times and had gone into overtime.

No, perhaps she wasn't attractive, but you couldn't've told that to her Orville, who also accepted her as perfectly normal. They'd met when he was stationed at White Sands. No Clint Eastwood himself, Orville Spangler was for the most part a good man.

Mrs. Spangler's eyes moistened. She had never felt so alone.

"Mr. Washburn," she said at a whisper.

"Huh? Spit it out. I ain't got all day."

"Mr. Washburn, it's Mrs. Spangler. I– I'm sorry to bother you, but you didn't come by and pick up the jumper."

"The who? Oh yeah, yeah, right, okay. I been tied up. I'll be right there."

"Right there" was 20 minutes. Mrs. Spangler huddled in the doorway, bony blue-veined arms wrapped tightly around herself. He could have pushed a buzzer, allowing her to enter and wait in the nice, warm lobby. But he hadn't. An awful, awful man.

Mr. Washburn finally shambled out of an elevator in a soiled jogging suit. He opened the door, filling the space, showing no inclination to invite her inside. His eyes were bloodshot and he was chewing a mint, a pathetic attempt to conceal the fact he was drinking.

She handed him the jumper she had carefully wrapped with paper and string. "I apologize again, Mr. Washburn. You always deliver and pickup at my apartment. You were late and I was worried."

"Yeah? How much?"

"What we agreed on. Not a penny more, despite having to let it out at the pockets too."

"Yeah, yeah, fine," he said, thrusting a wad of small bills at her. "I'm sure you did good."

"It would be helpful, I think, sometime, at her convenience, if I could meet Mrs. Washburn for a fitting. Alternations are so left to chance when I work only from measurements."

"Yeah, well, Bibi don't get out much. She's a big girl as you are aware and no spring chicken. She's under the weather too."

"Oh, I'm sorry. Nothing serious, I hope."

"She'll be okay if she stays off her feet, so she won't be buying clothes as far as alternations are concerned anything soon. I'll let you know when."

Mrs. Spangler began to say that was a shame when Mr. Washburn let the door latch in her face and plodded to the elevators, the crack of his behind disgustingly exposed above the waistband.

She crossed the street with a spring in her step. His behavior had confirmed her suspicions, him and the mysterious Mrs. Bibi Washburn. Balderdash! Mrs. Spangler had done alterations for obese women before. None were cursed with Bibi's dimensions. They retained feminine bust lines and hips, not the blobby roundness she had incorporated into the Washburn garments.

She went into her apartment with a smile on her face. She was picturing Bucky Washburn in that polyester-blend navy jumper. She pictured a hippopotamus at parochial school.

Giggling now, she made a cup of tea. It tasted as sweet as honey.

She sipped, thinking, rationalizing. She wouldn't have dreamt of doing such a thing if she weren't so poor and if Mr. Washburn weren't such a beast. Her Orville, not much of a planner, had left her with no life insurance, no savings, no pension.

If she had to take in sewing until she contracted arthritis or went blind, she might as well sew on the best machine. Two thousand dollars would buy her a spiffy new Singer or Pfaff with all the trimmings, and enough left to pay some overdue bills.

~ ~ ~

As a child, Buckminster Washburn had been too chubby and uncoordinated to play the sports he loved. In adulthood, he participated in the quasi-athletic

9

activity of golf, but had by no means mastered the game.

He had been a profound disappointment to his father, who taught PE and coached football at the high school Bucky attended until Coach Washburn was discovered under the bleachers on a tumbling mat with Miss Le Page, the French teacher.

Before and after the senior Washburn's dismissal by both the school board and Mrs. Washburn, Bucky devoted long afternoons at home to his mother while his envied classmates were in the gym and on the practice field, running and shooting and blocking and tackling.

Him and his mom were as close as he and his rugged, muscular father were distant. They talked and they watched soap operas together. Sometimes, he would serve as a sewing dummy. She was a difficult size, a physical double to her adolescent son. Nothing off the rack fit quite right.

Minutes passed like seconds as Bucky stood draped in wool or formless flowered print, him like a statue while Mom chalked and pinned hems. It was simultaneously mortifying and thrilling.

Memories of sewing-dummy afternoons with his late mom throbbed inside his aching skull as he fielded Ed in Edmunds, who said of yesterday's fill-in, "Moose is okay, Bucky, but he doesn't have your grasp of the issues and game situations."

"Hey, the Mooster is aces, but I gotta agree with you as far as smashmouth sports. Moose, he's more into baseball, you know, fresh-cut grass and tradition and whatnot. For me, the best thing about the national pastime is cold suds and a dozen hot dogs."

"Well, all of us here at Edmunds Auto Parts hope you're feeling more chipper."

Bucky shunted from his mind the past twenty-four hours spent mostly in the fetal position when he wasn't in the bathroom puking his guts out. "Let's hope she's feeling chipperer too and not too sore if you catch my drift. The party, it kinda spilled over into the next day."

Ed in Edmunds chuckled knowingly.

Bucky gritted his teeth and said, "We have the momentum."

"What's that mean, Bucky?"

"Whadduya mean, what's that mean?"

"Hey, don't get angry, Bucky."

"Don't talk to me about no angry, bozo. The station manager, *ex*-station manager, he told me I had to go take an anger management course. I told him, hey, I already know how to get pissed off. I don't need to go to some class.

"Next caller. And please, somebody, okay, who can ring up an IQ in triple digits."

~ ~ ~

Mrs. Orville (Alma) Spangler smiled. She put down her needle and thread, and turned off the radio. She had been sewing a separated lining into a customer's coat.

The repair could wait. It was time to make merry. She brewed a cup of tea and seasoned it with a teensy taste of apricot brandy.

Prudently, she had not retained an incriminating copy of the note she had made from newspaper clippings, but she knew it by heart:

TONIGHT. 6 P.M. SOUTHTOWN MEGA MALL. PARK IN EAST LOT. LEAVE MONEY UNDER DRIVER SEAT. SMALL UNMARKED BILLS IN PLAIN PAPER BAG. EAT DINNER AT FOOD COURT. TAKE YOUR TIME. CONFIRM ON YOUR SHOW BY SAYING "WE HAVE THE MOMENTUM." YOU ARE BEING MONITORED!!!!

And he had confirmed, after a day off work recovering from what she assumed to be a crippling hangover. She drank her spiked tea, amazed at her own audacity.

She had her late husband to thank for the confirmation inspiration. *We have the momentum.* Orville was an encyclopedia of sportscaster lingo. He'd probably approve of her foray into the blackmailing profession too. Orville definitely wouldn't approve of Mr. Washburn treating his Alma the way he did. No sirree. Orville often said that you gotta do what you gotta do.

Mrs. Spangler resumed repairing the coat. When she was finished, she'd take a short nap. It would be a long bus ride to that mall.

~ ~ ~

Bucky parked outside the Southtown Mega Mall food court entrance, taking two slots so some doofus didn't ding his doors. Anybody has a problem with that, tough shit.

He had time to kill, so he just sat there, thinking what a disaster. It was falling into place, though, who was behind it. *We have the momentum.* This was the syntax of the sports media pro. The extortioner had to be someone or something jealous of his success trying to run him out of the business, like a rival radio station or Fox Sports or ESPN. Had to be.

But how come only two grand? It was chicken feed.

Bucky thought of Mrs. Bibi Washburn. If she existed except on catalog order forms, she'd be one classy broad. But Bucky and the babes, it hadn't worked out. He was always afraid he'd blush and say something stupid, and sure enough he always did.

Not that he was fruity. He'd bust your chops if you ever said that to his face. Just cuz he liked to dress up elegant in the privacy of his own home, why was that skin off anybody's nose?

How'd they found him out? How, how, how?

Bucky scouted the scene. Only thing suspicious was the kids loitering outside the doors, cocky little pricks in baggy pants and ball club jackets and baseball caps on backwards. They were loud, smoking, blocking foot traffic, making general nuisances of themselves.

They saw Bucky glowering at them and responded in kind. He got out and swaggered past, eyes forward. He hated leaving his rig unlocked under any circumstances. The thought of two grand under the seat weakened his knees. Irregardless, he had no choice.

The smell of frying meat and potatoes bubbling in grease perked his spirits. He remembered he hadn't eaten since lunch. He went for his gutbomb standard — two double bacon cheeseburgers and jumbo fires. If his tummy still growled afterwards, he'd spring for one of them monster cinnamon rolls. He tore into his food. If things weren't gonna be hunky-dory, on a full belly they'd at least be semi-okay.

~ ~ ~

Mrs. Orville (Alma) Spangler wished she had a Swiss bank account like they did in the movies. She could have instructed Mr. Washburn to wire the $2,000 and that would be the end of it.

She hurried into the Southtown Mega Mall after her hellish 90-minute journey. A jouncing ride, rich with diesel fumes. A frigid wait at a stop. A transfer to another coach occupied by the deranged and the unwashed.

Mrs. Spangler had visited this mall shortly after the grand opening. She was appalled now as then by its monstrous size and tackiness. The icky fast food, the electronic gizmos, the jewelry that would turn your skin green before you fastened the clasps. Worst of all were the clothing stores. Lordy, where did this junk come from? Oriental sweat shops, probably.

If folks would just buy quality and maintain it. She grudgingly admired Mr. Washburn's taste. He bought nothing but the best for his fictitious bride.

At 6:05, Mrs. Spangler began skirting the outside of the complex. She presumed that if radio work had taught Mr. Washburn anything, it was punctuality. His motorized behemoth was easy to spot, a chromium bull among calves.

She edged toward it, a scarf and parka hood covering much of her face. She was afraid and she hoped he was too. She was also excited, quite an unfamiliar sensation.

When she reached the end of the aisle, the vehicle suddenly lurched out of its space, burning rubber and fishtailing, lights out. She skittered helplessly between parked cars to avoid being struck as it accelerated by.

After she caught her breath and boarded the next bus for home, shock shifted to terror. Mr. Washburn had no intention of honoring her modest demand. The stinker, he had tried to kill her.

~ ~ ~

"You say you know who took your vehicle, Mr. Washburn, and now you don't?"

"It was stole, is all I know."

"Mr. Washburn, you told the 911 operator, and I quote from the recording 'Them little punks out front with their caps on backasswards is who done it. They're in on it'."

"I didn't actually see nobody. I went outside and my rig was gone and so were they. I dunno, maybe somebody didn't like me taking up an extra space."

"What were you doing at the mall?"

"I went to window-shop and eat dinner. I love their burgers. So how come I'm getting the third degree? I ain't the fucking criminal. I'm the victim."

"You were adamant to the investigating officers it was those kids. Your vehicle meant a lot to you and you were insistent how we direct our investigation. Yet when we recovered your vehicle and notified you that it was stripped and partially submerged in a river, you seemed unconcerned."

"Hey, shit happens. That's why you got insurance."

"What were they 'in on', Mr. Washburn?"

Bucky shrugged. "Don't have the foggiest what you're talking about. My words that come across in the 911 call, they must of been miscomboobalated by the phone lines."

The detective gave up and left. Bucky slumped in his recliner and stared at nothing. He should have been dying to try on the jumper the nutty old bat across the street had alterated for him. Maybe some walls had ears. Maybe his had eyes too, maybe some kind of a high-tech radar laser vision kind of thing.

Never again could he slip into something frilly without wondering.

If he hadn't thought it over and clammed up about those juvenile delinquents, he'd be a dead man. Them hanging out at that mall, it wasn't any accident. ESPN or some high-wattage radio station, they wouldn't besmirch their own hands, they'd sub it out to lowlifes. They'd rattled him too, he didn't mind admitting just to himself. Otherwise, he wouldn't of been preoccupied and forgot to remove the keys out of the ignition.

And nobody squeezed you for a lousy two grand and walked away. This was only the beginning. The creeps, they'd bleed him dry.

~ ~ ~

Mrs. Orville (Alma) Spangler had a dream.

15

She dreamt of calibrated buttonholing, of automatic needle threading, of built-in rolled hems, of multi-color embroidery features, of dual feed, of a limited lifetime warranty.

She awakened with a start, looked at the ringing alarm clock, said "Oh my gosh," and scurried out of bed. She had tossed and turned all night long, and hadn't drifted off until after midnight.

It had been a great relief to see the newspaper piece on Mr. Washburn's SUV, the photo of it nosed into a river. Her presumed murderers turned out to be common car thieves. Mrs. Spangler had been caught in the middle of a coincidence.

The close call caused her to ponder her mortality. Outwardly, yes, she supposed she appeared a bit unusual, although well within human range. She knew her body and assumed there were significant internal irregularities. For that reason she had never visited a doctor. She had no desire to be a freak attraction.

Mrs. Spangler went out into a light drizzle, wearing the same parka, but a different scarf. The weather had warmed and the snow remained only in filthy patches. She walked the four blocks to the Mission Charities Thrift Store.

There was a great need for it in the neighborhood. Transients, bizarre street people, day laborers, and those like her on a meager income could not afford to buy new garments, even at the cheap discount chains.

So this was why she felt her plan and her next note was so sweetly ironic:

DONATE A DRESS WITH AMPLE BODICE. FILL LINING WITH $4000 IN UNMARKED BILLS. DURING NIGHT AT MISSION CHARITIES. LAST CHANCE. BETRAY US AGAIN AND SUFFER THE CONSEQUENCES!!!!!!

Sister Aggie, director of the thrift shop, didn't approve of people dumping things after hours. Often it was just trash. Nor did she like people prowling through the items, making even a bigger mess. She understood that there was desperation in the area, though, and didn't make an issue of it.

Mrs. Spangler wouldn't be noticed perusing the things. She'd wait for others, then be lost in the throng. She was intimately familiar with Mr. Washburn's secret wardrobe. She'd pick it out easily.

She turned the last corner, preoccupied, narrowing it down to the sequined red cocktail dress and the strapless taffeta evening gown. Neither should be worn by anyone that size, male or female. She couldn't have been too specific on the garment or he may have guessed the truth. The sight of a KJK All Sports Talk Radio van froze her in her tracks.

~ ~ ~

As befitting one about to hold court, Bucky picked the venue. The owner of the Weasel's Breath Brewpub meekly protested Bucky's choice of a window booth. He had hoped to seat such a personage in the center of his establishment, fronting the antique back bar. It came from a turn of the century hotel and had cost him an arm and a leg.

He didn't push Bucky or his luck, blessed that the KJK superstar was filling in for the scheduled radio celebs. Not that there was anything wrong with Moose and Dutch, but they weren't the legendary Big Bad Bucky Washburn.

Patrons bellied up for a porter or amber ale crafted in shiny copper vats visible at the rear of the pub. Wide screens on all walls blared with pre-game commentaries. As customers got their game faces on for the upcoming NFL doubleheader, Bucky riveted his eyes on the junk store across the street, two doors down.

Must be fate, he thought. Them doubling up the ante on him, then being dumb enough to set the drop-off on the same block as a KJK celebrity appearance. They didn't count on him pulling the rug out from under Dutch and Moose.

A guy wearing team colors from head to toe came up to him with a bar coaster to autograph.

Bucky sneered. "Get lost, dildo. I ain't on till ten. Can't you see that I'm mediating?"

The guy shrank off to his buddies, with a Big Bad Bucky story he'd be relating for months.

Bucky continued his vigil. Nobody out there but tramps and geezers shuffling along the sidewalks, and yuppies setting their car alarms before coming in for a Weasel's Breath microbrewski and an opportunity to be star struck.

He didn't have a clue what he'd do when he saw his red sequenced number snatched. He'd jammed the bills up where you'd stick falsies if you was so inclined.

At least he'd know who he was dealing with.

Bucky sighed.

It was his favorite outfit.

~ ~ ~

The tavern's reader board announced Mr. Washburn's imminent guest appearance. The stunned Mrs. Spangler had passed the point of no return. She presumed he was already there. She snugged up inside her raingear and minced ahead.

She thought of the last road trip vacation she and Orville had taken. Had it been 8 years ago or 9? Roswell was a stop, a *must* stop of Orville's. He hadn't been in the area since his White Sands days and their courtship. But Mrs. Spangler worried that he suspected.

Her worries proved groundless. Orville had merely developed a UFO fascination from television programs. He enjoyed the sights, the tours, the UFO museum. So did she, though absolutely nothing was familiar. Nothing except a feeling, a sensation.

She tugged at her hood so her face would lie deep in the cloth tunnel.

~ ~ ~

Bucky watched the losers rummage through the hand-me-downs. There must of been a half dozen bums and freakoids checking out the duds and some old folding chairs. A tall skinny dork with big earrings and a cape was even climbing on a beat-up bike. He looked like he was on something and about ready to fall on his keester. This neighborhood, he thought. The land of the fruits and the nuts.

Bucky couldn't picture ESPN or their ex-jock muscle mingling in this mob. But you never knew. Whoever put the arm on his finery, that'd be his man. He didn't know what he was gonna do then, but he sure as hell was gonna do something.

~ ~ ~

The discards were drawing the usual morning crowd. Mrs. Spangler knew the regulars. There were some others too, younger people whose styles were, well, eccentric. Should she try it now? Blend in and stick the dress inside her parka? Mr. Washburn couldn't recognize her if she stayed in the group, her back turned.

Then a peculiar gentleman on a bicycle lifted from a plastic garbage bag Mr. Washburn's tent-sized red cocktail dress. He was holding it, dangling, gaping at it as if it were something that had snagged his fishing line.

Mrs. Spangler quickened her pace.

~ ~ ~

The technician in the van told Bucky that they were up and running, and that they had 3 minutes until airtime. Bucky said yeah, yeah, yeah, hardly able to believe his eyes. The twink who could barely stay on the junk bike, he was holding what Bucky had shelled out $289.95 plus shipping for, ownership written all over his freaky puss. Not to mention the four grand inside. That was his boy!

Bucky erupted out of the booth off-balance. He knocked aside the technician and caromed into a waitress carrying a tray holding glasses and a pitcher of Weasel's Breath Oktoberfest Lager.

~ ~ ~

"No, dear," Mrs. Spangler told the strange young man straddling the bicycle. "This is much too large. You take a size twelve or fourteen long."

"It's for my mom. What the hell you think I am, lady?"

"Oh," was all Mrs. Spangler could manage to utter, although she had a firm grip on the dress's waistline she had so carefully let out.

"Leggo, Granny."

But Mrs. Spangler would not let go. She tugged harder as she glanced and saw Mr. Washburn thunder out of the saloon. He was drenched with beer and wore a most demented expression on his crimson face.

~ ~ ~

Some old hag with her back to Bucky was fighting over the dress with the freak. She ducked behind the bike, still yanking, almost pulling him off of it. He yanked too, harder, and — ah shit — ripped the tape Bucky had stuck on the underside. Twenties and fifties fluttered in the air. Everybody was grabbing. It was a fucking shark feeding frenzy.

Knees pumping like a blitzing linebacker, howling like a banshee, Bucky plunged into the fray. And almost ran smack-dab into a Harley Davidson. As it skidded to a stop, Bucky lost his clumsy stride and fell on his butt.

A towering gray-haired gal in black dismounted the motorcycle and extended a hand. Bucky had attended a Catholic elementary school. Though he was unhurt, his knuckles stung from the memories of all those ruler blows. The talk jock accepted the helping hand and was effortlessly jerked to his feet.

"Weren't you taught to look both ways before crossing the street, young man?" Sister Aggie admonished.

Big Bad Bucky Washburn lowered his gaze and softly replied, "Yes, ma'am."

"My stars!" Sister Aggie exclaimed, eyeing the green folding manna.

Her resonant voice put an immediate halt to the greedy, grasping chaos. The scavengers stared anxiously at her, clutching currency. The cocktail dress by then was in shreds.

"Does that – thing belong to any of you?" Sister Aggie asked.

Nobody answered. Bucky Washburn backpedaled to the Weasel's Breath Brew Pub.

"Well, does it?"

"No, Sister," somebody murmured.

"The money was in the lining," someone else said.

"Apparently a silver lining, a remarkably generous donation to the Mission Charities Thrift Store," Sister Aggie said, looking upward. "Thank you."

So that was that, Mrs. Spangler thought as she peeked around a Dumpster. The folks forked over what they'd grabbed, picked the rest off the ground, and gave it to Sister Aggie.

Perhaps Mrs. Orville (Alma) Spangler wasn't destined to have that Singer or Pfaff. Perhaps she had been preordained to perform good works late in her life. Perhaps she had been sent from a distant galaxy for this very purpose. The tabloids did speculate that the aliens could have good deeds in mind, and didn't necessarily come to Earth to enslave us or drive us into feedlots.

Perhaps at her guidance Mr. Washburn was meant to pay for his sins through donations to worthy causes, the instrument of her goodness.

Demand $8000 next time?

She'd give it serious thought.

KILLER THEME PARKS
FROM HELL

Monday mornings are mean, ugly and vicious. Factor in David Oakes' weekly staff meeting and I'm beat to my bloody knees before my 7 cups of coffee have had a chance to kick in.

Insurance company claims managers like Oakes are whipping boys. They take lashes from all quadrants. They need a release from that stress and abuse, a convenient release like the rest of the crew, myself included.

I stumble in late. I'm short and thin as a red herring, so I slip in behind Lander, who's 6' 4" and goes 250, 260.

No luck. David pauses in mid-tirade, glares at me, then continues, "I'm tired of excuses. I didn't write the policy on Nursery Rhyme Park. That's out of our control. What's in our control is handling of the losses.

"Sure, we know Unity Property and Casualty's motto. Everyone Is Insurable. We've heard the jokes a zillion times. How Unity wrote group life on the Seventh Cavalry. How we wrote hull coverage on the *Titanic*. Ha ha. We're having the worst quarter in history and who gets blamed? Who?"

"Who?" he demands again, wild-eyed.

"You," we obsequiously chorus.

"Good guess. Home Office decided that Unity's going to be the leader in insuring biomech theme parks. Well, boys and girls, the powers-that-be got their wish."

Consulting notes, he continues, "In Omaha, we had short-circuiting clowns. If you weren't afraid of clowns before, you sure as hell are now. In Tampa, software-glitched alligators on the loose during a matinee. Buffet time. That's small change compared to our local Nursery Rhyme Park exposure. I'm not talking random mechanical failure. I'm talking wholesale fraud!"

"Cooper versus Hightower," somebody in the front row whimpers.

Cooper v. Hightower stars in our worst nightmares. Hightower, Inc. is a biomech manufacturer and installer that caters to thrill-seekers with deep pockets. Cooper, a Hightower customer, came out of biomech surgery as promised, looking like a cross between Batman and a parasail.

Mr. Cooper rarely passed a tall building or cliff he didn't leap from. But something went haywire on the Golden Gate Bridge. A wing delaminated or tore. He corkscrewed down like Icarus. From that height the surface of the water is concrete. Cooper went splat instead of splash.

Cooper is a quadriplegic and the U.S. Supreme Court ruled that Hightower, Inc. was liable. Never mind the recklessness of consumers who have made biomech the hottest fad going.

"What do you expect *me* to do about nine imbeciles in black robes?" David screams, his face the color of a pomegranate. "Unity hired you people to adjust claims. I can bring winos in off the street to smile and write checks. Let's hit the bricks and do our jobs. Hudson, stick around."

As the gang scuttles out, I know that David has a dirty detail for me. My job's been dangling in the breeze for months, and I haven't helped my employment security a bit by failing to prove that Humpty Dumpty took a dive off that wall.

Dave hands me a file that has the heft of a tire iron. "Charles Evans Clounce is their attorney. I've been negotiating, but I can't be civil to the shyster bastard a minute longer."

I page through it. Two Nursery Rhyme Park performers sustained injuries in a fall (what else is new?). A young female had only minor abrasions. The other, a boy, suffered a mild concussion, but has had blurred vision and recurrent headaches ever since. Like Humpty Dumpty, they're suing the Park for damages, claiming negligence due to unsafe working conditions.

"Here we go again," I say. "Are any Rhymer claimants *not* represented by Charlie Clounce?"

"Some coincidence, huh?"

"Jack's and Jill's biomech profiles?"

"Soft mech. Hydrosilica padding injections under the skin. They're on puberty retardant meds too. You ought to be able to fall down without breaking your crown and come tumbling after, *no problema.*

"Home Office wants this one bought off, Hudson. They don't want Charlie Clounce rolling those kids into court in wheelchairs. Go over and settle it. By the way, the grapevine has it that there's an ownership change cooking at the Park."

"I'm unclear on the present owner."

"Join the club," Oakes says. "Nursery Rhyme Park, LLC. is buried in a conglomerate that owns Cayman Islands banks and Panamanian-registry cargo ships. Park officers aren't listed."

"Not your basic mom and pop operation."

"Speaking of coincidences, our flood of Rhymer losses started in earnest when the for-sale rumors began. Probe Clounce on it, Hudson. You're my senior adjuster. I'm counting on you."

I leave, wearing David's *counting on you* like a 500-pound albatross. I take the elevator down with Lander, who looks like a gigantic, pinstriped, melancholy pear.

"I overheard. Have fun with Clounce."

"Thanks. You're working a Rhymer file too?"

"Who isn't?" he says morosely. "The Three Blind Mice."

"Where do we stand?"

"I'm fighting tooth and nail on contributory negligence. But thanks to *Cooper*, contrib ain't gonna cut it. They shouldn't've been able to leave the Park unsupervised. They had opaque lens implants and those god-awful ears sewn on that match their black bodysuits. If you ask me, that's taking biomech to an extreme."

"Realism is the appeal," I say. "You can't just dress them up in plastic like the Disney parks do."

"Two streets from the Park entrance, the mice walk against a red light," Lander says. "Boom. Punted by an SUV into an espresso cart."

"A masochism defense?" I suggest. "Three shows a day, all running after the farmer's wife, her cutting their tails off with a carving knife. You gotta be a little sick in the head, you know."

"Too tough to prove. And they're claiming whiplash and other soft-tissue injuries that won't show on X-rays. They're contending that management didn't adequately warn them about the hazards of blindness."

On the sidewalk, we exchange a cynical "have a nice day." I walk the 11 blocks to Clounce's. If my company car will run that far, it won't stop. The brakes are metal-on-metal and Oakes won't approve repairs until our loss ratio perks up.

I knew Charles Evans Clounce when he worked out of a duplex by the railroad yards. His circumstances have greatly improved since he landed the Nursery Rhyme Park account. I ride to the top of a building so tall the upper floors have their own weather.

After Clounce keeps me waiting a fashionable 20 minutes, I swoosh into calfskin and spend another 10 listening to impassioned guano about Jack's and Jill's chronic pain, weakened extremities, permanent disability, et cetera. Charlie's good, I'll give him that. He looks the gasbag trial lawyer too, with rumpled suit, mottled face, and wild shocks of white hair.

"They're biomech'd Rhymers," I remind him. "Employees who accept certain risks inherent in the job."

"Under Unity's blanket liability policy, employees are entitled to recover for any and all negligent acts and omissions by the named insured. Period."

"Charlie, don't tell me how to read an insurance policy."

Clounce whistles through yellowed teeth. "Touchy, touchy."

We're getting nowhere. I switch tactics from reason to emotion, and whip out checkbook and pen.

He stares at the checkbook, moistening his lips.

"Run some numbers by me," I say.

"We can settle Jill today," he says hoarsely. "As for Jack, he's on hold pending an updated report from the neurologist and releases from their chiropractor, dermatologist, shrink and mechanophysio therapy clinic."

"C'mon, Charlie. He took a bump on the noggin."

"Fell down and broke his crown. That's the technical term," Clounce cries. "Cranial contusion and brain stem trauma."

"They're trained and well-paid to tumble down that hill for the paying suckers."

"They're not paid to be ruined for life."

"We have a witness who states he thought Jack was attempting an unscripted double gainer and didn't quite make it," I lie.

"States he thought? States he thought! I'd love to cross-examine your Mr. States He Thought, Hudson. Jack slipped because the hill hadn't been properly raked between shows. His feet went out from under him on loose gravel. He slid into Jill and she lost her balance."

"How much?"

"I think the world of those youngsters. If I can expedite them getting on with their lives, I'll bounce some bargain numbers off the wall."

His numbers strike with a leaden thud. High six-digits for Jill, $10 million for Jack, with an open-ended release, a Pandora's box if there ever was one. Home Office is eager to unload the case, but if I give away the store, Oakes will disembowel me with his letter opener. I counterpunch, lopping a zero off Jill and two from Jack.

He yawns. "Fine, Hudson, see you in court. You better hope Jack's having a good day, that he's not jerking and drooling, and that the tykes' hydrosil hasn't turned into petrified wood. There've been recalls on the material, you know. The jury will be out ten minutes, max. The judgment will blast Unity Property and Casualty right into Chapter Eleven."

"On the subject of corporate instability, Clounce, I hear Nursery Rhyme Park is on the block. Your leash-holder is changing hands."

"Nonsense," he says too quickly.

Interesting, but I let it drop.

We trade more unpleasantries, then I catch a bus for a south suburb and Nursery Rhyme Park, to see what there is to see. Anything to delay reporting back to David. Two transfers and 90 minutes later, I arrive at a garish, sprawling affair of molded plastic and primary colors. A polyvinyl funk clings in the air.

I'd been out once with my kids on a visitation day, but it'd been at least 6 months and 3 biotech generations ago. Seems like there's a new wrinkle daily. You keep up on the technology or fall by the wayside.

The place looks the same. It looks different too, in a way I can't put my finger on. The format remains the individual exhibit, at which nursery rhymes are recited and spectacularly enacted.

Old King Cole is holding court with his Fiddlers Three. They're loud, in a dueling banjos sort of way. A few moms and kiddies are seated, holding their ears.

On 10-minute intervals, Little Miss Muffet shrieks hysterically at a mechanical spider the size of a spaniel.

Jack Be Nimble seems the biggest hit with the handful of preschoolers in attendance. A flame licks at his privates as Jack and his spring-loaded ankles vault a propane candlestick.

I'm beginning to get a handle on the "different." Paint is peeling and trash barrels overflow. Also, lines at the turnstiles seem unusually short. The Park has an eroding, shabby feel to it. The polite term is deferred maintenance.

What this means to Unity Property and Casualty is murky. I follow the smell of rancid grease to a food counter just outside the entrance. I'm standing there, eating an oily, rubbery corn dog for lunch, hoping a clue will flap up in front of me like Four and Twenty Blackbirds.

I spot a pair of Rhymers. They're exiting the Park, holding envelopes, grumbling and shaking their heads.

One is short and stumpy. The other appears addled. I trail them to the employee parking lot. Before they get into a car, they compare the cash in their envelopes.

"Hey, fellas, what's the problem?" I ask.

"Who wants to know?" the short guy demands.

I know for a fact that Little Jack Horner is my age. Whatever they've done to him, Horner's the world's oldest cherub.

"Hey, I'm a big-time fan," I lie. "I hate the sight of an unhappy Rhymer."

Little Jack Horner looks at Simple Simon, who's in buckle shoes, tights, grungy cape, and a goofy hat that's pulled down over his ears.

"Not Rhymers, friend," Horner says. "Ex-Rhymers. They downsized us and cheated us out of some hours too."

"Why? You guys are terrific."

"Tell that to Management." Jack Horner sweeps a puffy palm. "They're pinching pennies. Look for yourself."

"I don't get it. You're headliners, not maintenance personnel."

"Tell me about it," Horner goes on. "They say we're not dramatic enough. Pulling a plum out of a Christmas pie's fine between Black Friday and New Year's Day. They said to come back then to apply for seasonal. Like I'm a goddamn department store Santa! You know what I went through to land this job?"

I cringe at the thought.

"Biomech compression and clamping to meet the minimum height. Pneumato-bloat to flatten the wrinkles." He cocks a thumb at Simon. "That's nothing compared to what they did to him."

I look at Simple Simon and his vacant expression. His buckteeth stretch his upper lip unnaturally: retro-orthodontia. The PC term for Simon is developmentally disabled.

"Lobotomy too?"

Horner nods. "They inserted a cerebro-switch, but it's on the fritz. They said they'd retrain him as a roving carny geek."

"Biting the heads off of chickens?"

"Exactly. I kind of look out for Simple, so I told 'em for both of us to go take a flying fuck at a rolling donut."

"I hear Nursery Rhyme Park is up for sale."

"So have we. We're talking distressed merchandise, pal. Management's running scared."

"Our glorious leader moved off-site." Horner angrily clutches his severance pay. "They maintain a two-bit HR office here at the Park to do their dirty work."

"Nursery Rhyme Park's org table isn't on the website. Who might your glorious leader be?"

"Mother Goose."

"That's been rumored. Isn't she your top act?"

"Yeah. Mother still emcees night performances, but she calls the shots too. She came out on top of a hostile takeover. The old board of directors is ancient history."

Little Jack Horner and Simple Simon give me a lift to a strip mall anchored by a supermarket and a discount pharmacy. In an adjacent wing of shops, sandwiched between teriyaki and a dry cleaner is:

MG PROPERTIES, INC.
SPECIALIZING IN LAND.

A brand-spanking-new BMW 750i sporting MTR GSE vanity plates is parked at the door. The receptionist is a lovely young woman, a petite work of porcelain with batting eyelashes and a synthetically enhanced bosom bursting out of a ruffled bodice. A crooked cane rests against the fax and a biomech lamb is tethered to the photocopy machine, pseudo-carpet grazing.

I give Mary my card and ask for the boss. She sweetly informs me that Mother receives nobody without an appointment. I politely inform Mary that if Ms. Goose refuses to see me, a senior claims representative of the Unity Property and Casualty Insurance Company, she is, in effect, throttling another goose, a member of the golden persuasion.

Mary rises and awards me a brittle-sensual-vulnerable-virginal smile, and says, gee, she'll try. Her hair is metallically lustrous and her metered fragrance is organic bath soap. I picture us in a shower together. My knees weaken. She closes the door of an inner office, then emerges in 15 minutes to say that Mother can see me.

Mother Goose flutters out of her chair and takes my hand. "Oh, Mr. Hudson, I apologize for delaying you. Insurance! Goodness! I telephoned Mr. Clounce. One cannot be too careful, you know. He said you were in his office earlier regarding Jack and Jill. Insurance? Oh dear. I haven't the foggiest about insurance. All that fine print."

I reply with a sneer, saying, "Cut the crap. Everybody knows your whole operation is in a kamikaze dive."

"Well, if that's what you crudely imply, I'm simply phasing out of Nursery Rhyme Park, while establishing a fledgling real estate agency. We deal in land, undeveloped tracts primarily, concentrating on glades, forests and anything else pastoral. How may I be of service, Mr. Hudson?"

Mother Goose is broad about the beam, has a large chin and a bent nose. She wears pince-nez glasses, a tall tall hat and a dowdy shawl. She looks like she'd been biomech'd by Frankenstein.

"Jack and Jill ran up the hill. It's all downhill from there, pun intended."

"Such darlings," Mother Goose says, clucking her tongue. "Jack is a worry, but his fate is in the hands of the best technical specialists and Mr. Clounce, a fabulous human being dedicated to the highest standards of jurisprudence."

Barf. "Humpty Dumpty?"

Mother Goose sighs. "Oh, I don't remember how often I instructed the grounds crew to affix nonskid pads to the top of that wall. It was raining that day, extremely slippery."

"Humpty is supposed to fall. That's why he's there."

"Not when he isn't ready, dear. Not when he's off-balance. Not to be crippled for life."

"We concede that his double canopy epidermal was brittle, that the pieces failed destructive testing, and that he has some nasty lacerations. But crippled for life is a reach. I hear he's recuperating in Bermuda."

"Warm weather and sunshine will speed his partial recovery."

I laugh bitterly. "Must be nice. If you can afford it."

"Mr. Hudson, what are you insinuating?"

"I'm on to your game," I bluff. "So let's cut the guano."

Mother Goose gasps. "Mr. Hudson, how dare you accuse me of nefarious –"

"Save it for the rubes. Nursery Rhyme Park is in disrepair and the turnout is pathetic. By the looks of it, I'll bet your cash flow is down to a trickle."

Mother Goose pauses, peering at me over her spectacles. She takes a package of rum crooks from her purse and offers me one. I decline. She lights up, drags deeply, and says, "May I speak frankly, Mr. Hudson?"

"That'd be swell for a change."

"You have four children, don't you?"

"How'd you know?"

"Two by each former wife, the second of whom you're six months in arrears on your alimony."

I don't answer.

"Her attorney is circling overhead. Compared to him, Charles Evans Clounce is Charles Evans Hughes. Your girlfriend moved out last month and David Oakes is on the verge of sacking you."

"Very thorough," I say with false calm. "How'd you know?"

"Mary."

"Your Mary out front?"

Mother points at her laptop. "She isn't just a pretty face. Dear sweet Mary came in to announce you and she also hacked into credit agencies and Unity's personnel records. Mary was trained by Bulgarians. Life is so unfair, Mr. Hudson, but being the eternal optimist, I do believe you are on the upswing."

I sniff. "Is that a bribe in the air?"

"Oh, such an ugly word."

"Know what I think, Ms. Goose?"

"Please call me Mother."

"Mother, the pastoral land business is slower than slow, isn't it?"

"Well, real estate is cyclical."

I say, "That doesn't matter. MG Properties, Inc. is a shell corporation, isn't it? It exists to complete one deal and one deal alone, the disposal of Nursery Rhyme Park."

Mother cackles. "How on earth did you draw that ridiculous conclusion?"

"Process of elimination inspired by a chance encounter with two unemployed Rhymers. Nursery Rhyme Park is worse than worthless. The only source of profit is fraudulent insurance payoffs. When the Park folds, from the cut Clounce kicks back to you on the damage awards, you'll have the capital to raze it and subdivide."

She replies by blowing a smoke ring.

"Correct me if you're wrong, Mother. Your mysterious corporate masters are breathing down your neck. The sooner the wheels come off Nursery Rhyme Park, the sooner they can charge a humongous tax write-off."

"Hudson, the reality is that biomech prices are softening. Soon, the most bizarre procedures will be affordable for the average person. The Chinese are in it now, full bore. They're lowballing everyone, like they do with everything else.

"In order to survive, the Park requires more than a broom and a bucket of paint. We'd have to upgrade our acts and our personnel, a doomed venture regardless.

"I have to save my babies. Do you think I enjoy the layoffs? I *do* feel like a mother to them. Most Rhymers are maimed. They aren't qualified to do anything else. They can't all have lucrative, insurable accidents. They need me. Without me, when the Park folds, they'll be on the welfare rolls."

Mother is tense, her eyes glassy. Her quasi-sincerity temporarily rattles me. "Well, what right does that give you to bleed Unity dry?"

"Situational ethics, if you like."

"I don't like." I get up. "You definitely won't like me blowing the whistle on your scam."

Mother pushes an intercom button. "Mary, dear, do you have that report? Oh, wonderful. Hudson, please resume your seat. Let's talk about you for a moment. Specifically."

"I am not for sale," I say, jaw thrust as I resume my seat.

"If Nursery Rhyme Park is to be saved, I'd need quality people to convert that mess into a *quality* theme park."

"I already have a job," I say weakly.

Mary flounces in, jiggling, pleats and frills rustling, trailing her intoxicating scent and a computer printout. She looks at me. I grow faint.

Mother peruses the printout, frowning, saying "hmmm" and "oh my." She underlines sections and frowning further. I retaliate by clearing my throat and glancing at my watch.

"You're antsy, Hudson. Do you have pressing work to do?"

"Thanks to you."

"Irrelevant," she says, giving me the printout. "Read it and weep."

Irrelevant is an understatement. Mary had hacked a sneak preview of Unity's demise: confidential Home Office memos, auditor reports, pending lawsuits, and the ilk.

~ ~ ~

A week later, Unity Property and Casualty's clichéd house of cards tumbles in a heap and the remains land in state insurance commissioners' laps.

You won't recognize Nursery Rhyme Park. Mother Goose has it sparkling. She's incorporating cutting-edge biotechnology and has added acts that are absolutely dazzling. Take the biggest hit, The Three Little Pigs. The porkers are state-of-the-art, a breakthrough involving DNA and titanium. Their shtick is closer to opera than to nursery rhyme.

Simple Simon and Little Jack Horner have been rehired, a nonnegotiable condition to my acceptance of a position. Simon is a cheap thrill, randomly lurching and slobbering, but you won't find a headless chicken on the premises. Jack is in his customary corner, plucking plums with panache. If he isn't a lesson to corporate leadership on the value of employee morale, I don't know what is.

As the Park's new risk manager, I use my pull to get Oakes and Lander on the payroll. They're working as Tweedledum and Tweedledee. Lander's bulk and anger gives him a comical edge over David as they push and shove. For real. I catch their routine whenever I can.

Since the Park no longer has an outside insurance carrier, I have an ample workload. This hasn't prevented me from wearing a second hat, bitten as I am now by the show biz bug. Despite the long hours, I have a fraction of the stress I had at Unity P & C. I feel 10 years younger and with the Park's resurgence in popularity, I'm a minor celebrity.

My children visit regularly, whether their mommies like it or not. I autograph programs for their friends. Further, Mother Goose pays me twice what Unity had. I've converted part of the windfall into back alimony and have thusly fended off summonses, liens, the slammer, et al.

Life is better than good.

I contemplate my blessings as I relax at the employees' meadow, a blade of grass in my mouth, tranquility in my soul. It's lunchtime and I await my Rhymer partner, who has become my true love.

She walks up the rise with our picnic basket. My heart rate leaps, partially due to a newfound sense of mystery. She's taken the morning off for an important and unexplained appointment.

She sits beside me with a seismic thud and doles out slivers of ham and a relish tray. While I nibble, she inhales a dozen donuts and a string of sausage. Her contract specifies a minimum daily caloric intake, mine a maximum.

"How long are you planning to keep me in suspense?"

She is weeping with joy as she hugs me so hard my ribs creak. Office work bored Mary, so she cross-trained. Curvilinear biomech layering supplements her weight gain, making her pleasingly plump, Erotically Rubenesque, if you will. Mother G. is attempting to extend our demographics deeper into adult territory.

"I'm pregnant. Isn't that marvelous?"

I don't even like to think about what they did to shave 50 pounds from my already-cadaverous frame.

"It is marvelous," I tell Mrs. Sprat. "I'm the luckiest guy on the planet."

SATAN ADAPTS TO THE TIMES, OFFERS LEASE-OPTION ON SOULS

Holding the car stereo, Vladimir said, "Jimmy, this word here after 'theft,' you know what it mean?"

It was late at night and they were at a gravel pit, standing by Vladimir's pickup truck with camper that he referred to as a "pop-up pawn shop."

Jimmy was short and scrawny. He had a wispy mustache, a bad complexion, and an 8th-grade education.

Jimmy, who did not read well, lied, "Sure. Who don't?"

Vladimir tapped a fingernail against the stereo. "Deterrent. Theft deterrent. What it mean is you yank unit out of dashboard, codes scrambles it up like omelet so it no work. It no good to nobody who don't have the code."

"This is a real nice stereo," Jimmy said. "Lookit. All these buttons. It holds I don't know how many CDs."

Vladimir shook his head. "It can hold a million disc. If it no work, it no work."

Jimmy said, "When the alarm went off, I had to go up over a fence and down the alley, this dog barking all the time."

Vladimir didn't know what that had to do with anything, but he had a second cousin whose teenaged son could hack and fix anything electronic. Slip the kid a bottle of vodka and he'd do the job. The stereo was a top-of-the-line unit. He'd get $50 for it, easy.

Vladimir gave Jimmy $10 and said, "This is piece of crap to me, but you try hard. You good boy. You deserve something for effort."

At the first bar he came to, Jimmy nursed a beer to make the ten-spot last, concluding yet again that the world was giving him a humongous headache.

A guy three stools down drinking a martini asked, "May I buy you another brew?"

Jimmy squinted at a sharp dresser with a gold watch, a dimpled chin, and cologne so strong it'd degrease a carburetor. He had a haircut that cost more than Jimmy's net worth. He looked kind of familiar too. "Yeah, sure."

The guy signaled the barkeep, then said, "I don't know about you, Jimmy. The world's giving me a humongous headache."

Jimmy blinked and the guy reappeared on the stool beside him.

Jimmy flinched. "Hey, do I know you?"

"You're an insomniac, Jimmy."

Jimmy sat up straighter. "Don't get no ideas. I ain't like *that*."

"Relax, Jimmy, relax. You do have trouble sleeping."

"So?"

"Night owl television. That little set you have plugged into the cigarette lighter in your Buick-slash-boudoir. Think, think, think."

Jimmy's eyes widened. He snapped his fingers. "That's you doin' one of them infomercials?"

"And you ask, can you get rich quick buying real estate for no money down? Or make a fortune in the stock market or on the Internet after shelling out for my package? Abs of iron too if that's your druthers. The miracle kitchen gadget that can julienne a Cadillac Escalade?"

Jimmy could only gape.

"The answer to all is, of course, you can't."

"Which one of them slicky-boys are you?"

"I am *all* of them."

"How come you know my name and what I watch?"

He tsk-tsked. "Jimmy, Jimmy, ten measly dollars for a dangerous night's criminality is, frankly, pathetic."

"Who the hell are you?"

"Oh, I think by now you know. 'Hell' is the operative word."

Jimmy's arms erupted in goose bumps.

"Satan, Lucifer, Beelzebub, et al. Take your choice. I do prefer the elegant, formal ring of Prince of Darkness."

"Them folks on your infomercials, I always wondered if they was real."

"They are, Jimmy. I am."

His grin gave Jimmy the heebie-jeebies.

He looked into his beer and said, "Let's say all this stuff you're saying is for real. You're hustling me to buy my soul? That's how the old story goes, right?"

Satan lit a cigarette from an arc between two fingertips. "On the contrary, I am asking *you* to temporarily rent *my* soul while I temporarily take custody of yours. A lease-option plan, if you will."

"The devil ain't got no soul."

His eyes glowed yellowish. Jimmy smelled brimstone.

"I do, after a fashion. Forget the Sunday school propaganda."

"Okay, so how come me?"

"I target my most faithful viewers. I hate to label someone arbitrarily, but you are, well, gullible. Witness Vladimir's flimflam regarding that stereo."

"He screwed me?"

Satan shrugged. "Water under the bridge. Let's move along, shall we?"

Jimmy gulped and thought, okay, he'd play along, see where this leads to. He nodded.

"I desperately need a sabbatical, Jimmy."

"A whozit?"

"Some time off, a well-deserved vacation. Again, I merely lease your soul, on a short-term, lease-option plan, I don't purchase it outright."

"How come you don't?"

"Consumer protection do-gooders have made the outright-sale plan a much tougher sell. I'm a victim of the changing marketplace."

"What's in it for me?"

"Our deal will be negotiated after a given period, an interim in which your cash flow will be, thanks to liberal usage of my soul, significant.

"I am thoroughly burned out, pun intended. Can you conceive how noxious an environment I oversee? On the whole, my clientele is rather unpleasant. It's not easy tormenting the collective damned for all eternity."

"That's a long time, huh?"

"Indeed it is."

"I don't know, man."

"Doesn't cash flow appeal to you? Cash flow being a popular infomercial buzz-phrase."

"Nah, not if I gotta take over from you and sell them phony real estate classes on TV and the other shit you hustle. That sounds like, you know, work."

"Perhaps an enhancement of your present career would be appropriate. Heaven forbid, another pun intended, that you should stray from your comfort zone."

"I got a career?"

"Indeed you do. You are a lifelong petty criminal. Does becoming a mob kingpin appeal?"

"I dunno. Let's say I agree. What's in it for you?"

"Well, my life hasn't exactly been a bed of hot coals lately. To tell you the truth, down there it's like herding cats. Dictators, CEOs, CFOs, COOs, televangelists, lobbyists, chiropractors. Not to mention the hordes of motivational speakers and self-help gurus. *Everybody* knows *everything*. It's impossible to get a word in edgewise or to properly maintain torture initiatives. The generic psychopaths, killers and rapists and whatnot, are the only ones who cause few problems. They knew where they were headed and accept it. And don't get me started on lawyers and politicians."

"Okay, I won't."

"Let's return to my lease-option alternative."

"You know, you're sounding like a used car salesman."

"Flattery will get you nowhere," Satan said, sighing sulfurously. "Once upon a time, Jimmy, you had your basic Good and Evil. No gray areas, no ambiguities. Simple superstitious folk accepted their fate and did what they were told at the orientation center. Now, they were just following orders or practicing situational ethics or it's their accountant's fault. It's allegedly this, allegedly that, yada yada yada. They rationalize and negotiate endlessly. It drives me up the wall!

"What about it, Jimmy? I lease your soul for a specified period of time while I have yours, at the end of which, you have the option of selling it to me. I'm mortal and free. I can goof for – shall we say – thirty days. It's win-win for you."

"I don't have to start no wars or famines or run for office, stuff like that?"

"Not even launch a locust hatch or a fifty-car freeway rear-ender. You'll still be a miserable loser, albeit a loser with a modicum of panache. What do you say? What do you have to lose?"

"You got a point there." Jimmy conceded. "Except for the change on the bar, I'm flat broke."

Satan extended a hand. "I rest my case."

Jimmy took it, expecting heat blisters. His grip was as cold as ice.

Jimmy blinked and the dude was gone.

Not totally believing what happened. thinking that you met all kinds in bars, Jimmy guzzled his beer and the one the guy bought for him, and went outside to the 1992 Buick Roadmaster he called home.

Instead, a brand-spanking-new mile-high SUV with privacy glass and JIMMY vanity plates idled in the handicapped slot where he'd parked the Buick. A no-neck loomed by the driver's door, arms folded.

"You ready, boss?"

Boss? Jesus H. Christ, Satan *was* Satan. Way cool.

Jimmy decided, what the hell, go with the flow. He got in the back and swooshed into soft leather.

"Awesome," Jimmy said.

"Where to, boss?"

"Wherever."

They drove around for a while. The Devil's soul felt funny. It was like a lump of iron in his innards. Jimmy had a similar feeling after one too many microwave burritos at the convenience store.

Bruno said, "We got us a problem, boss."

Jimmy stared at the outline of a square head and cauliflower ears. "Yeah?"

"The Ripugnantes, they been muscling in on the south side again."

Jimmy knew of the Ripugnantes. Robert (Bughouse Bobby) Ripugnante and his gang ran the town. You didn't mess with them.

"Yeah?"

"You know what means to us?"

"I do?"

"After you went to Bughouse Bobby and had a sit-down, he gave you his word that the south side was ours." Bruno pretended to spit. "That's how much a Ripugnante's word is worth."

"Yeah?"

"You give them Ripugnantes an inch, they take a mile, boss. Even though the Bughouse Bobby's funny in the head, not normal like me and you, that don't give him the right to disrespect you. What you gotta do, in my opinion, you gotta make a statement."

"A statement," Jimmy said. "Yeah."

"Let 'em know you don't fuck with Jackhammer Jimmy and get away with it."

Jackhammer?

They pulled into the driveway of a suburban ranch house. Bruno said, "We can do it tonight, boss. All you gotta do is say the word."

It?

Jimmy said, "Yeah, okay. You gotta do what you gotta do is what you gotta do."

"Sorry this ain't the Ritz, boss, but nobody'll know you're here. You'll be a hunnert-percent safe. The Ripugnantes ain't gonna take this lying down, you know."

Jimmy said yeah, no, okay, then got out and went inside. The carpet was skuzzy, the furniture flimsy, and the walls smelled of mold. Compared to the back seat of the Roadmaster, it was a royal palace.

"You comin' to bed, Jimmykins?"

On a creaking floor, Jimmy followed the voice to a bedroom and an angel. Big bleached-blonde hair, tattoos galore, and silicone implants bulging under a negligee, she was every go-go dancer he'd ever lusted for. He didn't have to be asked twice.

When she left in the morning she blew her Jimmykins a kiss and said he was incredible. Jimmy opened a cold beer and turned on the TV, almost believing her. There was a live news story from the airport parking garage. Some talking hairdo with a microphone stood by yellow crime-scene tape surrounding a car.

"The body of 64-year old Robert (Bughouse Bobby) Ripugnante, reputed patriarch of the Ripugnante crime family, was found in the trunk of this stolen Cadillac. Ripugnante had been bound and trussed and shot multiple times, executed gangland style according to authorities.

"Ironically, the airport is on the south side, the center of a power struggle that has been decimating the Ripugnantes and the rival Jackhammer Jimmy organization. So named for an alleged incident where he used a jackhammer on an alleged informant, Jimmy and Ripugnante were allegedly vying for control of lucrative air cargo theft and drug smuggling activities. Speculation is that this rivalry was the motivation for the killing. Law enforcement officials fear that the brutal killing may precipitate an escalated situation."

"Me the Jackhammer. I got credit for doing a stool pigeon," Jimmy told the TV, raising a bony fist.

Suddenly, bullets shattered windows, shredding threadbare drapes, chewing up plasterboard, and pulverizing the laminated-cardboard furniture. Jimmy dove and hit the floor, staying there until he no longer heard squealing tires.

He thought, why'm I acting like a weenie? Bullets oughta bounce off me, the clout the Devil's soul had to have. Jimmy pushed up onto his knees, puzzled why his hands stung. He looked at blood from the broken glass, thinking that maybe he'd been screwed on this soul-swap thing.

~ ~ ~

Bruno came for him.

"We went and whacked out the rat who give the Ripugnantes this address, boss. We're gonna go to your downtown penthouse condo and secure you tighter'n a drum. While me and the boys go take care of business, nobody's getting within a mile of you."

Jimmy had severe doubts where this was all headed, but didn't protest.

The penthouse condo was beyond his wildest dreams. Thick white shag rug, leopard-skin furniture, mounted animal heads on the walls, a velvet painting of Elvis over the fireplace, and a view of the docks and shipyard.

He couldn't complain about the company neither. The procession of ladies all had platinum hair, purple lipstick, and names like Trixi. The only difference was the flavor of the gum they constantly popped.

Jimmy watched a lot of TV. Cartoons and NASCAR were his favorites. A Trixi kept him occupied at night, so he didn't catch the infomercials. He also watched the news. He'd never liked the news before, but now he couldn't surf past without seeing himself.

Word was that the Ripugnantes were tightening their grip on the south side, while taking vengeance against the notorious Jackhammer Jimmy crime family for the alleged assassination of Bughouse Bobby Ripugnante.

The hairdos said that if the Ripugnantes didn't succeed in chasing the Jackhammer Jimmy gang out of town, the IRS reportedly had plans for Jimmy, multiple counts of tax fraud that would put him away longer than Al Capone.

The cops raided a massage parlor. Jimmy saw several Trixis in silk bathrobes being loaded into a paddy wagon. Drug-sniffing mutts discovered a big shipment of white powder in a cargo plane at the airport. A couple of Jimmy's soldiers were whacked out as they ate lunch at a restaurant not a half mile from the penthouse.

It was obvious to Jimmy that Bruno and the boys weren't taking care of business too awful good as there was a full-scale gang war on and he was losing. He wished he was somewhere else, boosting car stereos for $10, living in the filthy Roadmaster. The good old days.

Jimmy blew his top at more stories about him evading taxes and flung a beer bottle, smashing it against the King. Talk about illegal harassment! He'd never filed a tax return in his life, so how the hell could he commit fraud on one?

Then things got even worse.

Next day, the mile-high SUV blew up in the parking garage when Bruno started it. Jimmy had sent him out to fetch him a breakfast of a chili dog and a six-pack. Damn, he'd miss Bruno.

Jimmy missed his wheels too. A crime boss needed a fancy set of wheels. He saw a commercial for an SUV even bigger and cooler and fancier than his old one. He called a dealer. A salesman knew who Jimmy was and said he'd bring a unit right on over, with all the trimmings and the biggest engine they made. Jimmy loved how they jumped through hoops for Jackhammer Jimmy.

The salesman called in a half-hour and said to look out the window. Jimmy peeked between the drapes. The salesman was two blocks away, leaning on a

48

fender, cell phone to an ear, waving. He was fidgeting like he had to take a leak.

Nothing personal, he told Jimmy. He didn't feel comfortable coming any closer because of the, you know, situation.

Jimmy didn't want to be out in broad daylight himself, a sitting duck. He told the salesman to drive inside the parking garage and wait. Jimmy stuffed cash in his pockets till he thought he had enough. There was cash stashed all over the condo, flowing whenever he wanted it.

Jimmy took his private elevator to the basement, sidestepped around the crater left by Bruno and the SUV, did the paperwork, and gave wads of cash to the salesman, who tried to give Jimmy the keys, but kept dropping them.

After he was gone, Jimmy sat behind the wheel and made vroom-vroom noises. He wanted to take it for a spin in the worst way, but chickened out. The Ripugnantes could be parked on the next block, waiting to ventilate him and his rig like Bonnie and Clyde's. Jimmy skulked back up to the condo, thinking the life of a godfather ain't what it's cracked up to be.

Jimmy slept that night with a gun under his pillow, one under the mattress and two on the nightstand. Whenever he found more cash, he found guns. The guns were all he had in his bed. The Trixis were gone, in the slammer or too scared to visit their Jimmykins.

When the SUV car alarm went off at oh-dark-thirty, Jimmy lost it. He charged into the basement garage, a pistol in each hand, Ripugnantes or no Ripugnantes.

Satan stood by the jimmied driver's door, holding his stereo. He said, "Great ride you have, dude, and great tunes. Top of the line. Vladimir will pay me big bucks."

The Devil didn't look much like an infomercial slicky-boy anymore. A beer gut bulged under a dirty T-shirt, spilling over filthier jeans. He wore a baseball cap on backwards and had a three-day growth of stubble. His chaw that made him like look like he had the mumps.

"What the hell you think you're doin'?"

Satan spat tobacco juice and said, "What I'm doing, I'm having a ball. Shedding my soul took a huge weight off. I'm mortal for the moment, as vulnerable as any human, but, hey, it's the risk factor that rings my chimes, pumps the adrenaline."

"Well, your soul ain't done diddly for me. It's sittin' in my gut like a ton of bricks, doing nothing but gettin' me in trouble." Jimmy held up his hands. "Lookie at these cuts from broken glass. Ain't I s'pose to be – what's that word – in-something?"

"Invincible."

"Yeah, that's it."

"You get that only in the premium package, Jimmy. You should have read the fine print."

Jimmy was mulling that over when Satan continued, arms spread, "What did you expect, a ready-to-wear soul? What led you to believe our spirits could seamlessly interface? I made no such promise and you have been compensated handsomely. Is there any shortage of cash flow and good living?"

"Cash flow don't mean diddly if I can't go out and spend it without getting my ass shot off. All them Trixis bugging out on me too, enough is enough."

"Jimmy, Jimmy," Satan said, shaking his head. "You're temporarily *leasing* my soul. I didn't do a full install. If you pick up the option to sell, we can – "

"You ain't playing fair. You went and fibbed to me."

"Fair play and the truth? Think about it Jimmy," Satan said, sneering. "Who the *hell* am I?"

Jimmy muttered a string of obscenities and climbed behind the wheel of his rig to see how much more damage there was besides the stereo theft. At least he was able to start it.

"This is a crock, man," he said, pounding the steering wheel. "My thirty days is about up and I wanna quit now."

Satan shrugged. "I am a flexible demon. However, you lose all benefits that accompanied the deal."

Jimmy laughed bitterly. "So what? I'm basically a prisoner who's fixin' to be dead meat."

Satan thought what a lovely annual vacation this was proving to be. Adventure travel in the shoes of lowlifes. Last year's arrangement with an arsonist had been a blast too, four glorious weeks as a firebug. He'd reclaim his soul from Jimmy and head on home, rested and invigorated, eager to resume abusing the lumpen masses with renewed zeal. He was thinking ahead to next year. A lease-option with a serial killer perhaps.

Jimmy saw two guys step out of a parked car on the other side of the garage. They wore business suits and carried briefcases.

The IRS, he thought. Coming to serve tax fraud papers on him.

"Are you absolutely positive you wish to terminate our agreement, Jimmy?" Satan loved to goad them, to listen to their whiny complaints.

Jimmy's attention was on the suits.

"Last chance," Satan added, hand outstretched to finalize the transfer.

The IRS in the middle of the night, Jimmy thought? They're 9-to-5 paper pushers is what they are.

"Oh Lordy!" he said, peeling out.

Satan yelled at him to stop. Then he noticed the two men as they reached into their briefcases and withdrew pistols.

One fired at Jimmy, missing him as he fishtailed around a corner.

His partner cut Satan down. He was aware that he'd be dead before he hit the floor.

The Prince of Darkness would be heading on home, yes, but ignominiously, through the front door, into the orientation center.

Where billions of disgruntled clients awaited.

MIDGET MAKES MUCHO MOOLA FOR MOB

At the front gate of Flagford State Penitentiary, Jimmy (Feet) Brutto waited, right on time. Ralph Crazwell walked out, a free man. With his only piece of luggage, a duffle bag, he climbed inside Jimmy's SUV as if into a tree house. They weren't making them that big 4 years, 3 months and 9 days ago.

"Yo, Tom Thumb," Jimmy Feet said, giving Ralph a crushing shoulder squeeze. "You been drinking too much coffee in the pen. Stunted your growth."

Ralph smiled politely as Jimmy howled at his own stale humor. Not that he had much choice. Jimmy Feet was chief enforcer and all-purpose goon for the Ripugnante crime family.

Ralph had been tagged Tom Thumb for longer than he could remember. His full name was Ralph Jerome Crazwell. At 2' 11¼", which he rounded off to 3 feet if asked, Ralph was the world's shortest career criminal.

In a way, Ralph owed Jimmy and his organization. Flagford was full of psychos, but nobody laid a hand on him, aware that he was with the Ripugnantes.

On the other hand, in self-pitying moods, he blamed them for his latest incarceration. While pulling a Ripugnante job, he had gotten stuck in a heating duct that appeared bigger than it was.

Then again, Ralph J. Crazwell was pushing 40, an adult capable of making his own choices. Ralph kept his mouth shut and took the fall alone.

"So how'd they treat you?"

"Okay."

They drove in silence for a few minutes, Ralph craning his neck, gaping through privacy glass rather than steel bars. He watched Jimmy too, who wore gold chains and mirrored shades. Jimmy sported the lowest hairline Ralph had ever seen on a homo sapiens.

A favorite wisecrack of Jimmy Feet's was that Ralph could bobsled in one of the size-16s that earned him his nickname. Ralph expected Jimmy to spring that gag on him or to ask if he'd feel safer in a child's car seat.

But Jimmy got straight to business.

"There's this thing we need you for, Thumbo."

Ralph didn't think Jimmy Feet was playing chauffeur out of the goodness of his heart.

"Oh?"

"There's this pitcher we got a buyer lined up for."

"A pitcher?"

"You know, a pitcher some artist painted. It don't look like nothing."

Ralph didn't reply.

Jimmy handed him a page torn from an art magazine. The painting on it did look like something to Ralph — a salad bar that had been overturned on the floor. The caption identified it as *Pompeii Sunset* by Kennedy Scott.

"Pompeii is some country over there someplace. You make out what this is?

"No."

"Kennedy Scott was what they call an abstracted impressurist. Him croaking a long time ago is what makes his stuff worth a shitload of dough. This pitcher, it's on loan from some museum someplace to the modern art museum here in town. They're having this big la-di-fucking-da show."

This was not a swell moment to tell Jimmy that he didn't want to steal for him or anybody else. The penal system was a revolving door for Ralph Crazwell. One more bust and he'd be facing a habitual criminal sentence — life without chance of parole. Three strikes and he's permanently out of circulation.

"Museums have security as tight as banks, Jimmy, particularly during important exhibitions," Ralph said, hoping to discourage him.

"You talk funny, Thumbo."

"How so?"

"Big words. You don't talk normal."

Ralph had completed his GED during this stretch. To his astonishment, he enjoyed reading and cut a swath through the prison library, with a special emphasis on vocabulary enhancement.

Ralph shrugged. To confess that would be pointless. Education held no appeal to the Jimmy (Feet) Bruttos of the world.

Jimmy fluttered a beefy paw. "No sweat on security if that's what's worrying you. We got security in the bag. See, they just got the pitcher and haven't hung it up on a wall yet with alarms and guards and shit. We got a route in for you, on account of you're a dwarf."

Ralph was so accustomed to casual cruelty that "dwarf" didn't faze him. And this caper of Jimmy's was a larger problem than political correctness.

"It says *Pompeii Sunset is* like only three feet by three feet. We got us a guy on the inside who's helping us. According to him all you gotta do to yank the pitcher outta the frame is pop the staples. Then roll it up."

"When?"

"We're working on the details. Soon. Where you gonna be staying, Thumbo?"

"I don't know. Somewhere cheap."

"I know this good place and I'll spring for a week's rent." Jimmy slapped an ample gut. "Let's have lunch. Living on jailhouse slop, what're you hungry for?"

"Teriyaki."

"Nah," Jimmy Feet said, belching softly at the prospect. "Chinese don't agree with me."

Jimmy stopped at a sandwich shop in a strip mall. He ordered meatball subs and greasy fries for two without consulting Ralph.

Cheeks bulging with lunch, Jimmy Feet asked Ralph if it got any better than this, freedom and a fine restaurant. Ralph picked at his food, which was a slight step up from prison chow. No, he said, it didn't get any better than this. Jimmy said the job would be a nice payday and that he'd be able to eat whatever and wherever he wanted.

Ralph said he could hardly wait.

~ ~ ~

Jimmy Feet's "good place", a fleabag hotel hosting a cockroach convention, smelled like Flagford. Ralph's room was on the second floor, above a tavern. Noise and rancid odors seeped through the threadbare carpet. He hurried to the nearest teriyaki café.

Ralph yearned for teriyaki. Of everything absent in the prison's limited cuisine, he missed teriyaki the most. He devoured a steaming plate of chicken over sticky rice, then had the pork. The counter people smiled in amazement, wondering where he put it.

Ralph thought he might like working at a teriyaki café and eventually buy his own. But the only work he excelled at was crawling into impossibly small openings to steal. Who would hire him for anything else?

Jimmy (Feet) Brutto had made him an offer he couldn't refuse. If Ralph did, he'd wind up in the trunk of a stolen car in the airport garage. Ralph speculated on Jimmy Feet's final Tom Thumb joke: We had to stuff him inna trunk on account of he didn't quite fit in the glove box.

Ralph J. Crazwell's epitaph.

Ralph hoped that the museum scheme would simply go away. The Ripugnantes didn't have long attention spans. If the deal got shaky — the buyer changing his mind or the museum's inside man not coming through — they had no qualms cutting their losses and moving on.

All that scenario required was a little luck. Ralph thought he was overdue, but when he returned to his room, Dirty Dean was sitting on his bed watching cartoons.

Dirty Dean was blubbery and unkempt to the extreme. When in Dirty Dean's company, you did your utmost to stay upwind. He was a colleague of Jimmy Feet's.

A man of few words, Dirty Dean flicked off the TV and said, "Let's go."

They went.

Dirty Dean stopped at a bar between a pawn shop and a used appliance store, and said, "There's a guy in there you're gonna talk to. Don't worry. He'll find you."

Ralph walked into the dive and past a twangy jukebox. He attracted the usual curiosity, the swiveling barstools and self-conscious looks. A nervous, skinny man Ralph's age stood up by a booth and waved.

"I'm Elliott."

Ralph sat in the booth across from Elliott.

"They said you'd be, uh, short."

Ralph's chin just cleared the table. He looked at a cocktail glass, an ashtray mounded with butts, then up at Elliott, who was lighting another cigarette.

"They were right."

"I work security at the modern art museum. I'm off today," Elliott said. "Want a drink?"

Elliott wore flat-lens glasses and the cheesiest fake mustache Ralph had ever seen. He had thinning hair, an Adam's apple, and sunken cheeks. Ralph imagined that Elliott hadn't been sleeping well, beholden to the Ripugnantes as he surely was.

"No thanks. When's this to happen?"

"Tomorrow night. I'm laying a sketched-out map on the seat beside you and a staple puller. The director's office is on the second floor. It has a small upper window on the alley side. The director will be gone, at a meeting. We close at six. It'll be dark then. You can reach the window from a Dumpster. I'll make sure it's where it needs to be. The window will be unlatched. A filing cabinet on a desk underneath it will make stepping stones. You have to enter the building between six and six-thirty. That's when we make the rounds to make sure everything's locked up and everyone's out. I walk that wing. The building alarm isn't armed until we've made a final check."

"You've got it all doped out," Ralph said.

With a trembling hand, Elliott swigged his drink, took a drag of his smoke, and said, "We don't need any goof-ups."

"*Pompeii Sunset*, what's it valued at?"

"They say it's priceless, as are the few remaining Scotts are priceless. Starting here, *Sunset* is on loan from the family for a tour called the Past Century Masters Exhibition. Whoever *Sunset* ends up with won't be able to show it in public. It'll eventually find a home in a moneybags' private gallery. An Arab sheik or Russian oil thug."

"After I'm inside?"

"You wait in the director's office till seven-thirty. That's when I go on break. There are three of us. Stan will be across the street at the museum annex, which is devoted primarily to young people. Bob will be upstairs. The gallery where *Sunset* hangs is right around the corner from the office. You can't miss it. You'll have the place to yourself for at least fifteen minutes. I'll discover *Sunset* missing around eight, sound the alarm, switch on the lights, and notify the police."

"How do I escape?"

"Reverse direction."

"Don't tell me," Ralph said. "That window's high up and too small for an average person to fit through, so they didn't bother to alarm it."

"You're being a good sport."

"Do I have a choice? What do they have on you?"

Elliott lit a cigarette from the one he was smoking. "I owe them money."

Ralph nodded knowingly. The Ripugnantes made a fortune shylocking. Jimmy Feet was an efficient collector. Dirty Dean too. They were handy with baseball bats.

"I'll be even-steven with them."

Ralph had his doubts. "And if this doesn't work out?"

Elliott cringed. "I don't want to think about that."

Neither did Ralph J. Crazwell.

~ ~ ~

Next morning, Ralph visited the city's main branch library. His newfound reading interests were eclectic. He devoured books and periodicals as if teriyaki. This library was a wonderland compared to Flagford's.

The art books weighed a ton. He lugged those that included Kennedy Scott's work to a table and spread them out. In a few minutes he had a notion of the man, an abstract expressionist who painted color fields and soft-edged shapes. Ralph studied the paintings. While they bore bizarre titles such as *Dar es Salaam's Plutonium Gecko, Raising Chickens on Mars* and *Rangoon Roundup*, some weren't bad in their own way. Scott had a flair for color.

The bios said that Kennedy Scott was well on his way to drinking himself to death, but was convicted of murder, then fatally shanked in prison.

He left behind ex-wives and wealthy art patrons, often older women. He was a barroom brawler who behaved like a jerk even when he was sober, a rare occasion. According to the books, Scott came from a "turbulent and impoverished" background. There were sibling mouths to feed, and boozing by parents and stepparents. In a photo of Scott taken in his studio, he was bony and balding and intense.

Ralph located a pamphlet on the city's modern art museum. It wasn't as weird as Scott's art, but it wasn't an ordinary building either. It had four different colors on the outside walls and no right angles. Per the mysterious Elliott, his window of entry was on the backside of an end section that swooped skyward like a rocket fin.

This library devoted a room to computers. Flagford had a few obsolete machines. Ralph had taught himself the basics there. On the museum's home page, he clicked on The Past Century Masters Exhibition link and scrolled through the hype. Some of the samples on the screen had pretty colors like Scott's, some were outright disgusting.

He scrolled to the event's schedule.

Things began to smell funny.

The exhibition ran from January 25 through March 2. Today was January 23. The museum was closed from last night until the afternoon of the twenty-fifth to set up for the Past Century Masters Exhibition. Only the annex remained open to the public.

So why were they pulling the heist on the basis of a normal day, a 6:00 closing, when the museum was closed anyway? Ralph went to museum map link. He compared the map Elliott gave him. They didn't jibe. Not only was the exhibition going to be on the opposite side of the museum, it was on the ground floor.

Was Jimmy Feet setting him up? If so, why? Who was Jimmy's customer for *Pompeii Sunset*?

And who was this shylocked rent-a-cop in the dumb disguise? Elliott hadn't rung true in other ways he couldn't put his finger on.

Ralph left the library in a state of indecision and with such a nervous stomach that he barely finished his second helping of teriyaki.

~ ~ ~

He napped in his room and packed. However this evening ended, he wasn't returning. He took a taxi to a self-storage warehouse south of town. Before sentencing on his last rap, using an alias, he'd prepaid 5 years rent. Then as now, he took pains not to be been seen by employees and fellow renters.

The facility hadn't changed, but the surroundings had. He remembered trees and vacant lots. Now it was completely industrial, a sprawl of blockish buildings as ugly as Flagford's.

He'd rented the smallest unit available and hadn't filled a third of the space with his belongings. The fruit of a life's work, he thought sourly, inventorying a splayed recliner, clothes and blankets in a cardboard wardrobe, a portable TV, knickknacks and suitcases.

Ralph unzipped a suitcase for reassurance that his money was there along with his burglary tools. He'd squirreled away what hadn't been confiscated during arrests and blown on lawyers. His stash wouldn't set him for life, but it'd get him out of town pronto.

He stuffed bills in his wallet, deciding that he'd have to give the museum job a shot. If he was merely being paranoid and it went smoothly, Jimmy would take care of him. The Ripugnantes paid well for services rendered.

~ ~ ~

At 6 PM sharp, the alley behind the museum was dark and quiet. The Dumpster was where Elliott had promised. Ralph opened it against the back wall. He climbed to the top edge of the lid. On one precarious knee, the other leg free, he felt for the wall, blindly extending an arm upward, and raising awkwardly until he could grab the bottom of the window sill.

The window was unlocked. It was small, almost too small. He'd have to squeeze in headfirst and hope he could drop onto the filing cabinet without snapping his wrists or breaking his neck.

He froze halfway through the opening. There were no lights on in the director's office. He waited until his eyes adjusted and bent forward, his stomach muscles aching. He stared at carpeting, more than 10 feet down. All furnishings were on the other side of the room.

No way.

Ralph wriggled back out as quickly as he could, the window sash chafing his sides. His instinct was to immediately head to the bus station and buy a ticket to as far as the money in his wallet would take him.

On the ground, he calmed down. He went to a café two doors from the museum annex and had a cup of hot chocolate. He sipped at a window table, thinking of curiosity and dead cats.

At exactly 6:45, bells clanged and lights came on. Guards rushed around outside the museum like headless chickens, none of them Elliott. Cop cars arrived. Some beelined into the alley.

Ralph left the café. He knew he should follow his bus station instinct. But between the museum and the station, he caught a city bus instead. He rode southward and got off a quarter mile from the self-storage facility.

He was happy he'd paid extra for a climate-controlled building with wall sockets. Safely inside, Ralph turned on the TV and spent a restless night in his recliner.

~ ~ ~

He had breakfast at a coffee shop in a business park close to home. The museum burglary made the front page of the morning paper. Details were sketchy, but it appeared that a single painting had been stolen, Kennedy Scott's *Pompeii Sunset*.

"The crown jewel of the upcoming Past Century Masters Exhibition," lamented the museum director.

Ironically, the director said, the thief had moved furniture in his own office to access a tiny window and hand *Sunset* out to a waiting confederate. The director had left the window unlatched for ventilation and was inadvertently responsible for a security breach.

Furniture conveniently underneath the window was news to Ralph Crazwell.

The painting was valued at $94.6 million. Carlton Scott, brother of the late artist, who was traveling with the exhibition, was said to be "devastated."

The situation had gone beyond smelling rank. It stunk to high heaven.

Who'd moved the furniture into position and why? Elliott was the logical choice. Was Ralph to be trapped inside when the alarm sounded? And shot by a guard?

Since the painting was already gone, the real thief had presumably chucked it through the window to an accomplice. The cops would figure out or be tipped that a little person had recently been released from prison, an unrehabilitated criminal who could fit through that window.

Ralph stared at city buses as they passed by, working up his courage. However *Pompeii Sunset* got legs and strolled away, the Ripugnantes had used him up to take the fall. It couldn't be otherwise. He finally caught a bus into town. Jimmy's scheme involved the fleabag hotel room he'd sprung for. Had to. There were no other links. Nobody knew of the storage unit.

Ralph preferred operating in broad daylight. Today's winter weather of wind and icy rain was an additional advantage. Your head would be down and you'd be in a rush. If you glanced at him and his delicate features, you'd register: little kid. A second glance and you'd see that he wasn't, but kids didn't warrant a second glance.

Dirty Dean wouldn't be in his room today, watching cartoons. If the Ripugnantes hadn't already planted evidence, Ralph Crazwell was Paul Bunyan. They'd be monitoring the hotel entrance and the alley, no question. What better timing to phone in your anonymous tip than when the suspect and smoking gun were at the same place?

The entrance to the tavern under his room was around the corner on a cross street. Ralph went in waving the newspaper he'd read at breakfast, saying, "Read all about it. Seventy-five cents."

The bartender and a smattering of customers ignored the paperboy.

"May I use your restroom, sir?"

The bartender cocked a thumb toward a hallway that led to the hotel lobby. Ralph passed the restrooms and squinted through a filthy pane in the connecting door. The broken-down lobby sofa and easy chair were unoccupied. The desk clerk was leaning back in his chair, dozing.

Ralph scurried upstairs in a crouch and into his room. Nobody home. He peeked between the curtains for snoopers. There were more crumbling buildings and a parking lot. If the Ripugnante boys were covering the rear, they weren't being obvious.

There'd be a brochure on the Past Century Masters Exhibition in a drawer, he'd bet. And/or a copy of the map Elliott had given him, a big red X marked on *Pompeii Sunset*. The law would have circumstantial evidence coming out of their ears.

Wrong.

No such evidence in plain sight or hidden. Ralph ransacked the nightstand and the closet. He lifted the mattress and rifled the dresser. He searched under the bed and extracted a rolled canvas.

He unrolled *Pompeii Sunset*.

He tried to make sense of the find. The cops could come crashing in any minute and have their burglar and his haul. Open and shut case.

But what was in it for the Ripugnantes? If they couldn't eat, drink, fence or sell it back to the insurance company, they weren't gonna steal it.

Ralph stuffed $94.6 mil worth of fine art into his duffel bag.

~ ~ ~

The walls of the storage unit were unpainted plasterboard. Ralph stood on an upright suitcase and hung *Pompeii Sunset* with tape. He could think of 2 or 3 reasons why it was good for him to have the painting in his possession and 50 why it wasn't.

He thought of the original Tom Thumb, not the thumb-sized creation of English folklore, but a bona fide little person. His name was Charles Sherwood Wilson, a man who lived from 1838 to 1883. Ralph Crazwell felt a commonality with Charles, who had permitted P.T. Barnum to promenade him around the

65

country and Europe, displaying him to the paying rubes. Ralph had permitted himself to be used too, by Jimmy (Feet) Brutto.

At dinnertime, he went out to a nearby convenience store. They didn't have teriyaki, but their chili dogs weren't terrible.

He ate in the recliner, thinking.

At Flagford, he tried to learn at least a new word every day. One of those words was "proactive."

Proactive: Acting in advance to deal with an expected difficulty.

An idea popped into his head too, a proactive solution to his "conundrum", another word of the day.

~ ~ ~

Ralph had been using the restroom in the manager's office after hours; he could pick the lock in his sleep. He shaved extra closely. Stubble was a no-no for a youngster.

He sorted through his wardrobe for the right outfit. What were kids wearing these days? He'd seen floppy pants that bunched up on their shoes. Sweatshirts. Baseball caps on backwards.

He enjoyed a nostalgic moment with an old lunchbox. He wondered if the basketball star on it was still playing. It was an ideal prop for a midday B and E, and had once saved his bacon.

He'd exited a house with a gold watch, diamond earrings and matching tennis bracelet, and $300. A cop slowed alongside and asked why he wasn't in school. Dismissal wasn't for an hour. Ralph hung his head and whined that he wasn't feeling well. The cop said hop in, he'd give him a lift home.

Ralph rattled an address off the top of his head. In the squad car, they talked about the ballplayer on the lunchbox, the great season he was having, his huge contract. To the cop, the lunchbox automatically made him a child, a schoolboy. There was no further scrutiny. The lunchbox was handy too. His loot bulged inside.

Enough nostalgia. He'd try to slip in the tail end of a museum tour group, a youth whose day was being ruined in the name of culture.

~ ~ ~

The annex featured watercolors of animals and birds by well-known artists, an exhibition suitable for adults and the kiddies. A sign announced today's grand opening on the Past Century Masters Exhibition, a wine and cheese party at 4 PM by invitation only. Then admittance to the general public at 7. There were twice as many guards on duty today, none of them Elliott.

As Ralph dug cash out of his wallet to buy a ticket, he noticed a guy flick his cigarette into the gutter and quickstep into the main museum. The guard at the door opened it door promptly. The litterbug didn't break stride. A VIP, obviously. And he looked awfully familiar. The guy was lean and nervous, balding in front.

Elliott, sans mustache and eyeglasses.

No, not quite.

He remembered the art book photo. Kennedy Scott.

No, Scott was dead.

Confused, Ralph stepped out of the ticket line and ran to the main museum and waved his wallet until the guard opened a door.

"Mister, that man who went in a minute ago, he dropped this," he said, his voice raised an octave.

The guard extended a hand. "I'll give it to him."

"No sir," he said, pointing to the line. "My mom in line back there, she said not to give it to anyone except who it belongs to."

67

The guard said that was a good policy and told him to wait. The man came out and turned to stone when he saw Ralph.

"Come in," he said evenly.

"No thanks. Carlton Scott, I presume. The resemblance is, as they say, striking. You come *out*. We're gonna talk."

Carlton Scott came out, saying nothing.

"Have wheels, Carlton?"

"A rental."

"Let's go for a ride."

"Where to?" Carlton Scott asked after they were underway, putting a cigarette in his mouth.

"No smoking."

He threw the unlit cigarette out the window. "You're one of those nicotine Nazis?"

"Carlton, what I am is in the crosshairs of life without parole because of this flimflam of yours."

"What do you want from me?"

"Just drive."

They approached a shopping center. Ralph told him to stop and asked if he was hungry.

Soaked with perspiration, Scott said, "You can't be serious."

Ralph said he was and told Carlton Scott to go into the food court for chicken teriyaki takeout. Scott scrambled out of the car and was back in 15 minutes with the teriyaki.

Ralph dug in and said, "You're not eating? This is delicious."

"Where do you put it?"

"In a black hole. The same place your brother's painting is."

"Then it was you."

"After it was hidden in my hotel room, you mean?"

Carlton Scott didn't answer.

68

"How deep are you into the Ripugnantes, Carlton?"

"I'm not. There is a guard, although his name isn't Elliott. For all intents and purposes, they own him. I'm a partner with them in — this."

"Don't count on it. The Ripugnantes don't have partners. Did the guard rearrange the director's office furniture for my ingress and egress?"

"Yes. We didn't bank on your night vision being so good or your ability to reverse direction in the window."

"At my last home, they fed us a lot of carrots. What's your true story, Carlton?"

"To understate, we Scotts are dysfunctional. I have two living siblings and a herd of shirttail relatives. Everyone wants their slice of Kennedy. I was the closest to him and want my fair share before the jackals carve up this last piece. There wasn't much remaining before *Pompeii Sunset*. I deserve it. I'm not greedy."

"Mighty commendable of you, Mr. Scott. How did you connect with the Ripugnantes?"

"My sister's boyfriend did time for a drug conviction. They were recommended for this venture. I have connections to private art collectors that they don't."

"A synergy made in Heaven. I can think of one logical reason why the painting was not to be recovered when they nabbed me."

"You tell me."

"It's a forgery," Ralph said.

Carlton Scott chewed on a fingernail. He didn't rebut.

"*Pompeii Sunset* wasn't on the wall where you said it'd be, was it?"

"No."

"You or the guard the Ripugnantes own removed it prior to the fun and games, so it was just me and an 8-

foot-high window. After the guard activated the museum alarm, I'd be busted by said guard. He'd probably get a raise. I wouldn't have *Pompeii Sunset* since I'd tossed it out to a buddy in the alley."

Carlton Scott drummed his fingers on the steering wheel.

"I'd have to clam up and take my medicine. I'd either do life or deal the Ripugnantes to the authorities, in which case my lifespan would be inexorably shortened. Inexorably and some of the other words you heard were in my word-per-day program."

Carlton Scott looked at him.

"No denial?"

Scott shrugged.

"I didn't fall through the window into your lap, so you had to go from Plan A to Plan B."

"If you say so."

"You slipped the authentic painting out during the chaos. I'm snitched to the cops. They find the painting in my room. It's easily appraised as a phony. You're quote-unquote devastated. Parties unknown must have pulled a switcheroo at the museum, possibly the unfortunate guard, who may be slated for a fatal accident or a tragic suicide. Meanwhile, the Ripugnantes' buyer has the genuine article. Besides your fee, you and them and your happy family divvy up the proceeds of the insurance claim. Not bad for a guy who isn't greedy."

"I have a proposal," Scott said. "So there're no loose ends, I *have* to have the fake."

"How much?"

"Two hundred thousand dollars, which is a third of my advance payment."

Ralph whistled softly. Two hundred grand. He could open a teriyaki joint for $200,000 and have plenty leftover.

"Sounds good to me. Come to this address tonight at seven," Ralph said, writing his hotel and room number on an unused teriyaki napkin. "You have my money, I'll have the fake painting."

"Agreed."

"Don't think of showing early to ambush me. You'll never find me. You'll never find the painting."

"I'm a man of my word," he said huffily.

"And if you know what's good for you, you won't call in Jimmy Feet."

"Absolutely not. Believe me, the Ripugnantes are out of the loop now. They'll cut their losses after this fiasco."

What Ralph didn't believe was almost everything. He was thinking this at 6:55 as he mounted a barstool at a seedy sports pub cattycorner from the hotel.

The bartender scrutinized his ID as if it were counterfeit money. There was no teriyaki per se on the menu, just a teriyaki burger. He ordered one and a beer, and watched an NBA game on a big screen. To him, the players loomed like Jack's beanstalk giant.

The burger arrived. He took a bite and judged it as fair-to-middling. At 7:05, on his second beer, Ralph heard sirens. No reaction from the clientele. In this neighborhood it was the nightly symphony. The sirens grew louder and persisted. There was a throbbing glow of flashing lights.

A customer 3 stools from Ralph volunteered to check out the commotion.

The customer came back with a thirst and an odd story. The bartender drew him a free draught for his initiative, listened to the tale, and said he didn't understand how you could kill yourself jumping or falling out of a second-story window.

"Yeah, he's a mess," said the investigator. "They're sure it was a burglar. He had fake glasses and a false mustache that fell off when he went kersplat."

Either Carlton had sold me out, Ralph thought, or Jimmy Feet had been staking out his room. Jimmy didn't trust Carlton either, especially with no painting and no Tom Thumb.

Carlton had had *Pompeii Sunset* painted or he'd done it himself.

Who *couldn't* paint it, Ralph thought?

Otherwise, Carlton would not have wanted to get his hands on that forgery so badly, to cover his miserable ass and to avoid complications with the insurance company and its $94.6 million obligation.

Perhaps Jimmy Feet had also discovered that *Pompeii Sunset* was a sham. He would not be amused. He and/or Dirty Dean had no legit painting, but they had one less witness.

Ralph sighed. He didn't have two hundred large, but he still had his skin.

You couldn't trust anybody these days.

Myriad perfidy – two former words of the day.

The bartender served Ralph another teriyaki burger and asked where he put it.

EINSTEIN'S SPACE-TIME CONTINUUM IS A CAR WRECK

Chick Chipperfield arrived bright and early at the lot, around ten-thirty. With a throbbing head and without enthusiasm, he played back the answering machine that was blinking its little heart out.

"Mr. Chipperfield, this is Alma Spangler *again*. This time the car lost a wheel on the freeway. It was a terrible experience and very dangerous. I insist that you – "

Chick shut it off, thinking that he'd get rid of the damn thing if didn't stop being so negative. Alma Spangler was an old bat with weird eyes who said she'd come into a little money lately and wanted to "spread her wings behind the wheel."

She'd bought a 6-year-old sport coupe a few weeks ago. How many times had he already told her, hey, when you buy secondhand transportation you're in your basic caveat emptor mode?

The phone rang and it was Gordy from Channel 136. He'd had a change of schedule and was right up the street, taping a spot for Eddie's Discount Furniture. Eddie was having another of his closeout sales and Gordy was sweating bullets.

"I don't like the way he's acting, Chick. I normally do you and Eddie on Tuesdays but he bumped me up a day. I want the spot in the can and paid for and aired before he has a fire sale that's the genuine article."

"Yeah, yeah, okay Gordo, gimme twenty minutes," Chick said.

Chick dug out his devil's costume and slipped it on. It was made of plastic and as hot as you-know-where. He'd been out late, socializing with friends and acquaintances, and the outfit wasn't doing his hangover one bit of good. He grabbed his pitchfork and went outside to look for a beater.

Anybody who watched Channel 136's Midnight Movierama was familiar with Chick Chipperfield of Chipperfield's Pre-owned Automotive Elegance. This week he was a prime sponsor of the Troy Donahue Film festival, along with Last Chance Insurance Agency and Cut n' Chop Kitchen Miracles.

Behind the office was a blue mid-90s Chevy Caprice he'd never seen before. He assumed Bruno, his sales manager, had taken it in on trade late yesterday. The front end was cockeyed and tire tread was ancient history. It had so many dings and rust spots, it looked like it'd come down with the measles, although the rear-end was semi-okay.

Gordy pulled in and hurriedly set up his videotape gear. He was a kid with a bushy perm and the metabolism of a hummingbird. He kept glancing down the highway, past the muffler shops and fast food to Eddie's.

"Chick, I'd appreciate it if we could wrap fast. I gotta get Eddie's check to the bank. I swear I smell gasoline."

"Relax. They don't call me One Take Chipperfield for nothing."

Chick went through his standard spiel, going from car to car, marking down already low low low prices. Then the grand finale. He patted the Caprice on the trunk, pointed at the camera, said, "Chick Chipperfield has one *hell* of a deal for you", then proceeded to beat the living daylights out of it with his pitchfork.

Viewers loved his shtick. Ate it up.

Evidently Chick forgot his own strength because the trunk lid popped open. He looked inside, expecting to see soiled carpeting and a bald spare tire, but instead there was a corpse curled in the fetal position. Chick couldn't make much of the bloodied face, but he immediately recognized him from the clothing.

White patent leather shoes and matching belt. Green slacks, green and purple checkered jacket, radioactive purple tie. The threads were worn by the only gink who Chick felt could compete with him in terms of sartorial splendor: Sincere Sam Selkirk of Sincere Sam's Quality Euro Imports.

This was not good, Chick realized. Sam's lot was 4 blocks up the road. Him and Sam went way back together. They'd both broken into the automotive sales profession under the legendary Maniac Monahan. It was also no secret that they hated each other's guts.

Chick gently closed the trunk lid and turned to ask if they had a wrap. First things first. But Gordo had fainted dead away. Chick helped him to his feet and trudged to his office, deciding that he'd better think things out before he did anything rash, like calling the cops.

Somebody out on the highway was laying on his horn. Chick turned around and there was Sincere Sam, stopped, holding up traffic, behind the wheel of an old Mercedes 450 SL that was so trashed Rommel could've used it as a staff car at Tobruk.

Sam gave Chick a wide grin and the finger, and peeled rubber. Chick struggled into the office with the woozy Gordo, thinking that he'd better quit mixing his drinks, especially when he was eating Mexican food.

~ ~ ~

Meanwhile, Mrs. Orville (Alma) Spangler was at her wit's end. She'd just gotten off the phone with a 1-800 lawyer she'd found in the yellow pages, Alvin

Selkirk. Mr. Selkirk wasn't interested in taking the case on a contingency. Cash on the barrelhead, he'd said, asking for a deposit equal to what her deceased Orville made in a month.

Problem was, he said, there were neither witnesses to all the promises Chipperfield made, nor anything on paper. Without more to go on, an alleged verbal warranty wasn't going to do her much good. He ended by advising her to buy her next used car from his brother, Sincere Sam Selkirk, an honest man.

Alma already had copies of letters the Better Business Bureau and the Attorney General's Consumer Protection Division had written to the used car dealer. For what benefit they would be, she thought. Both agencies knew Chipperfield's Pre-Owned Automotive Elegance well.

She looked out to the street from her dingy apartment and sighed. The silver coupe with the racing stripes and alloy wheels and smoked glass was her dream car. It was the first major purchase she had ever made on her own.

Her only real income other than sewing had been blackmail of a cross-dresser who lived across the street from her. She knew that sooner or later the law would pounce if she kept *that* up.

Mr. Chipperfield was loud and he dressed garishly. His cologne was oppressively strong, his television advertising outrageous, but he had seemed *so* honest and genuine in person. He'd been so patient as he explained the attributes of the powerful engine.

He hadn't, however, explained how much a turbocharger cost when it went out. The little squeaking noise he claimed was in her imagination turned out to be brakes way overdue for relining. Which she couldn't afford after replacing the turbocharger and paying for the freeway mishap. Not to mention the rusted-out muffler and the turn signal malfunction that nobody could diagnose. And the leak around the sunroof. A mechanic who had been under the car said it had been in a wreck. An entire body section had been welded on, like some hideous Frankenstein experiment.

Mr. Chipperfield told her just to call if anything went wrong, and that he'd take care of it. Well, she had called and had received a torrent of abuse for her effort. On the occasions she'd driven by the lot, Mr. Chipperfield wasn't there and his second-in-command frightened her, a creature named Bruno. He looked like he should have become extinct during the last Ice Age.

Alma Spangler checked her makeup, got her purse, and took a deep breath. She was unaccustomed to confrontation, but today that was about to change. She was going to march right into Mr. Chipperfield's office and demand that he do the right thing by her. She was determined to stay there as long as it took.

~ ~ ~

"I don't get it," Chick whined. "Me and Sam were like brothers. That isn't to say we didn't have what you'd call your basic business rivalry going on, but we were pros and had a mutual respect, irregardless of any gossip you may of heard to the contrary."

"You don't have to convince me, Chick. I'm not the police," Gordy said.

They were in Chick's office, drinking bad coffee. It was a converted house trailer, made stiflingly hot by Chick's insistence on keeping windows and doors shut, and blinds drawn. On the wall behind Chick's desk were framed photographs of Maniac Monahan, Richard Milhous Nixon, and a Playmate of the Month. He hadn't mentioned the Sincere Sam hallucination.

"Don't say that p-word, Gordo. It looks bad for me. Bruno, you're sure you haven't laid eyes on the unit before?"

Bruno, Chick's sales manager, had reported for work a few minutes ago. If anybody ever accused Chipperfield's Pre-Owned Automotive Elegance of not being an equal opportunity employer, all Chick had to do was point out Bruno, whom he was mainstreaming back into productive society after a stretch for armed robbery.

"Nope. I folded the tent last night at eight sharp and it wasn't there. I checked it over. The engine hasn't been steam-cleaned and the odometer hasn't been rolled back. It ain't one of ours."

"Don't joke in front of Gordo. He might get the wrong idea," Chick quickly said, then stood. "Since it's not our car and we didn't whack out Sincere Sam, I'm gonna take it and him for a ride. Bruno, follow me to the airport. I'll dump it in the parking garage, the way it's done when the Mob's involved, and there's no reason to think they ain't. Sam, the disreputable sleazoid bastard, Lord rest his soul, he could have been mixed up in damn near anything."

"Chick, you can't just pretend it didn't happen," Gordy said desperately.

"The hell we can't," Chick said. "You didn't do a zoom into the trunk, did you? Let's see. Play it again, Gordo."

"I – can't look, Chick."

"Gordo, I'm a loyal advertising client who's gonna walk off into the sunset unless you help out. You can run *Palm Springs Weekend* and *Susan Slade* free gratis for all I care. I'll be out of your life faster'n you can say Connie Stevens."

Gordy stared through his viewfinder as he played the videotape. "I don't understand, Chick. Have a look."

Chick played the tape, then played it again. Bruno played the tape, and Gordy viewed it once more. Chick said, "So we're in agreement that it's a normal shoot, except at the end where it goes blurry on account of Gordo keeling over?"

"Yeah. The camera shows the trunk loud and clear," Bruno said. "There ain't nothing in it. You guys on something?"

"I can't speak for Gordo, but the Chickster may of gotten into some bad guacamole at Lucille's," Chick said, referring to the topless bar where he'd whiled away the evening. "I'm going out to see for myself."

"Since this is resolved, I'll be running along," Gordy said, literally running along.

"I got hoods to raise and air fresheners to change," Bruno said.

Sure enough, the trunk of the Caprice was clean as a whistle except for the filthy carpet and the rust-through in the floorboards. He rummaged through the glove box for a title, figuring he'd phone an auto wrecker and have the Chevy hauled away and put to sleep. Nothing there, nothing clipped to the visors either.

As he stepped out, Chick was startled by the metal-on-metal squeal of bad brakes. The silver sport coupe stopped bare inches from him, its turn signals blinking wildly. A middle-aged woman with short gray hair and creepy eyes jumped out and faced him. Not a happy camper, he observed; she'd be a sure bet for a gold medal in the Olympic scowling competition.

"You'd better have the front end looked at, lady," Chick advised. "Somebody could get hurt."

79

"That somebody could be you, Mr. Chipperfield, unless you do the right thing."

He recognized her now. She was that old Spangler broad who'd been harassing him on the phone. "Are you stalking me? That's illegal, you know."

She slowly shut her driver's door. The hinges sounding like a tortured mouse. She calmly raised both arms, her hands wrapped around the butt of the biggest, baddest revolver Chick had ever seen.

"Liar, liar, pants on fire."

By then, Chick Chipperfield was scramming down the alley. Going-to-rotund and not as young as he used to be, he was nevertheless picking them up and putting them down at a pretty decent clip. Alma Spangler's gun boomed like a cannon. Slugs zinged off the pavement and raised sparks on masonry walls.

Chick rounded the corner and stumbled onto the lot from the front, panting. "Bruno, gimme the keys."

"To what?"

"I don't give a flying rat's ass. This piece a shit here is okay."

"Something wrong, boss? Is that firecrackers being set off in the alley?"

Chick grabbed the keys, slammed the hood, and flung away the *ONLY $2999!!!! High Performance on a Low Budget!!!!!* sign Bruno had slipped under a wiper blades of a jacked-up Subaru with a spoiler and hood scoop.

He drove the rice rocket to the swank subdivision to the home of his mentor and guru, Maniac Monahan. Without question, the Maniac was a creative genius. Chick remembered him when he was a tiny little kid, squinting at his family's fuzzy 17-inch black-and-white Raytheon as the Maniac Reddiwipped sale prices on windshields, challenging anybody to beat 'em, flashing the evil grin that earned him his nickname. Man, you were hooked.

Chick parked in the driveway of the Maniac's spacious split-level, between two of Maniac's tail-finned land yachts. He loved old Detroit iron. It was a goddamn crime, Chick thought, that kinescopes of his spots hadn't been preserved and enshrined in the Smithsonian. Whenever he came out here, he felt he was on a pilgrimage, like those Buddhists who went to Mecca.

Maniac came out of a side gate and greeted Chick. He was a wiry little guy in his mid-80s with wispy gray hair and a big schnoz. He was wearing Old McDonald coveralls and carrying a bag of potting soil. It saddened Chick to see the Maniac like this. He'd been a giant in the profession, Mr. Cool if there ever was one.

When Chick was an automotive sales rookie, he fondly recalled jet-black hair slicked back, the snazziest threads imaginable, and a line of bat guano that gave every cocktail waitress in town weak knees and a severe case of hyperventilation.

"Chick, you okay? You look like you seen a ghost."

"I have, except unfortunately he wasn't."

"Boy, you better come in the yard and have a cold one. June and the baby are at her sister's for the day."

June was Maniac's latest future ex-wife. It had tickled him pink that at his age he could snag a young babe and procreate besides, although they were disappointed that June couldn't breast feed the munchkin on account of the silicone. For a wedding present, Chick had given Maniac a jar of potency enhancer he'd bought from an Oriental herbalist. It was guaranteed to out-Viagra Viagra. On that basis, he took some credit for the couple's bundle of joy.

Chick sat at the patio as Maniac mixed gin and tonics. The brick barbecue was a little cockeyed, but

Maniac had built it with his own two hands. Chick remembered the days when Maniac's crafts talents consisted primarily of unhooking a bra one-handed and squirting ether into carburetors of beaters so they'd start when some gink had the gall to ask for a test drive. Times, they do change.

Maniac brought the drinks and listened to Chick's story. He turned pale and stared at his shoes for a moment before saying, "Chick. You're thinking you were having a case of the D.T.'s? I'm gonna tell you you weren't. I'm gonna tell you something I never told nobody, including my wives. Remember how quicklike I retired from the profession."

"Sure do. Here today, gone tomorrow. It was about twenty years ago, wasn't it? We all figured you had bucks galore and wanted to enjoy it."

"Twenty-one years next month, Chick. You ever study Einstein's Theory of Inevitability, that $E=mc^2$ thing?"

"Nah. I never took philosophy. Algebra gave me enough trouble."

"That don't matter. How I'm gonna explain it to you ain't exactly the way it is in the books anyhow. Einstein was a whiz at math, but he was a nerd in other respects. He didn't grasp the real importance of what he'd come up with. I kind of doped it out for myself after my own experiences."

"Experiences like I just had?"

"Uh huh. One after another." Maniac ticked them off on bony, soiled fingers. "An auditor from the IRS paid me a call, a mean son of a bitch who said Al Capone got off easy in comparison to what was in store for me. A detective from Fraud Detail with so many arrest warrants he carried 'em in a basket. Mike Wallace and a *60 Minutes* camera crew barged in and asked insulting questions. A couple of goons with saps and piano wire who said I'd defaulted on a loan slapped me around and said it was my last friendly warning. All this happened in the space of a week."

"I still don't get it."

Maniac Monahan sighed and asked slowly, "Chick, you didn't off Sincere Sam, did you?"

"I swear I didn't."

"I had to ask. You and Sam were bad chemistry. You youngsters were at each other's throats from the git-go and've been backbiting ever since. That gal with the nasty disposition, she didn't pump lead in your direction, did she?"

"That don't mean she's not stalking me."

"Chick, try to picture flood water rising up against a dam that ain't designed to handle so much, so fast. Einstein said time was relative, but he was talking about galaxies and continuums and outer space, shit like that. He was mixed up on terminology and location. His theory was right on the button, except it shoulda been a helluva lot closer to home."

"How'd the dam hold up?"

"Piss poor. Water was lapping over the rim. See, I didn't do *all* them things those folks accused me of. Oh yeah, sure, some at one stage or another. Others, maybe I'd been considering in the back of my mind. These events were backing up super fast, like the water. Time got compressed somehow and went kablooey! If I hadn't of thrown in the towel, I'm convinced the dam would of burst and flooded the valley."

"Mike Wallace really didn't visit?"

"Nope, but you can bet your sweet bippy they had a segment scheduled on me. It was inevitable."

"Einstein's law quit dinking with you when you retired?"

"Instantly. You know what you gotta do, boy."

"I don't know if I'm ready for anything that drastic. But I'm gonna go by Sam's lot just in case I need to pay my respects."

"Promise me, Chick."

"I'll give it some real close thought."

Maniac Monahan shook his head sadly. "It could be your funeral, not his. You been forewarned. Your dam's a rising."

~ ~ ~

Alma Spangler's courage wavered. She drove around and around the block, hoping to see Mr. Chipperfield outside with his pathetic rows of clunkers. She was sure she couldn't just march into his office and lay down the law. Perhaps he isn't here, she rationalized; perhaps I should do this another day.

She made one last circuit, this time through the alley. Mr. Chipperfield's Neanderthal employee was standing behind the office, scratching a head that was far too small for his body. He was perusing a parking slot, as if something had fallen out of his pocket.

Alma gritted her teeth and steeled her nerve. She accelerated forward, then braked. The combination of grinding and flashing signal lights startled the man, giving Alma a momentary psychological advantage.

"Please have Mr. Chipperfield come out for a minute," she demanded. "I'm not leaving until he sees me."

The look on her face was serious, Serious with a capital C, like she was sucking on a lime, the typical sourpuss look of an unreasonable customer. She was kinda familiar, but Bruno couldn't quite place her. He had his mind of other things. Like where was that beater that had Sam in the trunk except it didn't. And those little bastards firing off the cherry bombs, where'd they gone to? And the boss, his face the color

84

of a rotten tomato, fishtailing down the highway in that hot-rod Subaru like a bat outta hell?

Bruno couldn't fathom any of it, but suddenly inspired, he said, "He ain't here. Chick said to refer complaints to a colleague in the business. He'll fix you up fine and dandy, no charge."

Bruno gave her directions to Sincere Sam's Quality Euro Imports and waved bye-bye at a rooster tail of blue smoke. If Sam was slick enough to rise from the dead, he could finesse her out of their hair.

~ ~ ~

Chick smelled something fishy as he drove to Sincere Sam's Quality Euro Imports. He was beginning to suspect an elaborate plot to scare him out of business. Him and Sam were like sons to the Maniac, but Chick always had a nagging hunch that Selkirk was his favorite. This in spite of Sam's bad genes, him having a local 1-800-WHIPLASH lawyer for a brother.

Confucius or somebody had said that you can't bullshit a bullshitter. In the automotive sales profession, 2 plus 2 equaled either 3 or 5, depending on whether you were buying or selling, and nobody knew the math better than Chick Chipperfield. He'd go pay a courtesy call on Sam and just see if a lowball offer for Chipperfield's Pre-Owned Automotive Elegance uttered forth from his lizard lips.

He stopped at the lot first, to check if anything was going on. There were no customers, but Bruno was on the sidewalk with some suit carrying a clipboard. The suit was pointing at the drain and Bruno was shaking his head.

The suit gave Chick a business card when he asked what was the problem.

"Henshaw. State Department of Ecology," Chick read. "You're lost, bub. Take the third left and go seven thousand miles. Chernobyl will be glowing on your right."

Henshaw pointed at the drain again. "Waste Water Management filed a report on your operation, Mr. Chipperfield. Engine oil and other fluids have been seeping from your, uh, merchandise. Your people on numerous occasions were observed pouring solvent on the lot and hosing the fluids into the drain."

How the hell else were you supposed to get rid of it, Chick thought?

"These stool pigeons, whoever they are, they're mistaken."

Henshaw tore a copy of a citation from his clipboard and handed it to Chick. "Well, you're perfectly entitled to tell your side of the story at your hearing."

Chick grinned and tore up the citation. "You can stick your hearing in a warm, dark place, pal. Einstein's dinking with me again. You don't even exist."

~ ~ ~

Alma Spangler could hardly believe her luck. Since she hadn't had much lately, she didn't, not entirely. She didn't reveal her mixed emotions to Mr. Selkirk, though. He seemed like such a nice man, but so had Mr. Chipperfield.

"I can hardly believe my luck," Alma said in Sincere Sam's office, as a contract lay before her to sign.

"Obviously Mr. Chipperfield lied to me. Your salesman with the charming accent sympathized with my plight and referred me directly to the top, to you. Not only are you offering me what I paid for that horrible coupe as a trade-in, you're letting me have that lovely red German convertible at a wholesale price."

Sincere Sam Selkirk wore an orange seersucker suit, black shirt, yellow tie and aviator sunglasses. He smiled sincerely, displaying a wide array of Chiclet teeth that contrasted dramatically with his close-cropped gray hair and deep tan.

Though he looked in the pink, he hadn't been feeling well. He feared something was going screwy inside his head. Last night he dreamt Gottlieb Daimler and Karl Benz were in his bedroom, wagging fingers at him and saying he was a naughty boy. One little problem: he was wide-awake at the time.

"*Nearly* wholesale, Alma. I do have to make an honest profit."

Alma sighed. "I wish Mr. Chipperfield adhered to that code. I swear, there are times when I feel like just shooting him."

Selkirk shook his head. "Chick and I entered the profession at the same time. I took one fork in the road. Sadly, he took the other. Now, Alma, will you want us to be financing the car?"

~ ~ ~

Chick parked across from Sincere Sam's to reconnoiter. The lot was as normal lined with Beemers and Benzes past their prime, units formerly owned by tight-assed yuppie housewives too wrapped up in their creative writing classes and fashion-show luncheons to quite get around to adding oil and water. Not to mention staying clear of neighboring fenders and doors at the mall.

No sign of Sam, though. Just his salesmen circling the lot like vultures.

They spotted Chick before he had both feet out of the Camaro. A couple of Hitler Youth types named Wolfgang and Hans exchanged nervous glances and hurried into Sincere Sam Selkirk's office, a fake Swiss chalet. Chick followed cautiously, aware that something was up.

~ ~ ~

Mrs. Orville (Alma) Spangler picked up the pen Mr. Selkirk had thoughtfully provided. It was heavy in her hand. The further she studied the contract, the larger the numbers appeared to be and the smaller the print became. Mr. Selkirk's glorious smile seemed to be locked, lowering the temperature of the room.

Alma really didn't know what to do, but was saved from the need to make an immediate decision when that nice salesman in the lederhosen and one of his colleagues came crashing into the office, red-faced and wide-eyed.

Sam Selkirk gritted his Chiclet teeth. He wanted buyers to feel they were at Stuttgart, at the cutting edge of German engineering. He hired salesmen not on the basis of intelligence, but for their resemblance to old photos of SS officers, and their willingness to slightly alter their names and to affect Prussian accents. These two, Wally and Hal, Sam thought; what a pair to draw to.

"What's up, gents?" he asked coolly.

"Ach, outen zee lot," Wolfgang/Wally said with a heel click.

Sam looked out and a window and saw Chick Chipperfield advancing. He was in that stupid devil's costume and was carrying his pitchfork at port arms, ready to use it.

"I call nine-vun-vun, boss?" Hans/Hal asked.

Alma Spangler took a deep breath. "Mr. Selkirk, I refuse to sign. The car is too expensive."

If he lived through this, Sincere Sam Selkirk would go sit at the knee of his mentor, Maniac Monahan, and see if he could make some sense out of the day. Not that it'd do him any good, he thought bitterly. Chipperfield was the Maniac's fair-haired boy.

"Mr. Selkirk, will you please answer me?"

If a civilian was caught in the middle and got hurt, he'd be in deep doo-doo with the fuzz, he knew. He crossed out the price, entered one for half that amount, and initialed the correction.

"Oh my," Alma said as she hurriedly signed.

"Boss?" Hans/Hal pleaded.

"Nah," Sam said, reaching into his desk drawer. "I'll take care of this myself. Chipperfield's been a thorn in my side for years. It'll be self-defense."

Alma screamed when Sincere Sam took a monstrous revolver from his desk. She grabbed her copy of the contract and ran out the door, nearly bumping into Mr. Chipperfield.

She brushed his temple with the revolver.

"Don't shoot!" he screamed.

"He has a gun and is going to kill you," she screamed, shoving by him.

Sam stormed outside and fired. He wasn't a crack shot; the bullet popped a balloon strung on a banner. The recoil from the shot sent his second round skyward, where it shattered the glass in his rotating, blinking sign.

Gun, gun, who's got the fucking gun? Chick thought helplessly.

"Drop the pitchfork, Chipperfield," Sam ordered, gun shaking in his hand.

"I wish I had it, you oily scumbag!"

A thunderous collision distracted both gunman and intended victim. A 1957 DeSoto Fireflite sedan the size of a locomotive bounded over the curb and sheared off the fender of a hapless BMW 320i that had been marked down to $6999. A CBS van stopped across the street.

Maniac Monahan climbed out of the three-tone land yacht and shook a fist at Chick. "I warned you, boy! See what you done? The Mob blew up my house ten minutes ago."

"I been telling you for years, Maniac, Chipperfield's rotten to the core," Sam Selkirk cried from the porch of his faux chalet.

"You got a lot to talk about, boy. Look out behind you."

But it was too late. Wolfgang/Wally and Hans/Hal were riding through the doorway atop an avalanche of lemons that buried Sam. Simultaneously, a horde of unhappy customers advanced on the lot, car keys in one hand, torches in the other. The ground began to tremble and lightning crackled in the darkening sky.

"The dam burst, boy," Maniac told Chick in fearful resignation. "And it wasn't your dam or my dam. It was *our* dam."

What Alma Spangler saw in her mirrors struck her as some sort of Biblical cataclysm, the booming noises and flashing lights and unearthly howling. But probably not. Something awful like a ruptured gas main that exploded, she assumed. Maybe she'd find out on the evening news.

The sky was blue above her. She pushed a button and the convertible top came down. The mechanism worked perfectly, just as Mr. Selkirk had promised.

BANANA REPUBLIC GOES BANANAS

The coup took place while Susan and I were having lunch.

We were at the Hotel San Augustin's outdoor café when a Jeep full of soldiers in green fatigues came around the corner and skidded to a halt. They piled out into the dust they had stirred, then began jabbering and pointing upward. They had been drinking and none looked to be older than 19.

"What on earth?" Susan said.

She was a statue: Blond Gringa Holding Mediocre Chardonnay.

"You tell me," I said. "They're fixated on that street sign."

After their conference, a soldier backed the Jeep to the signpost. Another, standing on a seat, steadied by his unsteady comrades, bashed the sign with the butt of his rifle until it broke off.

"Calle Mendoza. *Calle* is street," I said, paging through our *Guide to Tierrahermosa*. "Mendoza, if it's the same one, he's their president."

A soldier sat on another's shoulders and strapped on a crude replacement with duct tape: Calle de la Revolusion.

"Maybe Ex-president Mendoza," I said. "They misspelled *revolución*."

Susan said, "It wasn't supposed to happen, not this fast."

The soldiers cheered their handiwork and sped to the next corner. We heard a distant backfire, although there was no reason to believe it wasn't a gunshot.

"Well, I think I'm done," I said, shoving aside my plate. "We ought to go to the U.S. Embassy, see what's going on. You know, just in case."

Susan said, "There isn't one here, not even a consulate. The embassy's in Dulzura. If it's still open."

Tierrahermosa was a Central American backwater, the prototype of a banana republic. It was hot and steamy, landlocked but for a toe dipped in the Caribbean. A spiny line of hills ran along its curved spine. Dulzura was the capital, 20 kilometers to the south. We were in San Agustin, Tierrahermosa's second largest city. Dulzura meant sweetness, named for sugar cane, once upon a time the country's sole cash crop. San Agustin honored a 16th-century friar who had flogged the love of Jesus into the heathen Indians.

A protracted taxi ride to lunch had delivered us to San Agustin. Whoever was to meet us here hadn't shown, the subject of our latest argument. He'd been a contact of a contact of a contact, the blindest of blind dates without even a name, for God's sake. Our last tropical Americas visit was to Cancun, three years ago, a rare vacation. Cancun cabbies were slick, ready to accommodate you for a peso, but this was ridiculous.

Besides, we were here on business. At least Susan was. Sugar was still king in Tierrahermosa, but the veins of copper in the hills were gaining fast, thanks to the metal increasing slightly in value the past year. Meth freaks at home were snipping live power lines to steal copper, giving themselves permanent perms.

Copper was Susan's bailiwick: senior vice-president of a firm that consulted to the industry. She'd been dispatched to Tierrahermosa to take a reading on the political instability, to read between the lines as it pertained to the mining and exportation of copper.

I was along for the ride. I am a house husband. Since we have no children or even pets for which to care, "house husband" was a euphemism for chronically unemployed. I'd been a freelance housing consultant, but the wheels came off that gig and I haven't been able to latch onto anything since.

"It probably wouldn't be wise to go exploring today," I said.

"No, probably not."

"There could be roadblocks."

"Can you imagine?" Susan said. "This little country turned inside out and we were there."

"We should go somewhere," I advised, looking around, feeling naked under the frayed cloth umbrella. "All of a sudden, our waiter's gone and nobody's on the streets."

Susan placed her hand over mine, digging her nails in. "Upstairs, then. We'll get a room."

~ ~ ~

If you're thinking spontaneous passion, forget it. Those days are behind us. Susan tried to nap. I couldn't either.

We watched the ceiling fan laze around, paddling thick slabs of humid air. Then the fan stopped.

I turned on the TV. "It isn't working either. Power's off, but what the hell, the price is right."

Compared to Cancun it was. There, you could max out every piece of plastic in your wallet without half trying. The *Guide to Tierrahermosa* gave the San Agustin two stars. It had hot water, which we were advised not to drink. For $20 a night you couldn't beat it. That is, if you were on your own rather than on Susan's expense account.

She said, "When there's a coup, the first thing they do is blow up the utilities."

"You can take the peasant guerrilla out of the jungle, but you can't take jungle out of the peasant guerrilla," I said.

"That is not helpful. We should call somebody."

"If the room had a phone," I added. "Our cell phones haven't worked since we've been here."

I opened the wooden shutters a crack and looked down on the leafy central plaza. "Still deserted. Who can blame them? They're having a coup and it's also siesta time."

The ceiling fan began turning.

"Saved," I said, switching on the TV again.

The hotel offered cable television. A soccer game was on the only channel. There was toilet paper on the field. It was ringed by advertisements for cigarettes and beer, brands we'd never heard of.

The screen went black. A moment later, a small man in a white uniform with dark glasses stood at a podium, reviewing a raggedy column of troops. His shoulder boards looked like ingots. Scene shift to the jungle. The same man, in creased khakis, arms folded, mentored a rapt audience of infantrymen.

Next shot. The man in shortsleeved civvies, at a table, holding a cigarette, droning through a prepared statement. The camerawork was jerky and a caption read *en vivo*.

He was General Diaz. He read seemingly without punctuation, but Susan picked up bits and pieces. She had minored in Romance Languages.

"General Diaz is now President Diaz," she said.

"Leader of the coup."

"He calls it a revolution. Independence. Freedom from tyranny."

"I feel better."

"Diaz says the change of government was peaceful, with little loss of life. He promises to schedule free democratic elections once the situation stabilizes."

"Right."

"Essentially he's saying it's okay to come out. Nobody will be harmed."

"Would you buy a used car from that man?"

"I should be scared, but I'm not? Is there something wrong with me?"

I was scared because she wasn't. "Well, you asked for it."

"Leave it alone."

"How can I? You started again on the exciting combination of business and soft adventure when we got into the cab. How Ted and Marla rafted the Mississippi on whoopee cushions."

She knew I was teasing and softened, almost smiling. "No, Brie and Marc rafted the Colorado. Ted and Marla swam in the Ganges, actually only Marla."

I held up my hands and made a face. "And a week after they came home we ate a salad she tossed."

She grabbed a little finger and bent it back, a tad harder than playfully. "And you'd just love to finish out the week hanging around some palapa bar pounding down *cervezas*."

"That was always good enough for you too."

She released me, but not before a twist. "Let's calm down and decide what to do."

That was the first hint of physical abuse by either of us in our years together. I stared until she apologized and kissed my pinkie to make it well.

"This place, it's like some weird theme park I don't ever remember hearing of."

"Theme parks don't come with dust and guerrillas firing off guns."

We were certain it was too hot to sleep but didn't awaken until sundown. We wore our YUPPIE SCUM AND PROUD OF IT T-shirts, downstairs to the hotel's dining room, to dinner. Susan said they'd send a strong message that we were educated and professional

95

American citizens and weren't about to be pushed around.

We ate inside, figuring there might be rabble-rousers in the streets who hadn't gotten the word the coup was over. We ate tough beefsteak. I drank *Tigre Aureo*, a local brew advertised in the soccer game. Susan had a couple of shots of *aguafuego*. According to the guidebook, it was the national alcoholic beverage, distilled from some gnarled cacti that grew in the Tierrahermosan foothills. Since we were stuck here, Susan was determined to experience it in the fullest. She chased her second shot with water, so it didn't taste quite so much like kerosene.

The only other patron was an American, a large florid man with a gray ponytail, his name was Mike. He'd been reading a supermarket tabloid.

Mike worked for a Texas company that manufactured packaging for bananas. We bought him what he was drinking – Jamaican rum on the rocks – and Susan asked if the coup was really ideological, like Diaz claimed.

Mike laughed. "It's about bidness and power, and it's personal. Mendoza and Diaz are ex brothers-in-law."

"Nothing said about undoing the shackles of the workers, anything in that context?" Susan asked.

Mike laughed harder.

"I asked, "Who are the rebel leaders?"

"Lieutenant colonels and deputy assistant ministers who weren't getting a big enough piece of the pie. Forget the barefoot partisan crapola. Those soldiers whooping it up in the street are garrison troops."

"It isn't a communist thing?" I asked. "Backed by Havana?"

"That's pretty much obsolete, although Diaz'll probably carry on squeezing foreign aid out of us on account of the Cuban menace in the region. Mendoza had the knack too."

I could hear Susan's wheels turning. Reduced copper output because of the turmoil would give the metal's price a boost. "Is there a menace?"

Mike smiled, shook his head, and rattled the ice cubes in his empty glass. "Like most people, Cubans and Russians and Chinese don't know Tierrahermosa exists. What brings you kids here?"

"I wanted our travel agent to be creative," Susan said quickly. The subject of copper was between her and me. "Something untouristy and off the beaten track, yet warm and Latin. We've done Montego Bay and the rest to death."

Mike sipped his rum. "Well, you got it, you got your off-the-beaten-path."

"It's kind of fun how the Tierrahermosans stare at you, like you're Martians," Susan said.

"You been out to see the ruin?" Mike asked.

"Is La Ceiba really worth the trip?" Susan said.

"Definitely. You'll have the place to yourself. I definitely recommend it. Head out there fast. Who knows how this thing'll play out? Everything might be shut down for a while."

La Ceiba was a major pre-Columbian site, less than 60 kilometers from San Agustin. An entire chapter in the guidebook was devoted to the ruin.

I added, "You're sure it'll be safe out there in the middle of nowhere?"

Mike said, "Safe? Probably. This coup thing is spreading like an oil slick. It takes its time getting to the hinterlands. I didn't know anything had happened until I returned to town this afternoon. Mendoza and Diaz are peas in a pod, except Diaz loves Chinese food and Mendoza doesn't. Those dudes have no shortage of appetites. As far as La Ceiba goes, it's not Palenque or Tikal, but it's the best ruin they got."

"*El presidente* said little loss of life," Susan said, getting the coup topic back on track.

Mike shrugged. "I heard fifteen or twenty dead, more or less, and these were old grudges settled. Some others are missing. You can bet they've been disappeared."

"Not good," Susan said. "We'll do the ruin, then head up the coast to the beach."

Beach? I said nothing.

Mike looked at me, reading my hesitation, and said, "You know, you can sort of do a ruin right in town without going there. You've seen the main cathedral?"

I do believe he was reading me, goading me. "On the other side of the Central Plaza?"

"Yeah. The first big things the Spaniards built were cathedrals. You needed a proper house to convert the savages. They forced the Indians to tear down the tallest pyramids. The limestone blocks made terrific building material. Rub the stones on the east side and you can still feel the ancient glyphs."

Susan was looking at me too. There was a glaze to her eyes I'd never seen. It wasn't just the *aguafuego*. The manhood thing again. I had no choice but lift my glass in toast and say, "I'm game. To the ruins. First thing in the morning."

~ ~ ~

The Hotel San Agustin had rental cars. Susan arranged for one, a Nissan coupe so old it was a Datsun.

The parking lot at the La Ceiba Archaeological Park was potholed and empty but for a VW Microbus that had just unloaded a group of Asians bristling with cameras. An unsmiling woman in a shack sold curling postcards in a wire carousel and soda pop and beer in an old-timey chest cooler. Nobody was on duty at the gate to take our money.

"Could be a bad sign," I said, thinking ambush.

"A good sign," Susan said, taking my hand. "We're getting in for free. C'mon."

Susan had our guidebook open to a sketch of La Ceiba as we walked a narrow pathway. Jungle tickled our shoulders. If I were running the place I'd fire the maintenance crew in a minute.

Susan said El Castillo was the temple really worth seeing. A don't-miss. She said it was a kilometer in. When we emerged in a clearing at least 2 miles later, I was so hot my eyes stung.

El Castillo was a pyramidal stack of rubble. Weeds grew between the limestone blocks. Other stone – cubes and slabs and chunks – lay in piles at the jungle edge.

Susan examined a boxlike roof structure, saying, "A written language fifteen hundred years old that we haven't fully deciphered. Amazing."

The inscriptions carved in the stone were dots, bars, pudgy profiles, and plump squiggles. I couldn't help but be impressed. I wasn't totally ignorant of the ancient Maya culture. They knew astronomy and were terrific at math, understanding the concept of zero before Europeans did.

We sat on an edge, enjoying a breeze. It wasn't what you'd call cooling, but it held the worst heat at bay. We stared out at a verdant expanse flat as a tortilla except for bumps that Susan explained, "Those aren't little hills, they're unexcavated ruins. There'll never be the people or the money to restore everything."

I shrugged and kissed her salty cheek, thinking what an easy target we'd make. The jungle was as thick as a shag carpet. A sniper could take his sweet time dialing us in.

"It's hazy at the horizon, but I'll bet on a clear day you can see Nicaragua," Susan said.

It wasn't any secret that in these turbulent situations, whichever side you were on, you made brownie points by making an anti-American statement. Like zapping a gringo tourist. I heard a faraway rumbling. Artillery, I thought. I knew Susan would say thunder.

"Hey," I said. "Let's go to the beach."

~ ~ ~

Our *Guide to Tierrahermosa* sported color plates of turquoise water. Playa del Norte was only 9 kilometers wide., but the beach did have sand like granulated sugar.

We shared it with a scattering of upper-middle-class Tierrahermosan families. Susan eavesdropped and overheard complaints about lazy maids and high gasoline prices, and not a word about the coup.

We collected shells and bought T-shirts at a gift shop. We ate grilled snapper under a straw palapa and drank the house specials. The cocktails were loaded with fruit chunks and were as sweet as syrup, concealing their jolt. The entire evening cost a paltry $30.

We walked on wobbly legs to our unit, a stilted thatch-roof cabin with screens instead of windows. In bed, I listened to the roaring surf, thinking of Guadalcanal and the Bay of Pigs, of bayonets and gang rape.

At lunch the next day, we met a Canadian couple who had come to snorkel at the offshore keys, and asked about the coup.

"What coup?" asked the man.

"Well, we did see a lot of uniforms," the woman said, "but I thought that was normal in the Third World."

Susan noticed an American newspaper in the woman's bag and asked if she could see it.

"Here it is, buried in a teensy box on page seven," Susan said. "Listen to this. A military takeover met minimal resistance. Ex-President Mendoza is in Tegucigalpa, Honduras, seeking political asylum."

The man said, "Down here in these banana republics, these uproars are like our elections. When they're over, they're over."

"Until the next one," I said.

~ ~ ~

"We need to go to Dulzura and see what's going on," Susan said at sunset.

"Nothing's going on," I said quickly. "Nothing that's any of our business."

"We could see the new *el presidente*. Maybe even meet him, get his autograph."

Had she forgotten all about copper?

"Not likely," I said.

"We'd have something to talk about this time. Our friends will be *so* envious," she said, giving herself the giggles.

I caught them too. When we recovered, hoarse and weepy, I promised to sleep on it. Inside, in the darkness of the cabin, with the sea's relentless rush, it occurred to me that Mendoza could be mounting a countercoup at this very moment. A tank could roll right over us and we wouldn't even hear it coming.

~ ~ ~

Next morning, a norther blew in off the water. Wind and rain howled through the screens, and the floorboards vibrated as if the cabin were ready to lift off.

We put on damp clothes, shivering in 70-degree temperatures. Susan's hangover was worse than mine, but unfortunately, she remembered my promise to sleep on it. There was no point in staying, she argued. Unless we wanted to be washed out to sea.

I insisted on driving. We sped by banana plantations and villages, by sugar cane as tall as bamboo, and jungle that crowded the highway. I drove as fast as I could on the narrow, pocked road without shaking the Datsun apart. I drove with the windows up until Susan complained. There were no checkpoints, no roadblocks, no ambushes.

She kept her nose in the guidebook most of the way. When we entered the capital, she had thoroughly studied the layout. The Gran Hotel on the central plaza, the Plaza of the Heroes, was her hotel of choice. Most amenities, comfortable rooms, moderate-to-expensive, where the action is, she read. Three stars.

We checked in at a musty, baroque lobby with dark, Persian carpeting and parrots in brass cages. Susan insisted on a room overlooking the plaza. We had cable TV and one channel on which a soccer game played. Our air conditioner worked, but it sounded like an airplane in a World War Two movie. We had a tiny balcony with a wrought iron railing. Directly across the plaza was the National Palace.

Susan stood on the balcony, grasping rusty iron. "I can picture Diaz ranting and raving at his subjects exactly like this. I really can."

I noticed that our windows had no shutters, no protection against an errant grenade or a Molotov cocktail. The plaza and the streets seemed peaceful, however. People went about their business in their languid tropical style. The only disconcerting thing was all the Diaz posters and banners. It looked like the day before an election, which I didn't think some of these people would see again in their lifetimes.

Susan pointed to the National Palace. "I wonder if they allow visitors. Those doors are wide and inviting."

"Like the White House? Maybe they'll have a Mendoza Room to tour."

"You joke, but we'll never know till we find out."

There were soldiers at the wide, inviting doors. A sergeant raised his carbine to port arms and said, "*No turista.*"

I said, "What the hell. We can go shopping instead."

"After I check something first."

In the Gran Hotel's lobby, we paged through the Dulzura phone directory. "Remember what Big Mike said about Diaz loving Chinese?"

"A regular guy."

She sighed. "There're seven *restaurantes chinos.*"

"Now that he's the top banana, don't you think Diaz sends somebody for take-out? Let's go shopping."

The Central Market was exotic and pungent. Fly-encircled slabs of meat hung from hooks. Mounds of produce, familiar and unfamiliar, were for sale. Silver, blankets, leather, and pottery too. Vendors on the rear wall did a lively trade in obsolete Korean and Chinese electronics, Scotch whiskey, and American cigarettes. We bought a liter of *aguafuego* – we'd have some fun with our friends – and T-shirts.

"Our modest black market," a man said as I examined a belt. "Import tariffs are very steep."

He was a local, young and slender, with sly eyes and a hair-trigger smile. A hustler. I ignored him.

"They charge too much here, sir. Whatever you are searching for, I can take you to a better place and cut you a nicer deal."

"Your English is excellent," Susan said.

"I work very hard at it. We get few North American tourists and I wish to be of service. My name is Pedro, but you can call me Pete."

"Well, I am looking for sandals."

"Jesus H. Christ, Susan."

"Highest quality leather, I can do," Pedro/Pete said. "Cheap. Almost free."

"We'll follow you," Susan said.

I gave up and followed them. We were led to an alleyway stall. I smelled raw sewage. The old lady running the stall and Pete were chummy. Mother and son, I thought. Susan shelled out $15 for a pair. Now we could ditch Pedro. The sandals would fall apart tomorrow. She would chalk it up to experience.

Then Susan had to invite the little sneak to a late lunch. Pete recommended a cafe on the plaza. He knew the chef and insisted on ordering for us, a surprise. When our food came out, I had to admit that it was the best burger and fries I'd had in a long time. But it wasn't any reason to go gaga over him like Susan was.

"My friend cooks the tastiest *hamburguesa* in Tierrahermosa," Pedro/Pete said.

We brought the conversation around to the coup.

"I am twenty-four years old," Pete said. "We have had five presidents since my birth, and four of them were not chosen in the polls. The ones backed by your CIA are usually the worst, but you learn to stay out of the government's affairs. They will do what they will do."

"How about Diaz?" I said. "How does he rate?"

Pete sucked the lime wedge impaled in his bottle of *Tigre Aureo* and said, "He is no worse than Mendoza."

"Can he keep the situation stabilized?"

"As I say, they do what they will do. We cannot change what is, so we do not try. We live each day, trying to get along."

Susan started in on meeting Diaz or at least getting his autograph.

"My husband can't understand how I feel, Pete –"

"I'll drink to that," I said, lifting my bottle.

"I mean, history is being made before our very eyes. In my entire life. I've never personally seen our U.S. senators or even the mayor. Come to think of it, I've never seen *anything* happen. I've never even actually seen a car accident take place."

"Watch these drivers here on the side streets for a _"

"Will you please stop whining?"

The *Tigre Aureo* stuck to my lips for another pull. I was startled into silence. A drop of beer ran down my chin.

Pete said, "I do know people. Perhaps I can be of help."

Susan said, "We're told that President Diaz loves Chinese food."

"An excellent observation. I shall see what I can do. Give me one hundred American dollars, please."

I rolled my eyes at Susan.

Pete rubbed thumb and fingertips together. "It is not for me. It is for access."

Susan looked at me.

Whining. I folded my arms. I wouldn't look at her. Susan gave him five twenties. it. Pete pocketed the cash and called to one of the many vendors who sifted between the tables.

An old man with a Polaroid camera nearly his age snapped our picture. Pete said, "I will pay. For my memory book."

The photograph centered a smiling Pete and Susan, and half of an unsmiling me. Pete said he would leave a message at their hotel desk when he had word. I said sure. Susan said when did he think he might? Pete said perhaps tonight.

After Pete left, an excited Susan asked if we could sightsee in the immediate area so we could regularly check at the desk for messages.

"Whatever. Why the hell not? Far be it from me to whine."

"Sorry. I didn't mean it."

I nodded and said, "Keep one thing in mind. Little Petey could be with Diaz's secret police. He's big enough to use a cattle prod."

"Oh, he's harmless and a dear. He's just doing what he can to make a living."

We bored ourselves peering into shops, churches, and cafes. We bought a handmade blouse for Susan's mom and more T-shirts for ourselves. After the third stop at the hotel desk, I suggested we wait in the bar. Susan liked the idea. We might run into journalists covering the coup, maybe even a famous one from the TV networks.

The closest we came was a drunken travel and gardening writer for a California weekly. We watched television and drank *Tigre Aureo*. A soccer game and the same documentary on President Diaz were on. Maybe the same game too. I was becoming attached to the team in the vertical stripes. They were scrappy, constantly attacking the goal.

Susan returned from her umpteenth trip to the desk, gushing. "Nine-thirty at the Kung Fu. He's having dinner there."

"That's late."

"The guidebook says they eat late in Tierrahermosa, when it's cooled off a little."

"I'd never question the guidebook."

We drank some more, showered and changed, napped, and took a taxi to the Kung Fu. The restaurant was several miles from our hotel, in a commercial neighborhood, sandwiched between a beauty parlor and an appliance repair shop. A pagoda facade in primary colors was painted on stucco.

"Unassuming," I said.

"Don't be sarcastic. The Kung Fu's given four stars. Holes in the wall anywhere have great food. And don't you think the president of the country knows where the best Chinese is?"

I didn't feel like arguing. My head throbbed from the heat and the beer. Pete was waiting inside the door.

"The president was honored by your interest," he told Susan. "So few foreigners visit Tierrahermosa."

"Will he be arriving soon?"

Pete was beaming. "He is here."

Susan looked at her watch, her eyes widening. "And we're ten minutes early."

Pete snapped his fingers. A swarthy waiter materialized and swept us into a dining room illuminated by candles. We swooshed into a vinyl booth rolled and tucked like upholstery in a 1950s car.

"Is that guy Arab?" I asked.

"Syrian," Pete said. "The owner. He makes the tastiest shrimp in Tierrahermosa."

"Oh, that's him!" Susan said, squeezing my arm.

Except for three booths on the opposite wall, the restaurant was empty. Tables of men in dark jackets flanked President Diaz. They were not eating or drinking.

A large candle centered the new president's table. At a side was a champagne bottle in a silver bucket. There were two fluted glasses on the table. Diaz lifted one toward us. Even through the cigarette haze and dark glasses, I could swear I saw him wink.

"Would he autograph a menu for us now?" Susan asked Pete.

Pete ignored her and said to me, winking, "You and I, perhaps we can go. I shall show you the town. Anything you desire to see or do. Anything."

"Just me?"

"Come on," Pete said, cocking his head.

"What the hell is going on?"

"You researched *el presidente*," Pete told me. "You know his passions."

"Yeah," said a bewildered Susan. "Chinese food."

"He idealizes the blonde, the *guera*. Your picture enchanted him," Pete gestured to the presidential table. "Look."

President Diaz blew Susan a kiss.

That was it. I had Susan by the hand, towing her out the door.

Pete followed closely. "I thought you were modern people."

Outside, I maintained a hold on her, swiveling my head for a taxi.

"He will be considerate. Gentle, miss," Pete/Pedro/Pimp said. "You will have the memory of a lifetime."

Fewer than half the streetlights worked. The sidewalk was treacherous, cracked and uneven. There was no traffic. I pulled Susan into the street and began walking. She resisted slightly, but said nothing. On her face were the biggest Susan eyes I'd ever seen and a suppressed smile.

"What of me?" Pete screamed after us. "How do I justify your actions?"

I saw headlights.

"You will have to answer for your rudeness," he yelled. "You will not be difficult to find."

A taxi. A death grip now on Susan's arm, I hailed it by stepping in its path, frantically waving my free hand.

We got in and the driver asked where to.

I said, "To the airport. Hurry."

"Airport? We have no airport, *Señor*."

JFK ASSASSIN STILL ON THE LOOSE

The phone call was too intriguing.

I caught the first available flight to Mexico City.

I am chief historical and political affairs correspondent for the *Weekly International Tattler*. *The New York Times* we aren't, but nobody's snatching the *Times* off the rack in the checkout line.

The Mexican capital was an imposing sight from above. As we descended to land, solid habitation faded to the edges of mountains. The air was a yellowish pink haze, like that of Los Angeles and Mars. One of world's largest cities, it was just as intimidating on the ground, a raffish and exotic sprawl of pollution and chaotic traffic and danger.

Debbie Smith de Salazar, my mysterious caller, had made reservations for me at a downtown hotel. The cabby got me there by way of Guadalajara, I thought, but what did I know?

I barely had time to clean up before meeting her for dinner. The desk clerk directed me to our rendezvous, the Opera Bar, a 6-block walk. It was an older establishment, full of dark wood, alcoves, and white tablecloths. She met me at the door with a hug, and led me inside. I suppose I was easy to spot, a bleary gringo whose head was on a swivel.

Debbie Smith de Salazar was a youthful late-70s. Gray hair parted in the middle hung below her shoulders. Her face was triangular, like a fox's. She was a petite woman dwarfed by her clothing, trendy khaki safari garb. Her only adornment was a large silver coin worn around her neck by a length of twine.

"The Opera Bar is a watering hole for local businessmen, but once upon a time Pancho Villa hung out here," she explained after sipping her margarita. "Look closely and you'll see bullet holes from an evening when he was letting off steam."

Mildly interesting, I thought impatiently. "*Señora* de Salazar, you said on the telephone that you were a friend of Lee Harvey Oswald and that you know something about him nobody else does."

"Call me Debbie," she said leaning forward and dropping her voice. "Even today, one does not admit friendship to Lee. I presume you're aware he was in Mexico City in the fall of 1963."

"That is correct."

The JFK assassination had been a cash cow at the *Tattler* for decades. A keen fascination with cover-ups and conspiracies was a requisite in my profession, and I'd written on the subject a number of times. One of my finer pieces:

JFK AT ARLINGTON.
PUTS WREATH BY ETERNAL FLAME.

"And that Lee came to Mexico City in the hope of traveling to Cuba?"

"Yes."

"Lee so desperately wished to serve Fidel and the revolution. The Cuban embassy told him they'd issue a fifteen-day travel visa, but without a current Soviet visa the process could take weeks. The Soviet embassy knew he'd lived in the USSR. They read him as a kook and gave him the runaround. He bounced back and forth between the embassies like a ping-pong ball, raising a bigger and bigger stink. He never did get his visa."

"How did you come to know him?"

"In the nineteen-fifties I was a crazy, mixed-up coed, a wild child. After my sophomore year I went to Mexico for the summer. I changed majors monthly and my latest kick was archaeology. I did the major sites. Teotihuacan, Chichen Itza, Monte Alban, Uxmal. This was before you could drive to them in an air-conditioned bus. And I did something else."

I filled her melodramatic pause. "Which was?"

Debbie drained her margarita. "I married a millionaire A Mexican twenty years my senior. I turned twenty-four in 1963 and thought life was passing me by. Diego traveled a lot and we weren't getting along when he didn't. I had a brief affair with an American expatriate named Rollie D. Hoopsma."

Another pause for effect.

I retaliated by checking my watch.

"Rollie was Lee Harvey Oswald's double," she whispered. "*Exact* double."

The Second Oswald Theory was a staple of us conspiracy buffs. I urged her to continue.

"I'd fallen for Rollie, but this was before my divorce, so we were being cautious until Diego was out of the picture. But one day, as I walked past a small café near our home, there Rollie was. Pure happenstance. It'd been two weeks since our last tryst and I missed him terribly. I was still enough of a bubblehead to think this was fate. Kismet.

I rushed in and quickly recognized my error. It wasn't Rollie. It was a man we were later to know as the infamous Lee Harvey Oswald. He was arguing loudly with the manager over his bill. Rollie was easygoing. Lee was embittered and had an explosive temper.

"I interceded in Lee's behalf. The dispute was over a mere ten centavos on a one-peso check. I paid the difference."

"Oswald was a notorious tightwad," I said.

Debbie smiled and patted my hand. "I knew I chose the right journalist. I walked with Lee and told my story. Half the men in the world would have been curious to hear more of Rollie, the other half would've tried to seduce me, saying it was all in the family, et cetera. I was a looker those days."

"Oswald did neither?"

She shook her head. "Not only didn't he thank me, he hardly listened to a word I said. He was an angry, self-absorbed, little man."

"What did he say?"

"He complained and complained and complained."

"About what?"

"You name it. Mexico. The food, the heat, the filth. On his life in general, how he'd been given a raw deal. It was so banal. He gave me a monstrous headache."

"Nothing on his politics, his intentions?"

"That came later."

"I have to wonder where this is leading."

"To the truth," she said, staring at me. "I'm depending on you to write the story, the actual news."

The actual news was usually a synonym for boring. Too much "actual news" in my copy and I'd be downsized before you can say Loch Ness Monster. But perhaps she was properly twisting the phrase.

"Why me?"

Debbie Smith de Salazar smiled and withdrew an album from a large canvas purse. It was the old-fashioned kind with leather covers and pages of glassine on black construction paper. The glassine protected newspaper clippings, each one with my byline.

There was my Amelia Earhart piece. How she'd been the love slave of a Japanese general, then tragically vaporized at Hiroshima.

We came to my Jimmy Hoffa exposé, the union boss hiding out with Mengele in Paraguay, trading concealment for money, the Nazi death doctor's coffers having run dry.

And, of course, my ongoing Kennedy series. A recent headline:

JFK INSATIABLE IN HIS NINETIES,
STARLET CONFIDES TO FRIENDS.

I assumed my best humble-scribe expression. Debbie had created a portable shrine to me. I didn't know what to say.

"The *Weekly International Tattler* is the only publication in the world that prints the actual news and isn't afraid of controversy."

"We absolutely do not shrink from controversy. How may I help you, Debbie?"

"Rollie has some things he needs to get off his chest."

"What things?"

"I'd prefer that he told you. After the assassination he was forced to alter his appearance and lie low. Rollie became paranoid and frustrated. Through no fault of his own, he developed a personality rather like Lee's. Even prior to my divorce we drifted apart as lovers, but I tried to stay in touch over the years."

"Did Oswald and Hoopsma ever meet?"

"Once. I brought them together."

"Where is Rollie D. Hoopsma?"

"Tomorrow he'll be in Palenque."

"The Maya ruin in Chiapas State?"

"You're familiar with Palenque, aren't you?"

"Slightly. A couple of years ago, I filled in at the science and astronautics desk."

"Oh, don't you be so modest." She opened her album to my PROOF THAT ANCIENT ASTRONAUTS BUILT MAYAN PYRAMIDS. DEPICTION OF CRASHED SPACESHIP FOUND AT RUIN.

"My renaissance man," she said, beaming adoringly.

I do believe I reddened.

~ ~ ~

In the morning, we flew to Villahermosa, a city in southeastern Mexico. Our return flight to Mexico City departed at midnight; this was to be a whirlwind encounter. Debbie rented a car and we drove 2 harum-scarum hours in wild traffic on bad roads to the Palenque Archaeological Park.

Admittedly, my grasp of the ancient Maya civilization is superficial as it is about many things. They were as highly advanced as any culture during their heyday 1500 years ago, so it wasn't illogical to speculate that they had extraterrestrial help in the area of mathematics and architecture and their calendrical system.

Debbie Jones de Salazar felt otherwise. I let her prattle on. Of all the sites, Palenque was her favorite. Did I know that Lord Pacal reigned in the 7th Century for nearly 70 years? Did I know that Palenque reached the zenith of its sphere of influence over neighboring Maya city-states during his rule? Did I know that Palenque had a magical setting, the loveliest of any pre-Columbian Mesoamerican city?

I replied politely that I did, although I didn't remember precise details. Unless Madonna or Britney was carrying Lord Pacal's baby, it was none of my business.

We arrived late in the afternoon and Debbie said, "While we're waiting for Rollie, would you like to see the ruin?"

I acquiesced, although the only thing on my mind was Rollie D. Hoopsma, alleged doppelgänger of Lee Harvey Oswald. I thought of Oswald, the pathetic loser, on the sixth floor of the Texas School Book Depository with his $12 mail-order rifle and his grievances.

Or was it really he? If so, who pulled the strings? The Mafia, CIA, LBJ, Fidel?

Two utterances would bring you up on heresy charges at the *Weekly International Tattler*:

1. Elvis is dead.
2. Lee Harvey Oswald acted alone.

Neither had ever or would ever pass from my lips or my keyboard.

Palenque's limestone structures appeared to be impaled in the hillsides, crowding the jungle as if growing out of it. Low clouds docked against the hills. From the ground, tourists climbing the taller temples appeared to be walking into the mist.

I'd brought my camera on the off-chance that somebody atop one of those pyramids happened to toss a Frisbee at just the right instant, at just the right angle. A suitably fuzzy snapshot of the flying saucer and my trip wouldn't be a complete loss if Hoopsma-Oswald didn't pan out.

"I have a real treat for you," Debbie said, leading me up the precarious steps of a pyramid. "You have to see this. The Temple of the Inscriptions. It's an absolute must."

I suppressed a groan and followed her upward on wobbly legs. Twenty years older than I, she was bouncing along like an ingénue. The demands of investigative journalism left scant time for physical fitness. I dearly hoped that Mr. Hoopsma was at the end of this rainbow.

However, instead of him, I was met by a stairway that seemed 10 degrees steeper than vertical. It descended into the bowels of the pyramid. I began to protest, but Debbie coaxed me onward. Slick and smooth, the steps were perspiring as much as I. Bare bulbs dangling from a cord provided lighting. Illumination ranged from dim yellow to coal black.

"The final resting place of Lord Sun Shield Pacal," an awestruck Debbie said at the bottom. "That's his sarcophagus lid suspended above his tomb, a 5-ton slab of stone. Lord Pacal is sculpted into it, making the transition from this world to the afterworld."

Of course I immediately identified the lid, as would anybody in my profession. Suspended on an end, as it was in countless photographs, Pacal appeared to be at the controls of a rocket, the booster firing beneath him, proof positive of extraterrestrial involvement. The *Tattler* and every other tabloid worth its salt had used it.

"Interesting," I said, beginning my ascent.

Outside, I felt compelled to lay down the law. "Debbie, I have deadlines to meet."

"Oh dear, do you think this is a wild goose chase?"

"I can't answer that," I said flatly.

I *was* under deadline pressure. Next week's lead was to be my unfinished NIXON HAUNTS OVAL OFFICE. SECRET SERVICE REPORTS UNEXPLAINABLE INSTALLATION OF TAPING EQUIPMENT.

We walked toward the parking lot. She said, "I do owe you further background. I've aided Rollie throughout the years. We corresponded and I mailed him money. Rollie and Lee had numerous similarities. They had difficult childhoods and scrapes with authorities. Rollie was AWOL from the Marine Corps when we met."

"Oswald's stint in the Marines was less than distinguished too," I said knowledgeably.

"Rollie really never found his niche, but essentially he's a good man."

"But you and he —" I allowed my voice to trail off.

"The romantic part of our relationship was extinguished once and for all. We hadn't an iota in common. In 1963, our emotional states drew us together. I will admit, though, under present circumstances, the new anxieties, the urgency, creates a certain excitement. Where it leads, I cannot say."

"Please define urgency."

In the parking lot, she said, "He should. Not me."

"When?"

"There's his bus. Come. To our car."

I sat in the back seat as we observed tour coaches lined up in the bus lot. It was getting late and some were pulling out.

"Hoopsma's in a package tour?"

"Rollie's a driver. He was more or less in hiding for many years, moving from one Mexican city to another. Not only from the Oswald stigma — people can be so mean — but his own legal problems with the Marines. Time passed and Rollie has, well, changed."

"Isn't driving a bus the worst a person who desires anonymity can do?"

"I had misgivings, but Rollie had isolated himself so long, he craved limited human contact. Rollie drives Europeans exclusively."

"JFK was popular in the former West Germany," I said, proud of myself for recalling the opening sentence of his *Ich bin ein Berliner* speech.

Debbie blinked her headlights. An elderly man lumbered toward us. His gut overlapped his belt. He had gray stubble and wore a baseball cap over thick, black hair, obviously a rug; Lee Harvey Oswald was going bald at age 24. The pounds and the years could not alter the weak chin, the cold beady eyes, the tight perpetual smirk. You'd have to be looking for it, but if you were, the resemblance was startling.

Hoopsma got in the car without a hello. Debbie pecked his cheek. He cocked his head and said to me, "You the reporter?"

"Yes."

"Do you recognize this face?"

"I do."

"It was a lot worse just after the assassination," Hoopsma said. "The ordinary gringo on the street wanted to take a poke at me on account of the resemblance. I grew a mustache and put on weight. It gradually died down. Then the conspiracy freaks got on my case."

I found the use of "freaks" offensive, but held my tongue.

"The Warren Commission had them foaming at the mouth," he went on. "I was able to evade them and it died down again. Then in the seventies, the Senate Select Committee stirred up a hornet's nest, the jerks. That fizzled out too. Now they're on my case again."

"They?"

"With this job, I can keep on the move. Euros these days don't know Oswald from Adam. If they do, they don't care. But somebody last week phoned in to one of those tabloid TV shows you have up north."

Our electronic brethren. "Did they dispatch a camera crew?"

"No," Debbie said. "Serial killers and misbehaving celebrities are more their speed."

"Somebody in the legit media was tipped off too," Hoopsma said.

"What do you mean by 'legit' media?" I asked, concealing a defensive tone.

"You know, CNN, the networks, *Time, Washington Post*, one of them."

"They're hot on Rollie's trail," Debbie said, squeezing his shoulder.

"How hot?"

"It's a matter of time."

"What do you want from me, Mr. Hoopsma?"

"Print the truth, that I, Rollie D. Hoopsma, am alive and well, while that other person is not."

"Publish the actual news," Debbie said. "I can vouch that he's Rollie. Print that he is. Print the truth."

Print the truth? "My quid pro quo?"

He turned around. His bitter smirk sent a chill down my back. "No such thing as a free lunch, huh?"

Debbie said, "Here's that free lunch, an incredible story for you. I was so flabbergasted when I met Lee that I called Rollie. I arranged for the three of us to meet at another café the next day."

Hoopsma broke in, "This'll take all night at this rate and I have to load up my tourists and be out of here. Oswald and I talked for two hours. I'm not justifying what he did, but I could relate to his frustrations. I'd been kicked around myself. We'd both gotten a raw deal."

Debbie patted Hoopsma's arm as his voice rose. "Here was a bright, young man with unpopular political views paying the price, having his nose rubbed in the dirt by intellectual inferiors. Lee couldn't get ahead of the game."

"An innocent man who looks like a notorious assassin has his life ruined," I said. "Oswald killed Kennedy and Jack Ruby killed Oswald, and you've been paying for it ever since."

"There you go," Hoopsma said, nodding. "When Oswald and I parted company, he asked if I'd like to trade places with him in a couple of months. I asked why. He gave me a goofy grin and said that I didn't want to know why. I said no. I had a funny feeling. Oswald left for the States the next day and I didn't see him again until I watched Ruby plug him on TV."

"Lee Harvey Oswald returned to the States weeks before the assassination. But the Dallas motorcade route wasn't public and Oswald hadn't hired on at the Texas School Book Depository yet," I wondered out loud.

Hoopsma glanced at his watch and got out. "Draw your own conclusions. They're piling into my bus."

A circumstantial innuendo of a conspiracy. I was on fire from the excitement. "Debbie, is that your take of the situation too?"

"Oh yes. I sensed Lee was afraid. Somebody had given him his marching orders and was orchestrating his life. I'm sorry Rollie's so crabby. The stress, the relentless hounding."

"No apologies necessary."

Debbie held out the coin that dangled from her neck. I had a closer look. Dated 1963, a one-peso denomination, it was silver, the size of a half-dollar.

"Lee gave it to me."

"How generous of him."

"It was. Except for bus money and food for the trip home, this was his last peso, the one he and the restaurant manager squabbled about the change to. Besides paying the disputed amount, I gave Lee some extra cash. Somehow this coin wound up with me."

"You wear it for sentimental reasons?"

"I wear it to remind myself how random life is. The day after the assassination, I noticed it on my dresser with other change. I've worn it ever since."

"Fate, kismet?"

"Not for this girl. Rollie will be so happy you're writing the story."

It was dark now and stragglers were exiting the ruin. Vendors had packed their wares. Park employees were checking for dawdlers and locking the gates.

I pictured a circular spaceship hovering above the Temple of the Inscriptions. Silvery, with flashing lights. It flitted laterally for the briefest instant and vanished into the recesses of my imagination. We'll surely have a file photo that'd work.

Debbie and I drove to Villahermosa for our flight. We didn't exchange 20 words. We were too tired for small talk. However, something was troubling me, something I couldn't put my finger on. As we descended in Mexico City airspace, landing gear and flaps lowering, it dawned on me.

I'd been set up as a patsy. A *Catch-22* victim.

I was staggered by my naïveté. Debbie couldn't have more transparent if she'd brought Hoopsma to me with L.H. Oswald tattooed on his forehead. She and Hoopsma fully expected a *Tattler* headline such as JFK KILLER ELUDES JUSTICE FOR DECADES. ADMITS THERE WAS A CONSPIRACY. LEE HARVEY OSWALD BEHIND THE WHEEL OF A BUS ON YOUR DREAM VACATION?

It was so simple. The "legit media" would read my article and automatically believe the opposite to be true. A Palenque UFO sidebar would be the icing on the cake. Unwilling to be scooped by the *Weekly International Tattler*, not to mention being tarred by the same tabloid brush, they'd abandon their investigation. Rollie D. Hoopsma could live happily ever after.

Debbie and I said our good-byes in the terminal. I declined her offer of a ride to my hotel and hailed a taxi. I directed the cabby to the Opera Bar, hoping it was still open.

I was eager for a better look at those bullet holes. A caption was blocking out in my head:

SPECTER OF PANCHO VILLA
PARTIES AT OLD HAUNT.
PEPPERS IT WITH
MORE BULLETS.

REINCARNATED AESOP UPDATES FABLE

I get this crank call at 3 a.m. He asks if my HMO covers kneecap replacement.

So much for the sanctity of unlisted numbers.

Before I can tell him his mother made a major error being one, he says to go for the titanium, they last longer, and hangs up.

He thought he was waking me out of a sound sleep. He wasn't. Haven't slept a wink since confirming the rumor is more than a rumor: The tortoise is giving the hare a rematch. The official announcement's coming momentarily, which gives me until the end of that day to do the numbers.

The daily line you see on the sports page and on the boards at the casino sports books? That's me. I set the odds and the point spreads. Everybody locks into step. You're a high roller or you're making a friendly wager at the water cooler, you're picking based on my picks.

I stop pacing long enough to brew another pot of coffee. You remember how the first race went. I opened the tortoise at 200-1. The mother of all expensive mistakes. If I blow it again, the comedian on the phone will be predicting my future.

~ ~ ~

No preconceptions this time, no complacency; forget Aesop and his fable. Research is my middle name. Next morning, a supervisor of the high-priced detective agency I hired comes by. He plunks a thick binder full of reports and photos on my desk.

I cut to the bottom line: Is the hare keeping his nose clean?

Seems to be focused, he says. Adhering to a strict conditioning regimen.

Booze and babes?

Haven't encountered those issues. As far as we can tell, he's squeaky clean. No bar-hopping, no high-octane carrot brandy. Faithfully attends AA meetings.

Per your request, we also ran a detailed credit check on him and the tortoise. No problems there either.

I browse the pictures. They zoomed a lens into the hare's training camp. He's stretching under the direction of a personal trainer, he's running on the beach, he's pumping iron, he's gulping carrot Gatorade by the gallon.

Anything eye-popping on the terrapin?

He shakes his head. Predictable as sunrise and sunset. A yawner of a surveillance.

Staying in shape?

As well as can be expected. He goes out to the box for his mail. When he gets back to the house, it's time to go out for the mail again. He's steady.

Steady, I mutter. Don't remind me.

I tap my forehead and ask how the hare is that department.

Centered, he says. The attention deficit disorder issue has been addressed and treated.

Skeptical, I return to the photos, interested in the hare's entourage. I recognize some. Sports writers, his agent, family members, his clergyman, the SPCA ombudsman. Then a shot of a guy coming out of his house that gives me goose bumps.

I ask if the hare had visitors he shouldn't have.

Not on our watch. No sir.

After he's gone, I study that picture. The gentleman leaving the hare's is none other than Jimmy (Feet) Brutto, an enforcer for the Ripugnante crime family.

The shamus supervisor is young enough to be my son. He has suspenders and a $125 haircut. This fancy private eye outfit, maybe they have too many college grads on the payroll and not enough retired flatfoots.

~ ~ ~

If you want it done right you do it yourself. I go to my source on the shady side.

Understand one thing. I do not care who wins or loses, or how they play the game. I'm not gazing into a crystal ball. My objective is to equalize the action, half the money on one side and half on the other. We make it on our vig, perfectly happy with a consistent 5%.

Didn't work that way when the tortoise raced the hare. I bemoan this fact to Pauly Snoops. Okay, even whining a little.

Pauly says fuggedaboutit, you're dredging up ancient history.

We're sitting at a sports pub lit up by a dozen TVs. Paraphrasing the famous quote, I tell Pauly that history has a way of repeating itself, then dumping on the uninformed.

He points at a screen. A bulletin, he says.

So? I say, seeing frontal shots of the tortoise and hare. The second race is all they've yakked about for days.

You missed the lead, Pauly says. It's been officially scheduled.

I focus on a talking haircut who's calling the rematch Tortoise vs. Hare II. They're running a home movie of the first race they've captioned Tortoise vs. Hare I. It's all too familiar. I have my own copy I torture myself with when I'm feeling masochistic.

Way back then, the race wasn't even televised. They held it at a forest clearing alongside a river. The footage flutters and is scratchy. The sky's turned green from deterioration. Makes the Zapruder film look like HDTV.

Flash to the Tortoise vs. Hare II venue, a bankrupt amusement park. The promoters are hauling in fake greenery by the truckload, everything from high nap turf to tree-sized potted plants. There's an ersatz meadow of tulips every color in the rainbow and some colors that aren't. They've wound miles of plastic ivy and vines around the roller coaster framework. They're laying pipes and pumps for a river. They're erecting bleachers, a covered press box, and meadowside club seats that're already being scalped in the four-digits.

I palm a roll of bills across to Pauly and ask if he's heard anything on the street, anything regarding anything or anybody. For instance, Jimmy Feet. Who I doubt was paying the hare a social call.

Whadduya want, for me to get whacked?

Nobody's gonna be quoting you in the papers, Pauly.

Think back to what went wrong before, he advises me.

What didn't go wrong? It was a no-brainer, the mismatch of the century. There was below-average play at my 200-1.

Until the day before the race, Pauly reminds me.

Suddenly the action picked up, all on the tortoise, every last dime. Nobody could resist a bargain. I nosedived the odds to a 100, then 50, then 30-1, then 6-5.

Too late. It was a stampede. A few early birds made fortunes and a couple of casinos almost went under.

You're saying the fix was in?

Pauly just looks at me.

Not a chance, I tell him. We checked that damned rabbit out every which way. Yeah, he had a problem with the sauce and a hang-up on a hot little number named Cottontail Kate, but there was no hint of hanky panky or bad associations. Until now. He could have blown the doors off that turtle, blindfolded and hopping backward one-legged. But he didn't.

There's your answer, Pauly says.

Huh?

Could have. You said it.

Please explain.

He pockets my roll and repeats, *Could have.* There's your magic words.

~ ~ ~

A fine time for Pauly to go inscrutable on me. I seal myself in my office, and run and rerun and rerun the film of the first race.

You remember how it went. The tortoise trudged along, an agonizing step at a time. The overconfident hare goofed from the outset, shooting the breeze with his buddies, snacking and drinking, even taking a siesta.

Finally, one of the rabbit's groupies realized what was happening and nudged him awake. He went like a bat out of hell and lunged for the finish line a nose behind the tortoise.

So what was the true story? Was it a bona fide upset like the Jets over Baltimore in Super Bowl III? A Clay-Liston phantom punch? Or a Black Sox scenario? What?

Afterward, bad blood developed. The hare spouted off that the tortoise should be extinct, as pokey and ugly as he was. The tortoise responded that the hare was "burrowing, floppy-eared trash with the IQ of the carrots he binges on." Et cetera.

The trash-talking hasn't hurt interest in a rematch, not one bit. The money is staggering. Not only ticket and TV revenue and wagering, we're talking commercial endorsements, T-shirts and a mini-series.

I shut off the VCR and read the credit histories.

The hare made a few bucks crying the blues on tabloid TV and cutting ribbons at supermarket openings. He lives beyond his means, tossing money around and hitting the club circuit, but that'd always been his style. Evidently, he isn't so far in hock that he's gonna be guest of honor in someone's rabbit stew.

The tortoise's spending habits operate on a lower metabolism. He's frugal, conservative and generally maintains a low profile. The bulk of his purse was frozen in a tax-free foundation he established, a sea turtle nesting ground in Mexico they're trying to protect from poachers and tourists.

The hare's spending money he probably doesn't have. The tortoise too, even with the write-off.

Yet neither seems to be hurting. We got us a serious enigma here that inspires me how I'm gonna set my line, bringing it and my life into a comfortable equilibrium, and affording me a good night's sleep.

~ ~ ~

Ever shell out $49.95 for a pay-per-view fight? *Bam,* a minute into the first round, one pug's flat on the canvas? You've hardly settled into your recliner and popped the top on your brew. You feel cheated, right? Imagine how the suckers in the ringside seats feel.

Well, that's not too different a scenario than Tortoise vs. Hare II. The hare sprinted out of the blocks, legs churning, knees pumping high. He ran the forest slaloms and the riverbank cutbacks like a rabbit possessed. He broke into the homestretch clearing and pounded across the meadow wearing agony on his face, as if the tortoise were nipping at his heels. He wasn't. He hadn't even plodded though the opening glade before the fat lady sang.

I opened the hare at 3-2. Everybody knew the bunny was flaky. On the other hand, the turtle made molasses look like lightning. I didn't budge the line. Didn't have to. Caution ruled. Action was spread as evenly as warm butter.

Though I have no proof, I'm pretty sure somebody made out like bandits. I'm referring to bandits of the Ripugnante persuasion, who scattered a ton of money in small increments on the hare. At that volume, 3-2 is definitely worth the trouble and thin margin.

The hare's on the radio talk-jock circuit, baiting the tortoise into a rubber match, to show the world who's really tops, that the blowout was no fluke. The tortoise is in the Yucatán at his sea turtle preserve, thinking it over.

The promoters will be ready. They're taking the coaster and other rides out of mothballs, and making it into a year-round theme park. Naming rights to Hare-Tortoise Stadium are up for bids.

I'm visualizing the conversation Jimmy Feet had at the hare's: "Put them thumpers to good use unless you want one on my keychain."

He wasn't telling the hare to go in the tank. Just the opposite. Jimmy and his boys don't gamble, they invest.

And I get to keep my kneecaps.

$$$ IN PIRATE TREASURE BURIED OFF OREGON COAST

Harry tried to be a good sport, tagging along with Babs as she prowled the Chandler's Boot shops. He stayed with her until the 3rd. It offered the same trinkets and postcards and T-shirts and pottery and candles. It was the perfumed gift-shop bouquet that did him in. Woozily, he begged off, pleading a headache.

Babs knew her man. She released Harry with a kiss on the cheek after he promised to behave himself. He navigated around the ATM machine and out into a gloriously sunny day, in search of refuge.

Chandler's Boot was a seaside tourist community named for the shape of the big rock off the beach and the pioneer who settled the town a century ago. In Harry's mind, the boutiques and wine shops and espresso cafes and art galleries were insufferably cutesy, not to mention pricey. Visitors *dressed* for their seashore vacations here, their shorts outfits coordinated, their floppy hats cocked just so. Harry had never seen so many BMWs in one place his life.

On a side street, Harry found his oasis, a clapboard dive catering to locals. He entered to the comforting fragrance of stale beer. There was a moose head and a stuffed fish mounted on a grimy wall behind the bar. The jukebox sang of lost loves, pickup trucks, and dogs. The clientele wore coveralls with their names stitched above the pockets.

Being an outsider, Harry was ignored. That was fine with him. He could drink his beer in peace. But this

131

was not to be. Another out-of-towner came in and took a seat 2 stools to Harry's left, throwing down gin and tonics. He was quiet at first, but the sauce got to him. The guy would not shut up.

Roughly Harry's age of 40, he was a certifiable weirdo. Thick glasses, hair that went in every direction and a tweed jacket that hung on him. His name was Stan, a Ph.D. and college professor. That was easy enough to believe. Dr. Stan had pointy-head written all over him.

A few beers later, Dr. Stan didn't seem as obnoxious, especially when he started babbling about pirates and buried treasure. He asked what Harry did for a living.

"Quality pre-owned recreational vehicles. The marketing end. I'm executive sales manager for Chick Chipperfield's Pre-owned RV Elegance, a division of Chipperfield's Pre-owned Automotive Elegance. Say, would you happened to be interested in a – ?"

"Not real estate or excavation?"

"Sorry."

"A pity."

Harry had foxlike features, a hairline that was receding, and a midsection that was not. Sensing opportunity, he ignited his salesman's smile and said, "I can acquire those skills mucho pronto. What's up, Doc?"

"Oh nothing," Stan said, staring into his gin and tonic. "Sorry to be a bother."

"No sweat. Appreciate the company. My girlfriend is out there buying up the town. What were you saying about English pirates sailing up this coast?"

"Are you familiar with Basil Greenhenge, the legendary buccaneer? He isn't as notorious as Francis Drake and John Hawkins."

"Sure. Who ain't?" said Harry, who never wished to appear ignorant.

"Sir Basil raised so much havoc with the Spaniards, he was knighted posthumously."

"They can do that?"

"It was the late 1600s. The Spanish had increased their forces and were better equipped to deal with British and French privateers along the Pacific coast. Greenhenge became involved in a horrific battle near Acapulco and fared badly. He escaped and sailed north to California to lick his wounds. He met resistance and continued even farther northward.

"He reached the rock we see off this beach and moored. It was summertime. Game, fish and edible flora were plentiful. They repaired their vessel and sailed in the autumn with expectations of further plunder. Off Mazatlán, they were engaged by Spanish warships and overwhelmed. Greenhenge and many of his men were killed. The remainder were taken ashore and hanged."

"They didn't fool around in those days," Harry said knowledgably.

"The Spanish savagery was partially fueled by their disappointment at finding little of value on Greenhenge's ship. In his heyday he looted his share of gold and silver and gemstones."

Dr. Stan now had Harry's full attention.

"Sir Basil was a prolific diarist. However, his notations were fragmented. I have at long last assembled and translated a sufficient quantity to pinpoint him locally."

"This pirate wrote where he buried his goodies?"

"Not in so many words. A sample quote, 'I storeth for mine security until my life endeth'."

"Works for me," Harry said. "Kind of."

"It was a piecing-together process. Mapping beyond populated areas was rudimentary at best, but the description of Chandler's Boot was unmistakable. He used the rock as a landmark. Sir Basil lapsed into a sort of code, but once I deciphered it, I determined the location. He was precise in his distances and compass headings."

"Hey, I ain't doing anything. Let's go grab a shovel."

Stan shook his head. "I visited the site this morning. It's hopeless. All my work is for naught."

"How much work are we talking about?"

"Ten years of compiling, translating, analyzing. Colleagues ridiculed me. They claimed that pirates did not sail this far north and I will be unable to prove them wrong."

Harry whistled. "A long time. So if you found the spot, why's it hopeless?"

Dr. Stan either choked back a sob or hiccupped, and said, "Because it is in the heart of downtown, under a structure that has been inhabited for nearly a century. It was a Chandler's Boot original. The treasure could not possibly have gone undiscovered."

~ ~ ~

"You ain't gonna believe this, kiddo," Harry began.

Babs could believe that she would not believe, for this was her Harry speaking. They were at an RV park on the edge of town, in a travel trailer he'd taken as a trade-in at Chipperfield's scuzzy RV lot. Door and windows were wide open to combat the heat trapped inside the tin can. It took Harry 3 beers and Babs a rum and coke to get through his story.

"You don't believe him, do you?"

"He was dead serious."

"He was conning you, Harry."

"Don't you think I know a con man when I see one?"

"Yeah, whenever you look in a mirror."

It wasn't just the heat that made her grouchy. Despite the cleansers she'd used inside this trailer, one of the dealership's quality, pre-owned cream puffs, vague unidentifiable odors lingered.

Then there was Harry himself. They'd been an item for 4 years. Babs was no spring chicken. If she didn't see a ring pretty soon, the cookie jar was gonna to be closed. She was fairly certain he'd insinuated that a commitment could occur during this romantic week at the ocean. But Harry being Harry, nothing had happened.

"You oughta see the guy. He's one of these intellectuals. He knows his stuff."

"The poor man's deranged. Everybody knows there were no pirates this far up the coast."

"You're an expert?"

"I know when somebody's jerking my chain," she said, staring hard at Harry. "Usually I do."

Harry sniffed, his nostrils suddenly offended. He saw the source, a pile of bags on the bed, purchases made while he talked pirate and buried treasure with Dr. Stan. Babs had brought the smell of the boutiques home with her, in the form of figurines, dried flowers and I ♥ CHANDLER'S BOOT blouses.

Not that he was complaining. Incredibly endowed, Babs also had the world's biggest hair. By virtue of her makeup and manicurist professions, her nails always matched her eye shadow. The lady was pure class. He could even live with the matrimonial hints she had been dropping of late, even though they were as heavy as anvils.

"Yeah, you're probably right."

A horn honk interrupted Harry. An old Camaro slid to a stop, kicking up dust. Out piled Bubba and Junior. Both boys were seedy and lanky, with dumb eyes and jailhouse tattoos. Bubba was Babs' son by an ex-husband. Junior was either a son by the same ex or another ex or a pal of Bubba's from reform school. Harry couldn't keep the lineage straight.

Babs squealed in delight at the surprise, ran outside, and flung her arms wide for smooches and hugs. Harry brushed by and looked inside the Camaro. He saw a screwdriver dangling in the steering column where the ignition switch should be.

He said, "Hey Bubba, I thought you were on work release."

"It's the coolest halfway house I ever been in. They hardly ever take roll on the weekends," he said.

"Surf's up," Junior said. "Party time at the beach."

"Not on an empty stomach," Babs said.

As she rustled up a meal for her boys, Harry sat on a stump, thinking, the deep philosophical kind of thinking. Here he was, 6 weeks past his 40th birthday, the big four-oh, and what did he have to show for it? What had he made of his life? Basically zilch. Not diddly-shit. On a good month at Chipperfield's, he made four grand in commissions. Chicken feed.

He thought of Dr. Stan. Maybe he was loony. If he wasn't, Harry would never forgive himself if he didn't give the buried treasure a shot.

~ ~ ~

Kevin and Lori lay in bed after a typical 16-hour day in their shop, too exhausted to sleep.

"What's that noise?" she whispered.

Scraping, digging? Kevin didn't know. The constant, maddening, endless, nonstop rush of the surf muffled everything. Initially, it'd been so romantic, gazing out the window as the sun set beside Chandler's

Boot. But this apartment had become as much of a prison as the store below.

"Termites having a midnight snack," Kevin said. "Chowing down on the floor joists."

"Ha ha. Have I told you lately how this all sucks?"

For the 25th time today, Kevin didn't say. If he opened his mouth, they'd be at each other's throats again. Whose idea *was* this? Whose yuppie dropout fantasy? Whose naïve notion of empowerment? The serenity of quaintness and the thrill of entrepreneurship rolled into one?

"If our friends knew what our life was like, they wouldn't be so envious," Lori continued, barely managing the strength to raise her arms and make quotation marks at "life."

Kevin sighed. "Sometimes I think their envy is all we have. Them in their cubicles, tyrannized by downsizing bureaucracies."

Lori sneezed. The cloying reek of their merchandise had seeped up from Chandler's Boot Unique Gifts and Art Gallery to their living space. When she'd first walked into the shop as a customer, it had been so delightful, so captivating. Now she was developing an allergy to their inventory.

"Give me a one-hour commute each way in bumper-to-bumper traffic," she said. "The good old days."

"We thought a 20-step commute on the staircase was so nifty," Kevin said bitterly.

"Up the rickety, dry-rotted staircase a contractor said would take seven thousand dollars to rebuild."

"So how are we doing moneywise?"

Lori, an MBA and human resources professional, was in charge of the books. Kevin was a software whiz who had fits making change. A lot of good the education and oodles of IQ points did them now, she thought.

She said, "Three new shops selling what we sell opened their doors this spring. The markup on the hideous crap we sell is healthy, but the competition is diluting our customer base. We'll barely break even when the season's over in two weeks."

After Labor Day, you could fire a cannon down the main drag without hitting anyone, Kevin thought. He said, "And starve in the winter."

"Unless we continue to defer maintenance."

"We could sell," he said.

Lori laughed bitterly. "Dream on. We'd have to give the shop away and lose a bundle."

They had already lost a bundle, Kevin didn't have to be told. Their savings, the split-level, the 401(k)s they cashed in.

"Pray for an eager buyer," he said. "In the vernacular, a sucker, a pigeon."

Lori sighed. They had spent idyllic weekends in Chandler's Boot prior to their marriage. It was so enchanting, the town so *in*. "You're asking for a miracle."

"I still hear that digging noise," Kevin said.

Lori said, "I hope they eat the timbers evenly, so this dump doesn't collapse at a funny angle."

~ ~ ~

In the morning, Harry went to the OceanViewCrest Lodge, a motor court. He remembered seeing Dr. Stan's room key on the bar with his change. As luck would have it, he caught the good doctor checking out, his bags beside a ratty, old minivan.

"Hold it there, champ. I didn't take you to be a quitter."

"Excuse me, sir, have we met?"

Dr. Stan looked to Harry like he'd slept in his clothes without sleeping. His eyeballs needed tourniquets. His fingernails were filthy, very uneggheadlike. You'd expect chalk, not grime. Harry summarized yesterday's encounter, lowering his voice when Dr. Stan winced.

"Yes, of course. Please accept my apologies. I am unaccustomed to strong drink."

"Yeah, me too," Harry said. "Look, if what you said was true, you can't just flush ten years work down the ol' crapper."

Dr. Stan lifted his tailgate and gestured to a metal detector. "I rooted around the perimeter of the site last night. To no avail. I gleaned rusted bottle caps and tin cans."

"How about inside the, uh – where did you say it was?"

"I did not specify," Dr. Stan said, tossing in his bags. "The interior, the most likely burial site, is impossible. Construction of the building would have revealed the artifacts. This town is built on sand. There are no conventional foundations, no basements. They would flood. The place has a two-foot crawl space above concrete blocks."

"So why didn't anybody hear about this bonanza way back when?"

"The finders evidently were discreet."

"I don't know," Harry said. "Take me. I got ex-wives and their attorneys circling overhead for back alimony and my gal, the sweetest thing in the world, is putting on a full-court press in regards to holy matrimony. Despite this pressure, I cannot honestly say if I could keep my big trap zipped if I was knee-deep in goodies. Unless it was never there to begin with."

"No! I refuse to consider that option. Sir Basil was a precise diarist and my measurements are accordingly precise."

"Lemme ask one question. Did Sir Basil write how deep he buried his treasure?"

Dr. Stan opened his mouth. Nothing came out but halitosis.

"I thought so," Harry said, throwing an arm over a rounded shoulder. "It ain't over till it's over, guy. I think you need some hair of the pooch. You also need yourself a technical advisor."

~ ~ ~

At the bar, aided by the therapeutic effects of gin and quinine water, Dr. Stan lectured that the structure in question was one of the oldest. Elihu Chandler, a fur trader and traveling whiskey drummer, had been attracted by the massive rock offshore. A hundred years ago, within view of the boot-shaped monolith, he opened a saloon and general store alongside the well-traveled coastal trail. Folks bought overpriced staples and bad whiskey, and went up the steps to Elihu's second-floor brothel.

"One stop does it all," Chick said. "Your basic superstore."

Chandler's Boot enjoyed quiet, gradual growth until the 1970s. Tourists began to multiply the population of the town in the warmer, drier months. The powers that be decreed an artsy, gentrified atmosphere. No fast food franchises, no neon, no high rise. Visitors with disposable income came to Chandler's Boot in ever-greater numbers.

"Elihu got his paws on the loot?"

"Perhaps, perhaps not. The establishment was remodeled numerous times hence. Somebody likely spirited off Sir Basil's legacy."

Gary Alexander

"I'll vote for perhaps not," said the optimistic Harry. "Let's go check it out. Have you been in the joint?"

"Yes. It is a gift shop and art gallery owned by a young, professional couple."

"Have you *really* checked it out?"

"I don't know what you mean. I don't know what we could accomplish by simply perusing stock. We would soon arouse suspicion."

"If the goodies took a powder, *que sera sera*. What's the harm, Stan?"

"None, I suppose."

"By the way, what's the bottom line in respect to our boy, Basil? How much might remain down in the sand?"

"Hundreds of pounds worth of historical treasures."

Dizzying in the knowledge that gold was going for over $1200 an ounce, never mind the collectible value of coins, Harry signaled to the bartender. "We'll have one for the ditch, Stan. I got us a game plan. Today is gonna be our lucky day."

~ ~ ~

Harry couldn't recall whether or not Babs had dragged him into Chandler's Boot Unique Gifts and Art Gallery yesterday. They all looked alike. The shop had a square, old-timey false front of narrow siding and multi-paned windows, a swayback box with a peaked roof.

He carried Dr. Stan's metal detector in, saying out of a corner of his mouth that he'd do the talking. Chandler's Boot Unique Gifts and Art Gallery stocked the usual crapola. The shop wasn't exactly packed to the gills, but there were customers to keep the yuppie types behind the counter out of their hair for a few minutes. With Harry leading the way, the treasure

141

hunters pretended to browse. Harry held the metal detector close to his leg, its probe inches from the creaking, wooden floor. After a false reading by the ATM machine, the needle damn near wrapped itself around the pin.

Standing beside a display of clocks mounted in the bellies of ceramic seagulls, all they could do was stare at each other. The frenzied sputtering of the detector attracted the woman yuppie, who was health-club-skinny and tanning-parlor-brown. She asked if she could help them.

"Uh," Harry said, switching off the machine. "Do you repair these?"

She looked offended. "No."

"I love your store."

"Thank you. Is there anything in partic –?"

Harry said, "Hey, is your store on the market? This'd be perfect for me and my pard here."

The woman began to tremble, then bit her knuckles. Her eyes teared up and she called, "Kevin!"

The young fella who came running had gel in his hair and wore suspenders. "What's the matter, Lori?"

"Please, repeat what you said to me," Lori said hoarsely.

"Do you guys feel like selling out to us?"

Kevin cried, "Way cool."

He embraced his sobbing wife, who said, "Awesome."

~ ~ ~

On the beach, Babs sat on a driftwood log near the rock. The tide was out and families were examining the creatures that had been trapped in shallow pools. She'd asked Harry to come with her several times. He'd said, nah, he'd already seen the beach once. He didn't tell her where he was headed today, but she wouldn't be a bit surprised if it had to do with that buried treasure nonsense.

Babs wished they had a common interest like bird-watching or marine life, activities healthy and stimulating to the brain. If Harry was maddening, her boys were going to give her an ulcer. Bubba and Junior didn't return to the trailer last night, even after they said they would. They were frisky, rambunctious boys. She worried that they'd met bad company. Unsavory companions leading them astray, that was the root of their problems. The big lugs, they weren't rocket scientists.

Babs walked off the beach in the middle of town, figuring, what the hell, she'd

window-shop her way to Harry and the trailer, and pick up some moisturizer because of what the wind and salt air did to her delicate skin. But there Harry was, standing out on the porch of Chandler's Boot Unique Gifts and Art Gallery. They were shaking hands and hugging a young couple. A fourth member of the group, a geeky fella with thick glasses, no doubt Harry's nutty professor, stood off to a side, nodding and grinning.

Babs stepped into a doorway before she was seen. Those folks and their rustic store connected to Harry's latest pipe dream? Very interesting. Very strange.

~ ~ ~

It didn't set well with Babs that Harry asked his dorky friend over to lunch unannounced and treated her like a servant. She had to drop everything and throw together her world-famous egg salad, then have her intelligence insulted when they skirted the subject of the buried treasure except in the broadest terms. They were up to no good with those yuppies, who she'd learned were the gift store's owners. All she got out of it was a college lecture about pirates in the Pacific, the professor yakking with his mouth full of egg salad sandwich, which was *so* gross.

And Harry, the jerk, him not letting her in on the scheming. It was pretty obvious that he had no intention of popping the question.

She was thinking that things couldn't get any shiftier and weirder, but they did. Harry asked where those "fine strapping lads of hers" were.

"Huh?" Babs responded. When he wasn't pretending they didn't exist, Harry referred to her boys in barnyard language.

"They're the youngsters I told you about, Stan," Harry said before Babs came out of shock. "High-spirited pups, unafraid of hard work and always eager for a challenge."

Just then, Bubba and Junior trudged into the trailer. Babs took a gander at them and thought, Lordy, look what the cat drug in.

"Slept on the beach," Bubba said.

"Why?"

"Looking for chicks. It ain't like them old beach party movies you see on TV in the middle of the night," Junior said. "The ones here, they were with guys, husbands and stuff and their rug rats. A total bummer."

"We tried to build a campfire, like from, you know, Boy Scouts."

"You were kicked out of the Boy Scouts," Babs reminded them.

"Babs, hon," Harry said. "Can you excuse us for a little male bonding?"

Before she could repeat 'huh?', Harry pushed them and his goofy chum out the door. She watched them through curtains worn thin as tissue as Harry talked a mile a minute, his arms flailing. This was vintage Harry at the used RV lot, stroking a sucker on a moldy fifth-wheeler.

Well, maybe he could put one over on that overeducated schoolteacher. Her sons too. Anybody could with them, she thought as Harry reached into his pocket. Babs didn't know what he was cooking up, but she did know one thing. Blood was thicker than water. And it was thicker than any honey rolling off Harry's tongue and the few dollars he was giving to Bubba and Junior.

~ ~ ~

"It's mandatory that we become proactive," Lori said.

"They made an offer, didn't they?" Kevin said.

"Not exactly. Not in so many words," Lori said as she locked the front door of Chandler's Boot Unique Gifts and Art Gallery and hung the CLOSED sign. "I don't like shutting down an hour early. Why it's so important to do it this evening, I don't understand. You'd assume they'd prefer a structural inspection in better light."

Kevin said, "They're anxious, a good thing. And the only paying customer we had was the old lady who bought the macramé puffin. It's going to be a chore to pry open the crawl space lid. Nobody's been down below in ages."

"They are an odd couple. I don't trust the character doing the talking," Lori said. "We need to take steps to control the process."

"Yeah, if we can."

"Oh, we can," Lori said.

~ ~ ~

Another walk on the beach relaxed Babs, but it didn't cool her off. She returned to an unoccupied trailer. There was no room to pace, so Babs sat and stewed. A glorious sundown came and went. She and Harry should've been at water's edge, adoring it, hand in hand, planning their wedding.

~ ~ ~

When Harry arrived at the trailer, the nutty professor was with him. Odder still, Bubba and Junior were in back of Harry's truck. The boys hopped out, carrying paper bags.

"We had to do some shopping," Harry said matter-of-factly.

"For what?" Babs asked.

Her boys were already in the bedroom, behind the folding door, changing clothes. She repeated, "For what?"

"You'll see."

Bubba and Junior emerged in coveralls, carrying clipboards and flashlights. The unfamiliar sight of them in working garb took Babs' breath away.

"My, aren't you professional appearing. This errand wouldn't concern buried treasure, would it?"

Harry put a finger to his mouth. "A slip of the lip will sink our ship."

He took Babs aside. "Actually, you were right, kiddo. Dr. Stan was off-base on the pirate loot, but it's funny how things happen. Did you know he's a world-renowned expert on artifacts from the last century like beer bottles?"

"Why, no I didn't, Harry."

"There's a vacant lot in Chandler's Boot that used to have the town's oldest building on it. Dr. Stan's theory is there's stuff buried in it. Won't amount to much money if we do stumble onto anything, but what the hell, we can sell it to antique shops and recover part of the cost of this trip. Bubba and Junior are doing the digging. They need the money, and it'll build muscles and character."

"That's nice of you to think of the boys, Harry. Doesn't somebody own the land?"

"We'd cut him in if we knew who he was," Harry said sincerely. "Yessiree, we would."

Instead of asking why the project had to be done in the dark of night, Babs forced a smile and said, "You boys have a good time and be careful."

Harry impatiently pecked her forehead. "We will."

The boys were sitting in the truck bed, holding shovels. Babs called Bubba inside. "We're on a deadline," Harry yelled from behind the wheel, tapping his watch.

"He forgot his wallet, Harry. Keep your shirt on."

Inside, Bubba patted his pockets and said, "I didn't forget my wallet. I don't have a wallet."

"Bubba, you tell me what's going on. Harry gave you money earlier. What do you have to do to get more?"

Bubba's eyes widened. "How did you know?"

"That's how he operates, honey. He teases you with hope. You don't have to hit anybody with those shovels, do you?"

Bubba chuckled. "Mom. C'mon."

Harry honked his horn.

"Out with it, young man. The true story."

"Okay, okay. See, Harry and Four-Eyes, they go in this store first. Then Harry, he has us come in. He says for us to look official and don't say nothing. Then we go under the floor and dig till we hit something that ain't sand or rock."

"A store. Not a vacant lot?"

"What vacant lot?"

"What's he expecting you to hit?"

"Fossils and old bones and stuff."

"Oh."

"Yeah. Four-Eyes is a scientist, one of them architects."

"A who?"

"You know, they dig stuff up for museums, like King Tut. Me and Junior, we're s'pose to dig far enough to find out if anything's there. We get us a bonus if we do. Harry, he'll talk to the store people afterwards. He don't want to make no deal with them unless there's bones in the ground like Four-Eyes says there is."

Harry honked again. The creep, he'd con her boys into digging to China. Should the impossible occur, he'd pay them a few bucks for their hard labor and cut them out of a share of the treasure. Just like he was going to do to her.

Well, she'd see about that.

It hurt Babs to smile. She did, though, and kissed her Bubba on the cheek. "My Harry is such a clever man, isn't he? Run along now and have a good time."

~ ~ ~

Harry held the papers and wrinkled his nose as if they were something he'd stepped in. "What the hell's this?"

"An earnest money agreement," said Lori. "We believe that there should be a formal commitment on your part."

"Sign on the dotted line?"

Kevin snapped his suspenders. "We're on the same page on this issue."

"The sale here, it's contingent on the structural inspection we talked about," Harry said.

"The commitment, please," Lori said.

"Sure, what the hell," Harry said, passing the document to Dr. Stan. "Whip your John Hancock on the dotted line."

"It's too dark to read it," Stan said.

Harry handed him a pen. "No problem. I trust these fine folks."

As Stan signed, Harry waved Bubba and Junior out of the back of the truck. The yuppies squinted as the

148

boys loped onto the porch steps, Junior's shovel banging against a post.

"*They* are structural inspectors?" Lori asked.

"They're certified by the county and the state," Harry said, two thumbs up.

"What's the purpose of the shovels?"

"To root around inch by inch for dry rot. My inspectors are incredibly thorough."

Lori opened her mouth.

Before she could speak, Harry said, "I can read your mind. You break it, you bought it, right? Hey, with luck we'll be breaking our own stuff."

Kevin threw an arm around Lori and both winced at the tinkle of glassware.

"God, that would be *so* wonderful," she whispered in his ear.

~ ~ ~

Babs allowed Harry's scheme an hour to percolate, then walked to the gift shop and a commotion.

Her sons' white coveralls were every color but. Junior was holding what looked like a shot put, engaged in a heated argument with Harry. Bubba was looking around nervously, as they were drawing a crowd that might eventually include law enforcement. The young couple that ran the shop were looking at each other with question marks on their faces. The nutty professor was nowhere to be seen.

"I ain't paying you a red cent," Harry was yelling. "You were to come up the second you struck anything and keep your yap shut, not bring up what you found for the world to see."

"Yeah? Where's these old bones? All there is is these here, a whole bunch of them things and some rusted-out guns."

"Well, I'll be," Babs said to the yuppies. "There were pirates this far up the coast."

"Pirates?" Kevin and Lori chimed.

"Long story, kids. I'll fill you in later."

Dr. Stan stumbled out of the shop with a beatific smile, rusted musket in each hand and tears streaming down his cheeks. "I've been vindicated! My theory is correct. My research was not in vain."

Harry shoved by Junior and said, "Where the hell's the treasure?"

"This is the treasure! Cannonballs, muskets and harquebuses. The historical context is priceless!"

Harry said, "What about what you told me the old pirate wrote?"

"'I storeth for mine security until my life endeth.' Don't you see, Harry?"

"I don't see nothing but scrap metal that you couldn't even sell to a second-rate antique store."

"The armaments were Sir Basil's security. Should he be pursued to his new northern retreat, he would have a reserve. In hindsight, he should have taken them for his final voyage south. He could have used the additional firepower."

"So where the hell's the gold and silver? What use is it being a pirate unless there's gold and silver and doubloons and pieces of eight?"

Stan shook his head and smiled. "Had Sir Basil acquired a conventional treasure, he squandered it. Privateers were profligate. They lavishly dissipated themselves on wine, women and not necessarily song until the loot was gone, and headed to sea for more. As often as not, buried pirate treasure is apocryphal. Not every pirate became fabulously wealthy. For many, their life was a marginal and perilous existence."

"Harry, you give me and Junior the rest of our money," Bubba said. "We done our work."

Harry ignored him.

"Don't you see, Harry? This is a discovery of major, major historical significance," Stan continued.

"Mom, we gotta be back at the halfway house," Bubba said. "We really gotta."

Babs had a spare key to Harry's truck. She dug it out of her jeans, tossed it to Bubba and said, "Scram."

"Hey," Harry screamed, charging after them.

Babs sidestepped in his path.

Harry froze in his tracks. Babs didn't have to say a word. Harry looked into her eyes and saw a mother wolf defending her pups. He stood helplessly, jaw hanging, as the boys burned rubber and fishtailed out of sight.

"This is all mildly exciting, but where does that leave us?" Lori said. "How do we get out from under this white elephant? In two weeks, Chandler's Boot will be a ghost town until next spring."

"You are spectators to history," Dr. Stan raved.

"I got C's in history," Kevin said. "I can't relate to your subtext. A software generation is eighteen months."

"Shut the fuck up, Kevin," Lori said. "Our shop is a mess. Our earnest money agreement is worthless and the property will be classified as a historical site?"

Harry shambled off, arm around the professor's shoulders. "Dr. Stan, I need a cold one. I feel a headache coming on."

Kevin trailed the treasure hunters, saying, "Wait up, fellows."

When they were gone, Babs had an inspiration. "Lori, honey, I think your cloud has a silver lining that's solid sterling. As a historical site, you have a tourist attraction. They'll come twelve months a year, not just in the summer."

"Hmm," Lori said.

"We can notify the media," Babs said. "My favorite newspaper, *The Weekly International Tattler*, might like it too. This is something they can spin off into, well, who knows what? Aliens or whatever."

"Hmm," Lori repeated.

"Far be it from me to criticize, hon, but your fabulous merchandise isn't enough."

Lori sneezed. "Tell me about it."

"Although I am a licensed hair stylist, my true strength is in manicure and makeup. In the wintertime especially, the weather here must make it rough on a gal to retain her attractiveness. A lady's gotta look her best year-round."

"There are beauty salons in Chandler's Boot."

"Not in numbers like gift shops there aren't, and none smack-dab in a gift shop that's destined to be a leading tourist attraction. Nobody'd have a reason to go anywhere else."

Lori said, "Keep talking."

"Romantically speaking, there's nothing holding me where I'm from any longer."

"I may be joining that club shortly," Lori said, looking in the direction of the departed Kevin.

"A person can't set up and run a tourist attraction all by her lonesome. What's that bean counter word they have – diversify?"

"That's the word," Lori said.

"I wouldn't need a whole big bunch of space. In that corner where you have that darling display of watercolor paintings of seagulls."

"Not to worry. I can find another place for my art exhibits," Lori said, extending a hand. "Partner."

PRICELESS PAINTING PURLOINED IN PALACE

In 1961, a 34-year-old abstract expressionist named Kennedy Scott burst onto the art scene with a painting entitled *Raising Chickens on Mars*. Marguerite Hathaway Benning da Silva Greenhenge, a laundry bleach heiress, purchased the canvas for $7,500, a sum she could not afford. At the time, it was an impressive amount for the first sale by an unknown artist.

Raising Chickens on Mars was a polychromatic and puzzling scramble of pigments. Wags insisted that the 40ish Mrs. Greenhenge had purchased the painter as well. There was some truth in that. Four months later, she became Mrs. Marguerite Hathaway Benning da Silva Greenhenge Scott.

The couple lived in Hathaway House, a palatial estate overlooking Cape Cod Bay near Wellfleet, Massachusetts. They shared it with a dwindling domestic staff and David Benning Junior, Marguerite's only child. Kennedy Scott converted the rarely-used banquet room of the brick and stone mansion into a studio.

Although Marguerite and Kennedy drank and fought constantly, she was quick to defend him. "Would he be a genius if he were a milquetoast conformist? Without his passion and fury, Kennedy Scott would be a third-rate illustrator like his envious peers."

Marguerite's entertaining virtually ceased. The alcoholic oafishness of her new husband repelled all but her most Bohemian friends and hangers-on. The bleach company had long since been sold to a conglomerate and Marguerite's trust fund was depleted. The few people who genuinely cared for Marguerite worried about her predilection for violent gigolos, as well as her ability to match them drink for drink, shouted obscenity for shouted obscenity.

Her previous husband, Basil Greenhenge, an impoverished Yorkshire nobleman, had a fondness for riding crops. His marital predecessor, da Silva, Brazilian playboy and race car driver, kicked her down a flight of stairs, miscarrying David Benning Junior's last chance for a half-sibling. Only David Benning Senior escaped the wastrel label. A war hero, he'd been killed at Iwo Jima.

Based on his drunken boorishness and *Raising Chickens on Mars*, Scott's reputation grew. Admiration of his work varied widely. One critic commented that Scott's pigment did not merely meet surface, "it collided in a besotted rage." Even adoring journalists couldn't agree if *Raising Chickens on Mars* incorporated the solar system and barnyards or not.

As Scott's prestige increased, alcoholic rows with his wife did too. So it was no great shock when Marguerite Scott's body was discovered in the studio by the fireplace hearth. Her skull had been caved in by the bloody poker found by Kennedy Scott, who was passed out beside her, an empty gin bottle at his side.

The one person who did profess shock was the young man who found the Scotts, David Benning Junior. On holiday during his freshman year in college, he came home from a party and there they were. The fireplace smoldered and his mother was as cold to the touch.

Benning's report to the police was matter-of-fact. Scott and his mother drank too much, yes, and fought like cats and dogs, but he still couldn't believe it. He felt they loved each other.

The police wondered about the Benning kid. Why didn't he seem to have a tear to shed for his mama? And why did he think Scott was a good guy?

As David Benning explained it, he was closer to Scott than to the mother, to whom he was an "acquaintance." David enjoyed watching the painter, fireplace crackling as he worked. They actually conversed. His testimonial didn't help Scott, who received life in prison.

Interviews with classmates and professors revealed that the boy was a bit strange, awfully quiet at times, and a hell-raiser too. An undistinguished student, he was a budding black sheep in a family with a pasture full of them. Outsiders figured it was a miracle David was as normal as he was. Butlers, gardeners and cooks essentially raised him.

Gossip columnists and the tabloids had a field day. They learned of Marguerite's financial predicament before the courts did. One wag dubbed the duchess a "debtoress." A hyena pack of relatives and attorneys fought over what little property wasn't surrendered to satisfy liabilities.

There wasn't much left for 18-year-old David Benning Junior. His one valuable asset, *Raising Chickens on Mars,* which had hung above the banquet room-studio fireplace, vanished either the night of the murder or shortly before. David hadn't been in the room for several days. That Scott possibly sold *Raising Chickens on Mars* to an unknown buyer to grubstake his leaving Marguerite may have caused the deadly confrontation, but the painting's whereabouts remained a mystery. It wasn't in Hathaway House and it hadn't turned up in a gallery.

David Benning Junior horrified his relatives by enlisting in the army. Those who couldn't avoid military service with phony medical problems wangled commissions and Pentagon desk jobs. One of their own as a buck private was too mortifying to contemplate. Not that he would be a soldier long, they knew. The army would introduce him to discipline and spit him out when he refused to adapt.

David surprised everyone including himself by taking to military life. He didn't particularly like it. He didn't know anybody who did, even the lifers. Everybody was in for a reason. For David Benning, the army was family.

The army fed him three square meals a day; they didn't forget to make arrangements on cook's day off. They told him what to do and what not to do. David harbored no illusions that the army cared about him personally. He belonged to the army. He was government property. Belonging was a new phenomenon to him.

David reenlisted and was accepted in OCS, where he graduated as a second lieutenant. He was shipped to Vietnam as a platoon leader assigned to Cu Chi, where the ground beneath it was so riddled with tunnels it was like wormwood. For the first half of his tour, Lieutenant Benning followed orders. He sent his men into the tunnels to be drowned in water traps, bitten by snakes, and shot in the face.

After 6 months in-country, he concluded that his enemy was the United States Army, not the Vietcong. With flimsy justification, the army was trying to get him and his men killed. His new family was behaving as badly as his old family.

Lieutenant David Benning henceforth refused to order his men into the tunnels. Night patrols, fine. Paddy-humping up to their waists in muck, okay too.

But no more futile, suicidal tunnels. The army offered him the choice of a Section Eight or a court martial and the Leavenworth rock pile. David chose the loony route.

Not long after Benning's discharge, a fellow inmate murdered Kennedy Scott. Behind the painter in the chow line, he had severed his carotid artery with a shank fashioned of a soup spoon and toothbrush. It wasn't personal. Scott's murderer saw that they were having waxy, orangish macaroni and cheese for the third time that week and simply snapped.

Still doubting Scott's guilt, David attended his funeral, the only member of the clan to show. The sole Scott family representative was a maiden aunt who flew in from Omaha. The Hathaway House butler, a man named Tomlinson, and an art critic brought the mourner total to ten.

The art critic advised David that *Raising Chickens on Mars* was still missing. "I agree with the police theory that Scott took down the painting and sold it. Your mother got in his face. She paid with her life."

"So where's the painting?" David asked. "Kennedy Scott couldn't've slipped it out inside his raincoat."

"It doubled in value immediately after Scott was killed and is steadily appreciating. It's in the hands of somebody who can afford to wait," the critic said.

Because of the tainted discharge, David Benning had no GI Bill benefits, but enough of the puny estate in the bank to finance a return to college. David graduated in accounting. Thanks to anti-Vietnam War sentiment, his scarlet letter began to fade. A sawmill in Washington State ignored his service record and hired him.

David had had his fill of excitement, blood and turbulence. He married a college sweetheart who came from a volatile home too. They raised two sons and lived a stable, quiet life. After the boys were grown, there was nothing left between man and wife.

Two years after the divorce, the sawmill downsized David Benning. He had seen the signs — thinner stacks of shipping manifests, dwindling board feet to tally, short-term loans to meet payrolls.

He received two responses to his résumés. Both were from temp agencies. One wanted to know his typing speed, the other if he could lift 75 pounds and pass a drug test.

In very late middle age, former comptroller David Benning Junior was unemployed and unemployable.

~ ~ ~

"So the butler really did do it," Margo Hogan said, handing David Benning back the letter.

They were in their sweats, having just finished a 20-mile bicycle ride.

He said, "Maybe. Tomlinson — we addressed butlers by their surnames — was our last. I'd been away at school, so I didn't know him well. I saw Roland Tomlinson at Kennedy Scott's funeral. While Kennedy was a wild man and he and my mother had some legendary brawls, I never thought he had it in him to kill her."

Margo said, "Tomlinson attended the funeral out of guilt? His lawyer, this J. Robin Selkirk, says in the letter that Tomlinson made a deathbed confession. Your mother caught the butler stealing *Raising Chickens on Mars*. He clobbered her with a poker and placed it by Scott, who was passed out on the floor after a bender. Not a word in this lawyer letter on the fate of the painting. Nor whether he reported Tomlinson's confession to the police."

David took a hefty pictorial book on American painters from the bookcase and opened it to a page devoted to Kennedy Scott. There was a brief bio and a plate of his best-known work, *Raising Chickens on Mars*. Four other Scotts were known to exist, all smaller and less vividly colorful than *Raising Chickens*.

Margo said, "*Raising Chickens on Mars* is so famous there's a drink named for it. You'd think Scott had been to Mars."

"He had, in his head."

"Looks like potato salad with blue and orange stuff in it," Margo said.

"Be that as it may, the guesstimate of its value is eighty million. Wherever it is."

"The painting's noticeable, unique. How could you just walk out with it?"

"Scott painted oil on canvas. All you had to do was pull the staples on the stretcher bars and roll it up. It'd be doable if you had time."

Margo Hogan was a retired librarian who'd been dumped by her husband of 33 years for a big-haired, gum-popping beautician whose parents hadn't met when the Hogans wed.

Margo and David lived on 401(k)s and Social Security while they decided what they wanted to be when they grew up. They did love riding. And walking. And hiking and birding. Trim and fit, Margo and David were a striking couple on their bicycles, her long gray hair trailing. They'd found vigor and each other late in life.

"What are we waiting for?" she said.

"What are we waiting for?" he said. "We haven't taken a trip lately."

She said, "I'll pack. You make the reservations."

~ ~ ~

J. Robin Selkirk, Roland Tomlinson's lawyer, had a 2-room office in a Hyannis strip mall. Soft and pudgy, looking older than his 36 years, Selkirk wore a translucent comb-over and a sour expression.

Selkirk was wary of this pair of old-timers who had dropped in unannounced. He knew the type. Lean and tanned, they were fitness freaks. The ones who power-walked in shopping malls, getting in your way. Geezers determined to outlive you.

J. Robin Selkirk's uncle, Alvin (Ambulance Al) Selkirk, inspired him to go to law school. Wastrel that Uncle Al was, he knew how to enjoy life.

"Our firm does *pro bono* at the nursing home where Mr. Tomlinson lived," Rob Selkirk said. "My work there consists of writing and updating wills. It was a real shock when he called me in to hear his confession, as if I were a priest. He'd been moved to a hospital then and was on a respirator. I could barely understand him. Attempting to record the conversation would've been pointless. He died the next day."

"He didn't say what he did with the painting?"

"No. His desire was to purge his conscience of the murder. He felt terrible that an innocent man died in prison."

Margo tapped her temple. "How was Tomlinson upstairs?"

"He never was what you'd deem a Rhodes Scholar, but he was lucid. No dementia, no Alzheimer's."

Selkirk's condescending evaluation needled David. While Roland Tomlinson had little formal education, David recalled him as thoughtful and correct and articulate. "Did Tomlinson have any next of kin?"

"No. His tiny estate just covered the funeral service I arranged."

Margo asked, "Have you notified the police?"

"No. It'd be hearsay from a dying man on medication."

David said, "I'd like to check out the old neighborhood."

Selkirk smirked. "A fifty-acre estate is quite a neighborhood. There have been some changes."

"Don't spoil my surprise."

Rob Selkirk looked at David and said, "My mother remembers my grandmother buying Hathaway Bleach. It came in a gallon jug with a ring handle and cost a dime."

~ ~ ~

The sign on the iron gate of Hathaway House identified it as The Dharramaddaetyu Institute of Astral-Kinetic Healing.

"The landscaping is neater than my mother had it kept toward the end when money was running short," David said as they drove along the brick arc leading to the pillared entrance.

"Wow. You spent your childhood at Tara," Margo said.

"The Civil War was quieter," David said.

The front doors were ajar and nobody answered their knock. They went in and David led the tour, looking into bedrooms, studies and drawing rooms. Most were vacant. The rooms in use were occupied by people who sat cross-legged on mats, meditating and chanting.

"It's scary that nobody's challenged us," Margo said. "We must look like we belong."

David said, "The guys' hairstyle is Rasputin and women haven't jingled this much since the sixties. Hathaway House should be Halfway House."

They went into the banquet room-studio. The fireplace had been bricked in and the wood paneling was bare. The brickwork was old, some of the mortar cracking, and the paneling could use cleaning and varnishing. David shivered. It was a cold day and the room felt 10 degrees cooler to him than outside. He

161

stared at the fireplace long enough to concern Margo, who put an arm around him. "Are you okay?"

He nodded.

"Flashback?"

"I guess I wanted to feel or sense something."

"Don't go on a guilt trip. It's not your fault you can't."

"I did have a sensation."

"Of what?"

"I'm not sure. Something to do with temperature I can't put my finger on. Plus something else I missed that night, something I should've remembered, but don't. Something I may've blocked out."

~ ~ ~

"Did Selkirk say how long ago Tomlinson died?" Margo said.

David was driving. "Not that I heard. Why?"

It's peculiar he didn't."

"Let's check for ourselves."

David Benning Junior and Margo Hogan, ex-librarian, went to the nearest library, where they scanned newspaper obituaries online.

"Finally," Margo said. "Six weeks ago tomorrow. Rob Selkirk took his time contacting you."

David read, saying, "Survived by a niece, Cynthia Baxter. Selkirk didn't know Tomlinson had a next of kin or he's lying."

"Is Rob Selkirk associated with the old Hathaway family law firm?"

David shook his head. "The estate was picked clean. They terminated representation."

"Do you have any family left in the area?"

"It's highly doubtful any Bennings or Hathaways are anywhere. There was some serious dissipation on the Hathaway side. My father was an only child in a small family."

162

"He was and won what at Iwo Jima?"

"A Marine Corps captain. The Navy Cross."

"He was important to you. I have to pry him out of you."

"He would've been important if I'd have known him. I like to think he would've come home to a tickertape parade and gone on to become a spectacular black sheep."

Margo smiled and reached across the table to stroke his arm. "Should we pay a call on Cynthia?"

Cynthia Baxter was listed in the Boston-area directory. She lived in a clapboard apartment building that struck David as a candidate for a wrecking ball. Cynthia opened her door an inch and David introduced himself.

"Go away."

"We're not here to give you a hard time, Cynthia," Margo said. "We need answers."

After David mentioned J. Robin Selkirk, Cynthia let them inside her tiny spotless apartment. "I'm sorry about the grief Uncle Roland caused."

"It's not your fault," David said.

"We weren't aware Mr. Tomlinson had any relatives." Margo said.

"It's odd Robin didn't tell you. It must have been an oversight. He's an excellent attorney and very thorough."

Cynthia Baxter was a thin, pale woman in her 40s. David thought that Selkirk's name put a blush in her cheeks. He'd have to ask Margo if it was his imagination.

"Is Selkirk your attorney too?"

She hesitated, then said, "No."

"I suppose Rob spoke of *Raising Chickens on Mars*," David said.

"We discussed it."

"How about you and Mr. Tomlinson?"

"No. Uncle Roland and I weren't close."

"You were his only living relative?"

"Yes."

"How long had he been in the nursing home?" David asked.

"Three or four months. He was self-sufficient until recently."

"Self-sufficient as in independently wealthy?" Margo asked.

Cynthia forced a tight smile. "No. He lived in apartments smaller than mine and never owned a car. After your mother's murder, he worked domestic and janitorial jobs. Toward the end at Hathaway House, with the staff cuts, he'd doubled as a janitor. There wasn't much demand for a butler any more. If Uncle Roland sold the painting, he didn't reap the rewards."

David said, "Your uncle confessed to Selkirk to killing my mother to cover up the theft of *Raising Chickens on Mars*. The painting belongs to me."

Cynthia Baxter tensed. "If I knew anything about the painting, I'd tell you."

~ ~ ~

At their motel, Margo said, "Do I think Cynthia is infatuated with Rob Selkirk, you ask? I wouldn't be surprised if his class ring is under her pillow. Or she wishes it were, with him next to her. And, yes, I believe she truly knows nothing of the painting."

"Do you think *Mars* is still in the vicinity?"

"My instincts tell me it is," Margo said. "It isn't public knowledge. I think Selkirk has revealed Tomlinson's confession to as few people as possible, for whatever purpose. Any luck summoning that 'sensation' of yours?"

"No."

Their room had two beds. Their suitcases were opened on one. Margo pointed at them and said, "Do we pack or do we commit to the long term?"

"Eighty million dollars," David said. "We could spend some on ourselves and squander the rest by giving it to charity."

Margo took an old telephone book from the nightstand and paged to H. "The easiest research technique first. There's one Hathaway. George W. His address is North Truro."

David sat up. "That's along the bay, between Wellfleet and Provincetown."

"Do you remember George Hathaway?"

"Faintly. I had a shirttail relative by that name, a second cousin. He was younger. He'd come with his parents to summer lawn parties. There'd be bottles of French champagne iced in tubs like average folk would with soda and beer. A small kid. And quiet."

~ ~ ~

The adult George Hathaway was neither small nor quiet. He lived in a cabin verging on shack, on a lot too narrow and a beach too unprotected and rocky for profitable development. There was a faded FOR SALE BY OWNER sign staked in a patchy excuse for a yard.

George Hathaway bemoaned his real estate frustrations in a booming voice that David attributed to hearing damaged by a lifetime of living 20-feet from a crashing surf. "Nobody wants to give me my price. Realtors say it's tacky, it ain't appealing, the market's crummy, blah blah blah. I do odd jobs for a living. It's past my time to relax and enjoy. This dump is my Hathaway legacy and I intend to be paid fairly for it."

"My legacy was a Kennedy Scott painting," David said, summarizing why he was there, with minimal specifics.

165

"Ain't that something if it's true?" Hathaway laughed. "The butler did it. Get it?"

The interior of George Hathaway's hovel was a jumble of old newspapers, magazines, foul odors and worthless bric-a-brac. "Know of any other surviving Hathaways?"

"Nope. All dead and buried. I didn't know any of you Bennings still existed."

"I'd sure like to find the painting."

"You're the second person who's been snooping about that Mars thing."

"Who's the first?"

"A shifty little lawyer named Shelfkirk or something like that came out, interested in my property. Didn't say nothing about no picture. He visited twice. I thought I had me a live one. A week after, I was burgled. They turned it upside down."

"What was taken?"

"Nothing."

"You think it was the lawyer?" Margo asked.

"If he was sniffing for that picture, yeah, him or somebody he hired. If I had it, you'd be looking me up over there on the French Riviera."

~ ~ ~

Margo and David drove through the gateway of the Dharramaddaetyu Institute of Astral-Kinetic Healing, encouraged by Rob Selkirk's suspected burglary of George Hathaway's home.

"We can presume Rob Selkirk doesn't know where *Raising Chickens on Mars* is," Margo said.

"May we also presume that Selkirk finally wrote me because he presumes I may know where it is or know how to find it?"

"We'd be thinking the worst of the man, which is fine by me. What are we doing back here? Tickling that sensation of yours?"

As he parked, David said, "I'm hoping for enlightenment."

This time, a stout middle-aged man with a shaved head interrupted them in the foyer. He wore a saffron robe and a large earring that reminded David of a merry-go-round brass ring.

"You are not known to me. May I please see your enrollment cards?"

"Just looking around," David said.

"We're thinking of joining," Margo said.

"You should be accompanied by a counselor. I am Lan. What is it you seek?"

Margo said, "Raised consciousness and cleansed karma. You know, the usual."

"How did you learn of us?" Lan asked.

David said, "I used to live here."

"In a past life?"

"You could say that."

"Our healing is spiritually and holistically based. Auras are focused and transformed to facilitate multidimensional cleansing of the self."

Margo beamed and squeezed David's hand. "Oh, this is exactly what we are seeking."

"We do not recommend hasty decisions," Lan said primly.

David knew the game was lost. "Speaking of holistically based, how long ago did your organization materialize at Hathaway House?"

Lan folded his arms and became a standing Buddha.

~ ~ ~

In the car, David said, "He read us as phonies the minute we walked in. If that outfit is incorporated, there'll be a public record."

"I forget that you were an accountant a thousand years ago," Margo said. "This is a job for the library's computers."

~ ~ ~

"Buster Jensen of Dubuque, Iowa. Founder and former CEO of the Dharramaddaetyu Institute," David said, scrolling through screens. "In 1999, Buster had a vision. He ascended to a higher astral plane and became the Master Dharramaddaetyu. The former Mr. Jensen incorporated five years ago and sold his shares to a core group of members who run the organization today. Buster ran with the IPO cash. The planes he's ascending now take him to Waikiki and Cancun, in first-class."

"What color's their ink?"

"They're hemorrhaging. Permanent membership in the Institute has declined from seven thousand to three hundred. Without Buster's charisma, the flock drifted."

"I see mostly numbers and you're narrating a soap opera," Margo said, resting her chin on his shoulder. "How long has Dharramaddaetyu been headquartered at Hathaway House?"

"Three years ago, purchased from a failing bed-and-breakfast."

"What was Hathaway House before the B and B?"

"It has a history of marginal hotel and resort ventures. Our summer is short and the beachfront is as rocky as George Hathaway's. When I was a kid, Mother had started closing up rooms and sealing the fireplaces by bricking them in. It costs a fortune to heat the place. Hello."

"What?"

"Look. Under Dharramaddaetyu's board of directors. General Counsel, J. Robin Selkirk."

~ ~ ~

"How do we entice Selkirk out of the woodwork?" Margo asked David.

They were having a lunch of sandwiches and *a* Raising Chickens on Mars, a powerful and tasty concoction of red liqueurs honoring the Red Planet. The cocktail came in a stem glass, sugar on the rim.

David said, "Selkirk said 'our' firm does *pro bono*. Rob's a one-man band and he doesn't strike me as the philanthropic type."

"Is Cynthia Baxter in cahoots, perhaps unwittingly?"

"And did Roland Tomlinson first clear his conscience with Selkirk or with Cynthia?"

"She did pause when asked if Selkirk was her attorney, like she was being absolutely sure she had her story straight," Margo said. "Here's a scenario. Tomlinson confessed long before he died. That would explain Selkirk as a selfless volunteer at the nursing home. He cozied up to him and wooed Cynthia, thinking she had the painting."

"Painting, painting, who has the painting?" David said, throwing up his hands.

"We energize Selkirk into believing we do."

~ ~ ~

At the law office of J. Robin Selkirk, attorney at law, David described their meeting with Cynthia Baxter.

Rob Selkirk said, "Sorry. She slipped my mind. Tomlinson hardly knew her."

"Did she attend the burial service you arranged?"

He frowned. "I'm not certain."

David smiled. "Come on, Mr. Selkirk. This was no state funeral."

"I may've run into Ms. Baxter."

"A sweet lady," Margo said.

"Where are we going with this?"

"Just making small talk," David said. "I want to buy Hathaway House."

"Oh?"

"It's not what you're thinking," David said. "I've saved some money, made some lucky investments. I bought Microsoft IPO and cashed it in. I want my childhood home. I want it to be the home it wasn't when I grew up in it. You're the only attorney in town we know. I thought you could look into its availability."

Selkirk stared at David, then said, "I can do that. By coincidence, I represent the Dharramaddaetyu Institute."

"Really?" David and Margo chimed.

~ ~ ~

"He knows you were lying about your wealth."

"Unfortunately I was."

"He thinks *Raising Chickens on Mars* is your windfall."

"Cool customer, isn't he?"

Margo was driving. "Sociopaths are. There's a gorgeous silver Porsche 911 in Selkirk's slot. Do you agree with my plan?"

"I do."

"So we deduce this is as his destination," Margo said, parking a block from Cynthia Baxter's apartment house. "How long do we wait?"

"Detectives sit and wait as long as they have to."

Thirty minutes later, a silver Porsche 911 raced by them and braked in the loading zone at Cynthia Baxter's apartment building. Rob Selkirk jumped out and ran to her unit, using a key to enter.

Margo said, "Not a happy camper."

They heard loud voices and hurried into the apartment as Selkirk shook Cynthia by the shoulders.

"No, I didn't, Robbie, I swear," she cried.

"She's right, she didn't," Margo said.

"You're trespassing," Rob Selkirk said.

"Take your hands off her," David said.

"Butt out, pops."

Pops? David wrenched Selkirk free of Cynthia and shoved him toward the couch. Selkirk threw a clumsy punch that glanced off David's shoulder. David shoved harder and the attorney tripped, going down hard on the immaculately-polished floor.

"Please don't hurt him," Cynthia pleaded.

Margo restrained her before she could go to Selkirk's aid. "Honey, you and I need to have a gal-to-gal about Mr. Wrong here and men in general."

David told Selkirk, "We don't have the painting."

"That Microsoft IPO stock?" he said on his knees, rubbing a hip.

"No, Robbie," Margo said. "None of the above. The only thing we're in the market for is the truth."

Cynthia said, "Robbie, we should talk to them."

"Shut up!"

Margo said, "Cynthia, how on earth did you meet this little weasel?"

"At Uncle Roland's funeral. Nobody else came. We hit it off. I thought we had a whirlwind — Well, I thought we did."

"Cynthia, you said Roland Tomlinson worked domestic jobs following my mother's murder. Were any at Hathaway House?"

"Yes. Businesses tried to make a go of it as a B and B or a resort. Employers were impressed that Uncle Roland knew it like the back of his hand."

"Robbie, you told the truth about Uncle Roland's deathbed confession, didn't you?" Cynthia asked him.

"I did. Honestly."

"Which jump-started the present situation," David said. "You used me as bait or a catalyst to locate the painting."

"You're good at using people, Robbie," Cynthia said.

J. Robin Selkirk studied his fingernails.

"You swear you didn't do what?" Margo asked Cynthia.

"Tell you that we broke into George Hathaway's house. I'd told Robbie that you came to see me."

Margo's mouth fell open. "*We* broke in?"

"It was the stupidest thing I've ever done in my life. Robbie said he needed me. Two could search faster than one. He said there was an excellent chance George Hathaway collaborated with Uncle Roland and had the painting. Once we established he had it, we'd pursue it by legal means. I realize that he was using me as an accomplice, so I wouldn't be tempted to talk."

"George Hathaway was a kid when my mother was killed," David said.

"Yes, but we thought that if *Raising Chickens on Mars* hadn't been passed down, there'd be linkage, a clue. All we found was squalor. It's beyond me how anyone can live like that."

"It's logical that Tomlinson would be unable to dispose of the painting by himself. He was out of his league," David said. "Did Tomlinson approach an art dealer?"

"Or did he chicken out because of the murder and not sell the painting?" Margo said. "Did he stash the painting for the future?"

"What say we take a field trip there?" David said.

"Count me out," Rob Selkirk said. "There's nothing in it for me now."

David said, "I think you'd like to join us anyway."

Selkirk laughed and shook his head. "Why should I cooperate with you losers?"

"While we're playing detective, we won't be writing a letter to the Massachusetts Bar Association," Margo said.

~ ~ ~

Rob Selkirk's assignment was to handle Lan, the Dharramaddaetyu CFO. He did so sullenly, though without complaint. The foursome was escorted to the library and left undisturbed. At David's request, Lan had dispatched an underling to the coach house for a sledgehammer and a flashlight.

"Your temperature-related sensation?" Margo asked him.

"Yesterday, the room gave me the shivers. When I found Mother, the fireplace was going and the room was warm. Why that's important, I don't know."

"Tomlinson told me he disliked your mother and loathed Kennedy Scott," Rob Selkirk said.

"Is that true, David?" Margo asked.

"I wouldn't be surprised. A component of a servant's job is concealing class resentment. Tomlinson must have held in plenty throughout the years. I'll give him some benefit of the doubt on the murder. It wasn't premeditated. Mother went looking for Kennedy Scott. She found him passed out in the banquet room and caught Tomlinson removing the painting."

Rob Selkirk said, "Roland may have panicked after the murder, but he'd have the presence of mind to hide the painting on or off the premises. He didn't want attention drawn from Scott."

"The police searched the mansion?" Margo said.

"They ransacked it," David said.

"Shelves, nooks and crannies, drawers," Cynthia said, looking around. "This room would be a nightmare to dust."

"Selkirk, you're as familiar with Hathaway House as I am. Have any idea when this was bricked in?" David asked.

"Do I look like the resident historian?"

"David and I aren't going to file charges if you'll stop behaving like a horse's ass," Margo said.

David handed the sledgehammer to Rob Selkirk. "Me?"

David said. "If I were Tomlinson, I'd be worrying day and night that somebody would stumble onto the painting. I'd be afraid to walk out with it too."

"Bricklayers were called in. Tomlinson seized the moment. He may have hidden *Raising Chickens on Mars* elsewhere initially. He had intimate knowledge of the building and grounds. It'd be easy for the cops to miss, especially if they concentrated their investigation on this room and operated on the theory it was already gone," Margo said. "What's more permanent than brick and mortar?"

"This is a new suit," Selkirk said, taking off the jacket, looking at Cynthia Baxter for support.

She rolled her eyes and he began pounding. The masonry yielded stubbornly, coming apart in jagged chunks. Once Selkirk smashed an opening wide enough for his head and shoulders, David spelled him and finished.

Margo held the flashlight and her nose. "Yuck, what smells and what's that goo on the andirons?"

David poked at it with the sledgehammer. "Sticky, moldy and a dirty rainbow of color. There are fibers in it too."

"From the canvas?" Margo asked.

"Could be." David pointed his flashlight at the open damper. More of the material hung as if stalactites. "Tomlinson could've used an adhesive to hold it against chimney walls. But not in this one on the night of the murder.

"The temperature sensation. This fireplace was smoldering."

"Maybe from the ashes of the painting's wooden framework Tomlinson fed into it," Margo said. "With your mother dead and Scott out like a light, he had time to work."

"When the police were done in this room, Tomlinson moved *Raising Chickens on Mars* here from wherever. It's the largest room in the house, the most expensive to heat, so that fireplace was the first to be sealed with brickwork."

Rob Selkirk slumped against a wall, exhausted. Cynthia knelt at his side, wiping his perspiring forehead with a handkerchief.

Margo looked at her and sighed, then said, "So Tomlinson left *Raising Chickens on Mars* to molder for over forty years?"

"Whether guilt-ridden and/or afraid, he couldn't bring himself to follow through," David said. "After the opening was bricked in, he may've been comforted, knowing his secret was safe."

"Knowing it was there for him too," Rob Selkirk said.

David said, "It didn't occur to him that they only bricked in the opening. They didn't seal the chimney cap."

"Decades of melted snow and rainwater dripping down," Margo said.

"Beside your 'temperature' sensation, is there that 'something else' you missed?"

175

"Mother on the floor. The expression on her face, in her eyes, was surprise. When she was with Scott her face usually registered anger."

"You have something in your eyes, David," Margo said, dabbing them with a tissue.

CINDERELLA'S DREAM BECOMES A NIGHTMARE

Alas, she was not living happily ever after.

Her marriage to the Handsome Prince proved to be less than idyllic. It was soon apparent to Cinderella that his parents were driving a wedge between them. She supposed it was a combination of her barrenness, her less than regal pedigree, and lack of a classical education. The romantic magic of a perfectly-fitting Lucite™ slipper could maintain a shaky marriage only so long.

The Handsome Prince didn't stand up for her either. As well as being a wastrel, he was turning out to be something of a mama's boy and a serious boozer. When Cinderella considered the trouble the King and Queen endured to find him a bride – a nobleman with his looks, his position, his money – she should have wondered then. The clincher was when she perused his wing of the Royal Palace and found empty whiskey bottles and the unopened Viagra™ container she had purchased for him.

One night, a clique of army officers stormed the Royal Palace. They were led by a field marshal with shoulder boards and mirrored shades. Cigar in hand, he promised democracy and free elections as soon as the situation stabilized.

The upheaval saved her from having to make a painful and scandalous decision: to file for divorce. The course of events accomplished that.

The Royal Family went into exile to the Cayman Islands, for the sunshine and to be close to their money. They took their entourage and servants, but left her behind. She got up in the morning and they were simply gone, no note, no nothing, not even from her husband.

Almost as heartbreaking, Cinderella's Wicked Stepmother and Mean and Ugly Stepsisters had betrayed her, the ungrateful bitches.

After the Lucite™ slipper revelation and her betrothal, Cinderella had offered forgiveness for years of abuse. She'd appointed the Stepsisters as her maids of honor in the grandest wedding the now-defunct kingdom had ever seen.

In addition, Cinderella had recruited husbands of minor nobility for them, giving the reluctant beaus the alternative of the guillotine, a highly-effective bluff. She installed the newlyweds in luxury condo suites with mother-in-law rooms, so Wicked Stepmother could alternate between making each daughter's life miserable.

But Cinderella's treacherous step-brothers-in-law switched sides during the coup when offered obscure ministry posts for their cooperation. There was talk of a show trial for Cinderella, wife of the playboy who squandered the national treasury on his expensive hobbies: car collecting and car racing.

You *supermodel* skank, the Mean and Ugly Stepsisters screeched at her from the Royal Palace lawn.

Scapegoat City, she thought as locked the door of her wing seconds before rifle butts slammed against it. She hurried down a secret stairway in her spacious closet to the basement and the alley, tearing out of there in a Mercedes SL65 AMG with HNS PRNC vanity plates.

Cinderella fled to her Fairy Godmother's. Her suburban cottage was in bad repair and the golden coach in the driveway was tarnished, with one tire flat.

Fairy Godmother answered the door, disheveled and tipsy, holding a martini glass in her liver-spotted hand. The coup was on every television channel, even those with Fairy Godmother's favorite infomercials and reality TV shows.

It's a goddamn Chinese fire drill, she ranted to Cinderella. Free elections and democracy? Gimme a fucking break. How many times have we heard that line of bullshit when Third World governments played musical chairs?

After her tirade and a digitalis under her tongue, Fairy Godmother dyed Cinderella's flaxen hair black, gave her flat-lens glasses, and applied heavy makeup. Her magic wand was in a half-full martini pitcher. There was just enough juice left in the batteries to materialize a phony passport.

Cinderella slipped out of town just ahead of pursuing soldiers. Adopting the assumed identity on her counterfeit passport, she crossed the frontier and spent weeks in a refugee camp before being granted an entry visa to a faraway land.

Penniless except for a niggling portion of her allowance that she had squirreled away into offshore accounts of her own when her marriage started to founder, Cinderella arrived on the foreign shore all alone. She had never held an actual job. Her only employment experience consisted of exhausting scullery-maid duty at the mercy of her Wicked Stepmother and Mean and Ugly Stepsisters.

Cinderella hired an efficient and grabby immigration lawyer who wangled for her proper papers and a green card. In her mid-30s and incognito, she was still a babe.

Cinderella fell back on her one marketable skill, a tenuous one at that: art. She'd tired of pining at home while her prince-husband was pursuing his true passion: cars. Racing them, collecting them, and hanging out with his parasitic, car-crazed buddies. She filled the void with painting classes. She'd always loved to sketch and doodle.

Cinderella enjoyed doing still lifes and impressionistic seascapes in various mediums such as oil, tempura and acrylics. Dabbling in abstract expressionism and surrealism, she broadened her tastes. She possessed a degree of talent and had been on the verge of becoming a semi-polished amateur when the rebels seized the Kingdom.

She went by Cynthia Eller, the name on her bogus passport, and landed a job with a sign-painting company that specialized in furniture and automobile showroom windows. Her employer was an expatriate who fortunately didn't recognize her. Cynthia learned that a number of her countrymen had fled to this land to become entrepreneurs. Her employer had extensive connections in that community.

Cynthia was a whiz at the car dealerships, slathering on HUGE CLEARANCE SALE, NO MONEY DOWN, ONLY $199 PER MONTH, and BAD CREDIT? NO PROBLEM! She had a knack for color and old-country curlicues in the script. She could work in a multitude of fonts too, Bookman Old Style, Times New Roman, and Engravers MT among them. Not only was Cynthia Eller good, she was fast.

Cynthia was given a sizable raise and all the work she wanted. She primarily worked late evenings and early mornings, when the businesses were closed. She enjoyed the solitude, the freedom to express herself, although she did not delude herself that her painterly swaths were in the same league as Monet or Dalí.

One night after closing at an expat-owned dealership, she heard loud noises in the body and fender shop. This surprised her because employees normally knocked off for the day at 5. Yet overhead doors rolled up and down, up and down. The grinding and cutting of metal was nonstop. Cynthia continued working, minding her own business, until the metalwork suddenly ceased.

Then she heard voices, two men shouting, one in her native tongue. It was difficult to distinguish the full conversation through walls and doors, but words in her language were angry, threatening and profane.

She tiptoed closer to investigate. Through a small window she saw cars not normally repaired at this, a domestic-model dealership. There were Audis, Porsches, BMWs, Jaguars, a Ferrari, and a doorless Maserati Quattroporte. She had a queasy memory of her husband. These were models fancied by him and his worthless chums. Some were intact, others were in pieces. Cynthia didn't understand.

The man yelling in her language fired a gun point-blank at another man, who lurched backward as if he had been hit by a club, fell on the hood of a Jaguar, and slumped to the floor. Other men in coveralls dove for cover under hydraulic hoists and behind dismantled fenders.

Cynthia screamed.

The gunman wheeled and aimed at her. He looked vaguely familiar.

He fired and spidered the window glass above Cynthia, who ran outside. The cold, abrasive pavement reminded her that she was barefoot. She had taken off her brand-new sneakers to work, lest they be spattered with paint.

She didn't stop running until she waved down a taxi. She got into it and went home, her feet throbbing and bleeding. Cynthia packed and caught a bus to the next state. She fought tears as she rode to the unknown.

Cynthia Eller changed her eyeglass style and dyed her brunette hair red. She was developing spilt-end frizzies, but this could not be avoided. Her life was in jeopardy.

A chic art gallery in the state's largest city hired her, few questions asked. They adored her appearance, her exotic accent, her hands-on knowledge of fine art. For several weeks she was happier than she could remember being. A quick learner, she mastered the myriad tasks associated to any small business: inventory, accounts receivable, moderately heavy lifting, and taking out the trash. She loved every bit of it.

Cynthia was a hit with customers. She surprised herself by selling paintings while barely trying, including dreck she heartily disliked, works composed entirely of negative space.

She devoted long hours to an upcoming exhibition. It was to be the breakout show for a young minimalist who surely must have been a blood relative of the owners. They were organizing a full-blown Brie and chardonnay pre-opening party for him.

Cynthia thought him so minimalist that activity on his sprawling mostly-white canvases did not exist. The painter's boorish personality was unfortunately not as minimal as his art. And she wasn't looking forward to entertaining a bunch of freeloaders.

On the morning on the party, a handsome man her age walked into the gallery. He had a kind face and wore a suit, but it was not cut of the fine cloth many of their gallery customers wore.

A bulge in his jacket puzzled Cynthia until he addressed her by name and presented identification as an INS special agent named Jose Maria Principe.

She took a deep breath and informed Agent Principe that her papers were in order.

I'm sure they are, said he. We are investigating a homicide we have reason to believe you have information on. The alleged perpetrators are in the country on student visas and they have not attended a class.

What schools were they to attend?

Harvard, South Dakota School of Mines and Technology, Downtown Barber College. They run the gamut.

What on earth do you mean by homicide, asked Cynthia?

A person fitting your general description was seen running from an automobile dealership. The body of a man with organized crime ties was found inside the building. He'd obviously had a disagreement with somebody. We traced a sign painting project in progress to your employer, who reported that you had disappeared. You do very nice work, by the way. Those empty promises on the windows indicate a certain flair.

Thank you. By organized crime, do you mean gangsters?

I'm afraid so. This is a newer outfit, from a country that recently changed hands. Their closest counterpart is the Russian Mafia, he said. In fact, this country, the nation of your birth and of these gangsters, is on our SCL.

What is that?

Shithole Country List. All SCL immigrants are subject to immediate deportation.

Cynthia gasped.

Have no fear. I am flexible.

He, then gave her a photograph, asking if she knew this man.

Cynthia gasped again at the front and side profile pictures of the gunman. The long scraggly hair, the grim jaw set, the hard piercing eyes. She realized now why the monster was familiar to her. He was a car-enthusiast chum of her husband's. She had seen him and her husband together at a distance, in the Royal Coach Yard.

Terrified, she said that she knew him not.

I don't blame you for being frightened, Jose Maria Principe said gently, advising that they are truly heartless people.

He paused. It wasn't only a holstered gun causing the jacket bulge. He removed one of her sneakers from his jacket pocket and asked her to please slip it on.

She obeyed and the dainty footwear slipped on easily.

Nobody else in the entire world could possibly have a foot so slim and petite, so lovely, he said in a voice she read as pure admiration and compassion, with not a scintilla of foot fetishism.

She sighed, thinking the good news was that this time the man practicing the craft of a shoe salesman was not a self-absorbed pretty boy. The kind and handsome INS agent seemed to genuinely care. Cynthia asked him to follow her to the chic gallery's office, where she related her life's story and confessed what she had witnessed.

You are lucky to have gotten away, said he. This hombre was head of the King's secret police. He fled following the revolution and has done okay by himself as godfather of a network of old cronies. They were running a stolen luxury-car ring and chop shop out of that car dealership and others.

Cynthia was keeping current on her homeland's travails. She had been shocked to hear of the secret police apparatus, the profiteering, the ineptitude and corruption that precipitated the revolution.

The new regime was far worse than its predecessor. It had sunk into economic and social chaos. Its transition to democracy was slower than slow. The leading industry was the black market. The bad news went on and on and on.

Cinderella asked if the monster was coming after her.

The INS agent shrugged and said that he had numerous irons in the fire and that his bosses are unconvinced he is. Frankly, he was not so confident. Her positive identification of him is the only concrete thing that will put him away for a long time.

She felt if not safe, at least safer in the presence of this man, and asked what she should do.

He asked if he could put her on ice for a while until they can throw a net over the creep.

Hide? No! I have run long enough.

Agent Principe couldn't guarantee her protection. They didn't have the budget or the personnel.

She said she'd be careful, convincing neither him nor herself.

He wrote on a business card and gave it to her: his home and cell phone numbers. He said to call him anytime day or night.

Later, as she busied herself during the boisterous party, she couldn't get it out of her head how kind and concerned Agent Principe was, not to mention how gorgeous and studly. She felt secure tonight at the show, though, with all the guests.

Safety in numbers, she thought as she went into the storeroom for another bottle of mediocre white wine. She would keep people around her until the killer was in police custody.

She was thinking that as a large coarse hand clamped onto her mouth. She smelled garlic, perspiration and cheap liquor as she was dragged to the rear of the storeroom as if a rag doll.

Speaking in an unschooled dialect of their native tongue, he told her to promise not to scream or she was dead.

Cynthia Eller nodded numbly as he shoved her against the cloakroom wall. Even in the dim light she recognized him and his cold eyes in an instant.

He pointed a craggy finger and said he knew who she was.

You have mistaken me for somebody else, she said.

Brandishing a knife, he side-armed an athletic shoe at her and ordered he to try it on.

Her other sneaker.

Cynthia knew if she screamed she was dead. She knew if the shoe fit she was dead. She slipped it on and, before he could react, aimed a swift kick at his most sensitive region. He flinched slightly and sneered.

Cynthia's purse was on a shelf beside her. She quickdrew her pepper spray and gave it to him point-blank as he approached. He blinked, mildly irritated, and continued, calling her unspeakable names in their language. He loosened his belt, a snaggle-toothed grin on his face, saying that they were going to have a little fun before they went for a ride.

His head abruptly jerked backward. A gun barrel appeared at a temple. He dropped his knife. Using the assailant's hair as a handle, Jose Maria Principe spun him around roughly, snapped on handcuffs quicker than a blink of an eye, and knocked his feet out from under him.

Jose Maria and Cynthia collided in each other's arms before either realized that it had happened, even before the heroic INS agent Mirandized his prisoner.

After the police came for the suspect, Jose Maria told Cynthia that he had planned to guard her as long as it took, on his own time, vacation and floater days and whatever until she was out of danger.

She told him that eventual resolution of her problem was no excuse for him to leave.

They married the day after her divorce from Handsome Prince was finalized. Cynthia Eller Principe became immediately pregnant (her barrenness was not *her* fault.) and took maternity leave at the gallery. She was promoted to assistant manager when she returned. Agent Principe's arrest of the killer broke the stolen car and chop shop ring wide open. He was also promoted.

By and by, a bloodless counterrevolution occurred in her homeland. A group of foreign-educated software engineers hacked into the new government's computers and froze all bank accounts. Soldiers were not paid. Impoverished, they threw down their weapons and walked away from their barracks. A coalition of intellectuals, reformers, social democrats, and freelance idealists gained control. They muddled about, but meant well.

Cynthia could go home if she desired, the only Royal welcome to do so.

No thank you.

She liked her anonymity and loved her life. She ran the gallery now – no more minimalism, thank you – plus a new branch in an upmarket mall. She began acquiring obscure postimpressionists. Such rich textures, such color saturation. They sold as fast as she could display them.

Promoted again, Cynthia's kind and handsome husband assumed the Area Directorship the day she and their third child killed the rabbit.

They lived happily ever after.

INVISIBILITY RAY CLOAKS FUGITIVE'S NEW CLOTHES

There was once a heartless embezzler named Vance Popkirk. He was an attorney at a law firm that administered trust funds. Attorney Popkirk advertised himself as an "investment counselor with legal expertise." He rummaged in his clients' funds and stole with both hands. He rationalized his behavior thusly: many of the clients were old and wouldn't live long enough to exhaust the balances anyway.

One day, a senior partner acted on his suspicions of Popkirk's extravagant lifestyle and called in auditors. A secretary who foolishly believed Popkirk cared for her tipped him off. Popkirk defended his integrity and swore his devotion to her. He said it was a monstrous misunderstanding. He said he needed to go for a walk to collect his thoughts, to assuage his hurt feelings.

Popkirk kept walking. He had cleaned out a safe deposit box and made first-class reservations to Rio. But, alas, his passport was at home. Vance Popkirk commuted from an island a 60-minute ride to the city, where he owned a luxurious waterfront home several hundred feet from the island's ferry landing.

As the boat docked, he observed squad cars pulling into his driveway. He cursed the efficiency of the nosy bean counters and scuttled out of plain view. Popkirk presumed that search and surveillance would be equally aggressive at the other side of the water. His office, clubs, associates and acquaintances, the airport. They'd cover all the bases.

In a former life, the ferry had been a small cruise ship that plied other islands in the sound. Staterooms

189

on the inside of the main deck were now either empty or used for storage. Popkirk casually tried the doorknobs.

One turned. Popkirk slipped inside and locked the door behind him. He flicked on the light. Boxes were neatly stacked in a corner, a portable television atop them. There was a bunk and a tiny bathroom. Not exactly the comforts of home, although better than he could've hoped for.

Popkirk settled in. Other than avoiding apprehension, he had no plan. Stretched out on the bunk, he watched TV in the dark, sound muted.

They were interviewing the firm's senior partner on the local news. He jabbered on, shaking his head in disgust. You unctuous old windbag, Popkirk thought; if you had my refined tastes, you'd enhance your income too.

At one a.m., the boat shut down for the night. Popkirk's ears rang in the silence. They were at the city dock. He was exhausted, but too hungry and too paranoid to sleep. He heard voices and footfalls. Probably the night maintenance crew, he thought.

A key twisted in the lock. A young man holding a broom entered. He wore overalls and a gaping stare.

"Uh, who are you?"

Vance Popkirk rose from the bunk, lean and tanned, lawyerly in pinstripes if a bit disheveled.

"The question is, who are you?" Popkirk said, stentoriously.

"Billy, sir."

"Billy. What do you do, Billy?"

"I, uh, work graveyard. I work lower deck on the last runs and then I help clean up the boat. I must of left the door unlocked this morning."

Popkirk detected a tinge of guilt in Billy's dumb eyes. Standing half a head taller than the deckhand, he winked and said, "Well, Billy, this is a pretty nice place to goof off."

Billy studied his grimy fingernails and said, "Sometimes, you know, it's slow and we don't have a lot of passengers, the work's kinda easy."

"Billy, Billy, Billy," Popkirk said, raising a hand. "*No problema*. The issue isn't you enjoying a well-deserved break. The issue is how you and I can coexist while causing a minimum of inconvenience to you."

"There's this other stateroom that ain't jammed full of stuff I guess I can go use."

"I appreciate your cooperation, Billy. Believe me, it won't be forgotten."

"It won't?"

"No indeed. I value those who assist me and I'm not bashful about rewarding them. Know what I value to the utmost, Billy?"

"Uh uh."

"Discretion."

Billy looked at him.

Popkirk held a finger to his mouth. "A slip of the lip can sink a ship. Famous old wartime saying."

"Okay."

"Do you live in the city or on the island?"

"Uh uh. In town. With my mom."

Popkirk patted his stomach. "Have you eaten yet? I'll buy."

Though Billy didn't answer, he took Popkirk's money. When he returned, he knocked. Popkirk was elated. Knocking before entering meant that the dimwitted boy had yielded to perceived authority. It was conceivable that Popkirk could sit it out for a week or two, until the heat diminished.

Problem: How to maintain control without divulging anything substantive? Billy would eventually spill the beans to his mother and who knows who else.

Popkirk had a sudden inspiration.

He let Billy in and unwrapped a vending machine candy bar. "Billy, do you know what a parable is?"

Billy chewed his candy and looked at him.

"No matter. I'm going to tell you one based on a children's fable. Do you remember as a child your mother reading *The Emperor's New Clothes* to you?"

"Sorta. Ain't that where these guys sold this king new clothes that weren't really clothes? He didn't want to act dumb and pretend he couldn't see them cuz the guys said only smart people could see the clothes and dorks couldn't. He went bare-ass naked in this parade on account of they weren't really clothes. Nobody said nothing cuz they were afraid to tell the king he'd been suckered."

"Excellent, Billy. Then what happened?"

"I think somebody went and told him he was naked."

"Yes. An audacious young man whom, instead of being punished, was praised by the emperor for being the only person in the kingdom courageous enough to speak the truth.

"In a sense, Billy, you have the opportunity to be that person. In the same sense, I am the emperor. You know, Billy, in real life, the fable would end differently."

"It would?"

Popkirk shook his head and said somberly, "As soon as the parade ended and the emperor was in his castle, the crowd would tear the lad from limb to limb for making them appear cowardly and stupid."

"I guess," Billy agreed, mouth full.

"The moral, Billy, is that nothing is necessarily what it seems. Don't let your eyes and your assumptions deceive you. You are the rare person perceptive enough to realize that despite uncertainty of what I wear, in terms of my mission, you recognize the vital importance."

"Yeah?"

"And that loose talk will surely result in dire and unforeseen consequences."

"Uh huh."

Popkirk held a finger to his mouth again. "Bottom line, Billy. Dis-cretion."

"Uh, what is your mission?"

"Billy, Billy, Billy."

"Top secret, huh?"

"National security, Billy," Popkirk said grimly.

"Gotcha."

Popkirk gave Billy more money for food and toiletries, and said to keep the change. Billy promised he'd be by before going on tonight's shift. He did one better, bringing Popkirk hot coffee and a breakfast sandwich when he got off that morning.

A few days passed. Popkirk was feeling a connection with the ferryboat's hourly rhythm. The vibration and droning of the engines. The throttling back and gentle collision at the moorings. The ebb and flow of vehicle and passenger traffic.

However, by the 4th day, the cycle seemed interminable. Much more of this and he'd go crazy.

That night, Vance Popkirk sent Billy for casual clothes and sunglasses. He trimmed his whiskers into an embryo of a beard. He was already a new man. To hell with his passport. He'd stroll off this tub and purchase a new identity. He had all the money in the world. He could buy whatever and whomever he pleased. He merely needed freedom and access to the funds.

The next night, Billy came in with the clothes and a sappy grin. He said, "I figured out why you're here, you know, on the boat."

"Oh?"

"Uh huh. You're not no spy."

"I'm not?"

"You're trying to get in the *Guinness Book of World Records* for the most crossings in a row on a ferryboat without getting off."

Vance Popkirk digested the boy's ludicrous epiphany. It was perfect, though. He shrugged and smiled tightly.

Billy's grin widened. "Me and my mom, we got last year's *Guinness* at home. The most ferry rides in a row ain't even listed. You're a cinch!"

"Yes, Billy. How incredibly clever of you to deduce the truth. Kudos."

Billy blushed.

Popkirk continued solemnly, "Only if nobody discovers what I'm doing."

"Uh huh."

"Are we on the same page in that regard, Billy?"

"Uh huh."

"A world record," Popkirk said. "Won't that be special?"

"It'll be totally awesome is what it'll be," Billy said.

The following night, Billy knocked once, paused, then knocked twice. Popkirk had given him a code. Billy loved playing secret agent.

He entered with fresh fruit and a concern.

"I'm kinda worried," he said. "These *Guinness* people, how're they gonna know your record is legit? They're super careful. I haven't seen anybody who looks like they're checking you out."

Popkirk winked. "Oh, they're around. You know the British, Billy. Very subtle."

Billy nodded blankly.

"Trust me. They're monitoring my presence. They will reveal themselves when I'm made sufficient trips to justify inclusion in their book."

"How long's that gonna take?"

"Weeks and weeks. And you'll be mentioned. I'm sharing the glory. I would be unable to accomplish this feat without you, Billy, my main man."

"Wow!"

Wow, indeed, Popkirk thought later, perched at the boat's lunch counter. He'd been overcome by a case of claustrophobia, of literal cabin fever. He craved natural light and fresh food. Though the salad he munched was not right out of the garden, it was nonetheless satisfying. Billy's cuisine of choice leaned toward the carbohydrate, sugar and grease portion of the nutrition pyramid.

The midday crossings were sparsely occupied. Popkirk's beard had grown beyond the stubble phase. In slacks, T-shirt and lightweight jacket, he resembled just plain folk on an outing to the big city.

A dangerous impulse on his part, yes, but worth the risk. The public's attention span was short, as evidenced in the newspaper he read as he ate. Vance Popkirk had been relegated to page 13, to two small paragraphs on his estimated take.

Popkirk bit his lip to keep from laughing out loud. The number wasn't two-thirds of what he'd already spent and squirreled in offshore accounts. The boat decelerated and the city skyline loomed.

He was so tempted to put on the shades and disembark.

Now.

The tiny stateroom was becoming what he so desperately feared: a prison.

He resisted, hand tensing around his fork.

Only two or three or four more days, he told himself. Billy and his cockamamie *Guinness* notion should ensure him toeing the line that long. The emperor's new clothes were morphing into a changeable yet effective ensemble.

But, later, when the boy rapped once, paused, and rapped twice, Popkirk sat bolt upright on the bunk. His gold Rolex said 5:10. Billy was hours early.

He opened the door a crack.

"Lemme in," Billy said.

"Was your shift changed?"

Billy pushed inside and said, "I'm gonna see that you don't get cheated out of your world record."

Before Popkirk could protest, an attractive young blonde with helmet hair followed Billy. A burly man resting a video camera on his shoulder trailed her.

Popkirk saw the decal on the side of the camera:

CHANNEL 6

EYEWITNESS NEWS

INSTANT LIVE COVERAGE

The woman thrust a microphone in Popkirk's face. He thought she asked his name and how long he had been in quest of a world record.

But it was hard to hear with his jacket pulled up over his face.

RIDING HOOD PARK RIPPER AN ENDANGERED SPECIES?

Red was small as a child and small as an adult. When he joined the police force, he knew deep down he was compensating. But that was 10 years ago. He found that he enjoyed his work and performed it well. Size and brute strength did not talk the gun out of someone's hand or chase down a drunken driver.

Regardless, Red resigned himself to his height being an impediment to promotion. Nobody would admit discrimination, but he remained frozen on the sergeant's list for one flimsy reason after another.

Red *usually* enjoyed his work, but not tonight. The Riding Hood Park Ripper had struck again. On 12 instances in the past two months, he came up behind people in the park and pressed a knife blade to their throats, and demanded their valuables.

His victims were all lone women, such a mix of average citizens and hookers that there was no discernible pattern of preference. He hadn't demanded anything else of them, which everybody thought was really bizarre.

The Ripper, as the media eagerly tagged him, hadn't ripped anyone yet, although the last two victims had felt the pinprick of a knife against their necks. Red wasn't alone in thinking that the Ripper coverage had escalated his aggressiveness a notch, that he was savoring the "Ripper" tag. It was a matter of time before a victim was seriously hurt or worse.

Bugsy's Ghost Terrorizes Vegas...

After stealing their purses and jewelry, the Ripper disappeared, apparently fading into the foliage. Since the Ripper attacked from the rear, no useful descriptions were provided. Witness reports and confrontations of suspicious characters by police led nowhere.

Riding Hood Park was thickly wooded and by far the city's largest. Newly and expensively refurbished, the park was the city's jewel. The Ripper's reign of terror was a major embarrassment to the powers that be.

Every female officer in the precinct and several recruited from neighboring precincts had pulled decoy duty. Not one of them had been attacked. It was if the Ripper knew. Policemen possessing a slight build were then sought. Red volunteered before he was volunteered.

There were the expected snickers. Red waited for the *Little* Red in Riding Hood Park cracks. They never came. Red held a black belt in 4 martial arts and did 500 pushups a day, 50 of them one-handed.

The Ripper made the front page and the local TV news lead story nearly daily. Naturally, the mayor and public safety commissioner and chief of police were anxious for results. This anxiety passed down the chain of command.

Red dabbed his lipstick with a tissue. He slipped on fishnet stockings and hoped the stiletto heels he'd gotten from the property room weren't as uncomfortable as they looked.

~ ~ ~

Earlier in the day, a wolf sat across a desk from his warden, who conducted the wolf's exit interview.

"You realize," the warden said, "that it you recidivate to my institution, we throw away the key.

Our state's habitual criminal statute makes no exceptions."

Exit interview, the wolf thought in disgust; this was a lecture.

He said, "Oh, yes sir. I'm completely rehabilitated."

The warden looked at him hard. "Do you continue to harbor the fixation you have with those three pigs? Brothers I believe they are."

"A problem that is in my past, sir," the wolf said. "Counseling you generously provided me was extremely beneficial. I've learned my lesson."

"I do hope so. You're in my institution because of your attempt on their lives."

The wolf bowed his head. "I live with the shame of my actions."

"You'll be leaving us today with some baggage, you realize."

"The restraining order they have on me, yes sir," the wolf said. "I'm taking it very seriously."

"You're not to go within five hundred feet of them or their properties."

"No sir."

"You're a registered culinary predator, you realize."

"I deserve to be, sir, but thanks to counseling, I'm conquering my compulsion." The wolf sighed for effect. "One day at a time."

"I do hope so," the warden replied skeptically.

He thanked the warden for everything and walked out, a free wolf, pondering his future. That hollow feeling wasn't only in his stomach. Where would he go? What would he do?

He could take his chances in the woods. In the little forest surviving suburban development, that is. If he were lucky, he might chance upon a wild boar. But he might ultimately be unlucky. He was not getting any younger and boars tended to be grouchy. The wolf's prison counselor would say they had "anger management issues." If his potential dinner snarled and bared his tusks, how would he handle it? A no-win situation.

No, there was nothing in the forest for him. He decided to head toward "civilization", despite the burbs being the site of his last bust. Three pigs on a

cul-de-sac, respectively occupying straw, wood and masonry dwellings. The wolf had planned to eat his way from house to house, but the campaign went sour and he copped a plea.

Newly developed areas supplied bad memories and zero opportunities, so the wolf went straight into town. Muggers and petty grifters he met in the pen recommended Riding Hood Park. You could literally get lost in there if you got into a bind, the park was that big.

Mugging was not an option to the wolf. He regarded himself as a carnivore, not a criminal. Totally misunderstood and abused by the criminal justice system, he wasn't about to compound the stereotype.

Panhandling was another matter. His fellow cons said it was also fertile territory for a guy on the skids with a tin cup. Begging was definitely beneath the wolf, but it'd be a start. He hoped to cadge sufficient pocket change to buy a late-night breakfast of ham, bacon and sausage, hold the eggs and potatoes and toast.

Also, he knew that city folk kept every manner of strange pets in their apartments, including Vietnamese pot-bellied pigs. If he became genuinely lucky for once in his miserable life, one of them would get loose and wander into the park. A swine was a swine was a swine.

The minute he stepped into Riding Hood Park he knew that something was wrong. Cons he did time with weren't gonna win any awards for accuracy and honesty. The sun was setting on a balmy summer evening. The park should've been teeming with families and couples other panhandler and mugger bait. It wasn't deserted, but empty enough that the wolf felt conspicuous.

He noticed a scattering of guys on benches, pretending to read newspapers and a petite, unattractive, red-haired woman, all tarted up, sashaying along a pathway, wobbling on stiletto heels. The lady and a couple of those guys looked vaguely familiar, though the wolf couldn't place them.

How did it ever get started that wolves were man (or woman) eaters, the wolf wondered? You couldn't sink your choppers into a critter that unappetizing, you couldn't! You'd have to be starving! You could, however, tiptoe up to her and say, "Lady, can you spare a -- "

Next thing the wolf knew, he was seated on a steel chair, at a steel table, nursing a headache. The bare light bulb that lit the room had to be a thousand-watter. The homely

red-haired woman was now a homely red-haired man. The park bench guys were standing by the carrot top, casting a shadow over him and the wolf.

"Just can't stay out of mischief, can you?" Red said.

"I don't know what you're talking about."

The wolf had said that often before, but this time it was true.

"Remember me?"

The wolf nodded.

"You were stalking a truck driver and I picked you up for questioning."

"That was a misunderstanding."

Red frowned in deep thought. "He drove for a — what — rendering plant?"

The wolf shook his head. "The meat packer south of town. Porcine Pork Processing. I wasn't stalking. I happened to be in the neighborhood."

"Happened to be in the neighborhood constantly," Red snarled. "You're looking good as the Ripper, my friend."

"What ripper?"

"Don't you read the papers? The Ripper's created a reign of terror in Riding Hood Park."

The wolf shrugged. "It ain't me. I've been out of town."

Red laughed.

"Admit it, you're prejudiced against wolves."

"Don't start that bleeding heart crap with me. You're barking up the wrong tree, no pun intended."

"See. You made my point. We don't bark, we howl. And haven't you heard? We're an endangered species."

"Make it easy on yourself, pal, or we're gonna throw away the key on you."

"Where've I heard that before? Look, I've got an alibi for two months and then some."

"It should be a dandy."

"The best."

Red left the room and returned glumly a few minutes later, a plump computer printout wadded in a hand. He skidded a chair by the wolf and sat in it backward. "I spoke to the lieutenant who spoke to the captain who's been talking up the line to the head shed. You're not off the hook for obstructing justice tonight."

The world-weary wolf began to protest his innocence, but experience told him this wasn't the proper moment. "Okay, what's your deal?"

Red leaned forward. "The restraining order, your culinary predator registration, the whole nine yards, they could go away," Red said, leaning forward. "The paperwork could get lost, computer data mysteriously deleted."

"I'm listening."

"Hungry?"

Ravenous was the word. Tongue hanging out, drooling, he nodded.

"That's disgusting," Red said. "Let's go."

A vegan, Red took the wolf to his favorite restaurant.

"For some reason, the Ripper's made every single decoy," he said. "People are terrified to go into the park. Aside from the obvious, this is a political football. Voters shelled out a bundle on a bond issue to spruce up Riding Hood Park and there's still fallout from that situation. We're catching mucho heat."

Stomach growling, the wolf picked at his tofu and cheese omelet, half listening. He finally said, "Excuse me, but what's the bottom line as far as I'm concerned?"

"We send you out in the park tonight."

"Come on," said the wolf. "Me?"

"Sure. We've got plenty of nice duds in the property room. We'll cover you up and it'll be easy to hide a wire in all that fur."

"Why do I need a wire?" the wolf asked suspiciously. "When at least twenty cops jumped your alleged perp, namely yours truly."

"It'll be just you and me out there," Red said. "Too much police presence is scaring him off. We collar the Ripper, your life improves."

"I'll think about it," he lied, ready to bolt.

Red, being no fool, let him think about it at Headquarters, in the holding tank. When the time came, Red brought in a box of clothes and said, "We're glad you decided to do the right thing."

"I did?"

"Yeah. We talked to the district attorney. He likes our obstruction of justice beef. Are you up to speed on the habitual criminal statute?"

The wolf groaned and looked in the box. "Whadduya got?"

They selected a long red cape with a full hood, and a matching ensemble of shoes, purse and bracelets.

"That'll cover you up. The Ripper will never know the difference until it's too late."

"Swell," the wolf said. "Where did this stuff come from?"

Red spritzed cheap cologne on the cape and said, "We raided a strip joint. The headliner wore it when she walked on stage."

"I can see why she didn't keep it on long," the wolf said, cinching the hood.

Red told the wolf to shut up and do what he was told, and that he'd be nearby. The wolf wandered into the park, certain he looked like a mental patient in the get-up. He walked from one end to the other. It turned from dusk to darkness. The park lights cast funny shadows, so it seemed to him. The wolf wasn't particularly afraid of the dark, so why was a panic attack coming on?

He should be able to handle a guy with a knife and not come out of it too badly, a ripper who hadn't ripped anybody. It was the uncertainty, he figured, the total lack of control. The maniac might slash him to ribbons before he could react.

Worse, *nothing* would happen to him. After the commotion last night, if the Ripper had half a brain he'd back off temporarily. Or, while the cops were monitoring their decoy, he'd strike in another part of the park. Either way, they'd blame the wolf.

He said to hell with it and veered into a narrow, brushy path. He'd shortcut through and out an opposite corner, and go on the lam, take his chances.

It was pitch black. Bushes encroached, forcing the wolf to slow. A sudden jerking on his cape forced him to stop. An arm went around him and he heard more than felt a sharp object against his neck fur.

"Drop the purse."

The voice was a growl the wolf envied, the breath sour.

"Now!"

The knife pressure increased. Though the wolf's fur was not at its healthiest due to the prison's high carbohydrate diet, the blade didn't penetrate his thick coat. He shrugged free of the Ripper's grip.

"Turn around and you're dead."

The wolf turned around and faced a little old lady clutching a nail file. He bit his cheek, lest he laugh. Ugly as sin, she fit the profile of a witch. The last thing he needed was a spell cast upon him.

"What big eyes you have," she said.

"All the better to pick you out of a lineup."

"What big teeth you have."

"I'm not going there. I'm not that desperate for a meal."

The little old lady wrinkled her wrinkled nose. "You stink."

"I agree." The wolf flung off the cape. "Chanel Number Zero. What are you doing back in action after last night's ruckus? I was sure you'd be cooling your jets."

"What ruckus?"

The wolf told the entire story.

"Goodness," she said. "Perhaps I should read the papers. Last night was my bingo night."

The wolf was fairly confident now that neither spell nor curse was forthcoming, so he asked, "What's a little old lady like you doing being the Ripper?"

"Bosh. That Ripper silliness is exactly why I don't pay attention to the news."

"Nevertheless," the wolf said.

"I'm doing a public service," the old woman said. "I'm teaching young ladies how foolish it is to be out by themselves at night, lessons they shall never forget."

"Ahem, the money and trinkets."

"That damned park bond issue boosted my property taxes beyond my budget. I'm on a fixed income and was just getting by. The park taketh away, the park giveth."

"I hope you saved your loot. Your Ripper days are done."

The old woman wagged a gnarled finger at the wolf and said, "They'll have to catch me first."

Then she turned and bumped into Red, who cuffed and Mirandized her.

Recently, prior to her retirement, she had temped at police headquarters as a file clerk during the summer vacation season and had gotten to know the personnel. On the witness stand, she feigned memory loss and confusion, and her court-appointed attorney managed to have this premeditation tidbit stricken from testimony.

Because of her age, previously clean record, and courtroom con job, the old lady was given a light sentence at a minimum-security institution, where inmates were frequently bussed to pick up highway and park litter.

Red was promoted to sergeant and kept his word to the wolf. His rap sheet vanished into cyberspace. If he were confronted by a cop and ran on the computer, he'd be a cipher, as innocent as a newborn pup.

The wolf relocated to the suburbs for a surprise reunion with the three pigs. He had expectations of living happily ever after.

JACK'S BEANSTALK GIANT WINS RECORD SIGNING BONUS

When Coach Götterdämmerung said on the postgame show that "there was more to life than football", I knew I had to fire him.

This followed our 31-3 shellacking at the hands of Philadelphia. At home. I couldn't tolerate that attitude. Not when frustrated fans had themselves a mini-riot in the south stands, not when a guy outside the stadium was raking in a small fortune selling paper bags in the team colors with eye and mouth cutouts. Not when we were going from the frying pan to the fire, playing at Seattle next Monday night, where we were expected to be humiliated before a national audience.

My first bold stroke after being promoted to general manager was hiring Einar Götterdämmerung. He was the first ex-kicker ever to coach in the league. I should've had my head examined. What did kicking have to do with football? His standard game plan was to get in position for a 50-yard field goal attempt.

Our owner was a 31-year-old software zillionaire who liked to hang around the locker room and snap towels at the players. He reminded me of the son I'm glad I never had. He called me after the postgame show and asked if he could believe his ears, what Einar had said, and what was I gonna do about the situation.

I'd wanted to wait until after the last game to make a change. The season was shot anyway and there'd be less disruption. I'd been given no choice now.

Götterdämmerung was my boy and either he went or we went.

I met him in the parking lot. Einar came up to my nose and had legs like Popeye's. He'd once booted 34 consecutive field goals for our ball club. Back in the glory days when we were perennial playoff contenders. But that was ancient history.

I shook my head and he nodded. Just like that, the deed was done. I told him it wasn't his fault, not entirely. Fifty players, a dozen coaches, and a front office staff. When you're 1-9, there's plenty of blame to divvy up. Our ineptitude was a team effort.

Einar took it like a man and why shouldn't he? He'd have his life outside of football and a sizable chunk of a three-year guaranteed contract. His agent and our bean counters would work out the specifics.

I drove home, knowing in my heart I hadn't talked down to Götterdämmerung. It was everybody's fault. Our biggest problem was the offensive line, the league's most porous. We were puny up front in the trenches, barely averaging an anorexic 300 pounds per man. We had 4 quarterbacks in the hospital and our current starter last called signals on his prison intramural squad.

Because there wasn't *anything* more to my life than football, I arrived at an empty house. I'd never admit it out loud, but Einar had a damn good point. Right now, he was receiving loving consolation and a home-cooked meal. The comforts I'd once had and squandered because football was everything.

I checked my mail and opened a padded envelope, figuring that after the Seahawks handed us our hats, the fans would be howling for my job too. From then on, any letter this size, I'd call the police bomb disposal unit.

Out came a bunch of dried beans that bounced all over the table.

The Laird Kau trade. I should've known.

Laird Kau was a veteran strong safety, the same position I'd played many years ago. I had a soft spot for Laird, but halfway through last season he blew out another ACL. I forget how many operations that made. The surgeons would've been smart to put zippers on his knees.

His rehab was behind schedule and he'd gotten off to a slow start in training camp. Jacksonville offered their 5th round pick in the draft and we jumped on it. That rookie they shipped us was an overweight wideout who couldn't remember plays or where the practice facility was. We cut him after the second preseason game. Meanwhile, a fully-recovered Laird Kau is leading the league in interceptions and is a cinch to make all-pro.

Around the time of the trade, I'd let a remark drop that Laird wasn't "worth a hill of beans." It was just an expression related to his ruined knees, no disrespect intended. Somebody passed it along out of context to the sports writer who did the comeback kid piece on Laird:

Kau Traded For Beans.

I scooped up the legumes and flung then into the back yard. I sure as hell didn't need them around as a reminder.

I didn't sleep worth a damn in my cold, lonely bed and don't know how many times I was awakened by what I thought was thunder. I saw the next morning that it wasn't thunder. One of the beans had erupted from the ground, producing a beanstalk as thick of a tree trunk that disappeared into the clouds.

I didn't know what to believe. I was from the old school who tackled helmet first. I thought I'd retired from the league with all my marbles, if not all of my teeth. I went over and touched the thing to assure myself that I hadn't gone crazy.

This I did know. I'd have to go into the office and name an interim head coach. Both coordinators and the special teams coach had been lobbying for the job. Nobody liked one another much. Feelings were bound to be hurt, further killing morale. Then there'd be the next press conference from hell.

Up the beanstalk I went, with nothing to lose. I climbed and climbed until I reached the top of the clouds. A path led to the front door of an old, ramshackle house, something right out of the Addams Family.

An intense, wiry, gray-haired woman in a flowered dress answered the door.

"Where am I?" I asked.

"Where you are is in trouble if you don't go away, Mister. My son doesn't like strangers."

Suddenly the earth (or whatever it was) rattled under my feet. I scrambled inside the house.

"Quick, hide in here too," the woman said, hustling me into a closet. "My boy's surly after a workout and I don't want your blood on my hands either, although you probably deserve to be torn from limb to limb too."

I was wondering what "too" and "either" and the second "too" meant when I smelled cologne. Then I heard a cell phone chirp. A person beside me cussed under his breath, said his office knew better to call when he was recruiting, and shut it off.

My eyes were adapting to the light that knifed in around the doorjamb. I recognized the guy I shared the closet with and he recognized me. He wore a sport jacket, mirrored shades, and a heavy gold necklace inside an open collar.

"Jack," he whispered. "How ya doin', guy?"

"Fine Print Fowwler," I said.

"C'mon, Jack. Jeez. My name's Maurice. Don't call me that, okay?"

I'd negotiated contracts with Fine Print, the world's oiliest sports agent. He was notorious for holding players out and hiding injuries. More than one client had taken him to court for charging unreasonable fees. They'd lost because it was all there in what they'd signed, in the, well, fine print. "What are you doing up here, Fine Print?"

If he'd nudged me in the ribs any harder, I would have sent him through the wall. "Same as you, Jack. Don't play dumb."

The earth shaking started again and the front door slammed.

"Fee-fi-fo-fum, I smell the blood of a charlatan!"

We heard the woman speak softly and settle him down.

"He's off steroids," Fine Print hissed. "But he tends to be grouchy after pumping iron. The endorphins, I think. His mother has a way with him. She's a stabilizing influence. Take a gander."

I peeked through the keyhole and saw an enormous young man in his a20's listening obediently to his mother, lips locked in a pout. He had to be 7' 6" and at least 500 pounds. His hands were the size of catcher's mitts and his neck was wider than his head. He was gorgeous, absolutely beautiful.

When he lumbered into another room with her, quivering the timbers, I said, "Looks familiar."

"He was smaller when he played at Alabama," Fine Print said. "And he's still a growing boy."

I snapped my fingers, remembering scouting him when I was traveling with our director of player personnel. He'd made all-SEC offensive tackle in his freshman year, then dropped out of school and out of sight.

I said, "Didn't he lose his eligibility because some sleazy agent slipped him money under the table and slipped him into the seat of a leased SUV?"

"All clear," Fine Print answered, avoiding my question.

He opened the closet door and we walked out.

"Anybody you know, Fine Print?" I persisted.

"That was a misunderstanding, Jack. People are too eager to cast stones. But, hey, listen to this. I've been making amends and putting him through the paces." Fine Print showed me a stopwatch. "The kid runs the forty in four-six, has a thirty-two-inch vertical jump, and can bench-press a Hummer."

He patted his coat pocket. "Got him signed to a personal services contract. He's an unrestricted free agent, open to the highest bidder, and all roads lead through me, Jack."

"How's his mother feel about that?"

Fine Print gave me a thumbs up. "She's one hundred percent behind the lad moving on to the pros. She wants what's best for her boy and, frankly, she'd like to be able to relocate to a better neighborhood."

"Any other reason why he's so crabby, Fine Print?"

"Possibly he has a mild case of seller's remorse, nothing that we can't iron out."

I smiled. "The giant won't let you out of here alive with the contract, will he?"

Fine Print Fowwler fluttered a hand. His pinkie ring glinted. "He has a few minor issues regarding language in various clauses. But, Jack, hey, listen, you being here is a godsend for both of us. You, as a gee-em, give currency to my situation. Our situation. Did I mention that he's an unrestricted free agent? We'll sit down with him and Mama, and, presto, you'll have him in uniform and everybody lives happily ever after."

It was tempting. Though the giant wouldn't be ready for the Seattle game, we could have him on the field the following Sunday against Green Bay. We'd have pass protection and maybe even a running game.

Something else bugged me about this picture. "I have a vague feeling there ought to be a magic hen popping out golden eggs."

"The giant *is* the magic hen, Jack," Fine Print explained, rubbing thumb against fingertips.

We walked into the kitchen, to the giant and his mother having milk and cookies. He glared at us, neck veins throbbing, nostrils flaring. That'd be great to see in a pregame locker room, but I wished he was a little calmer right now. Fine Print introduced me and began his pitch.

The giant's mother had a magnifying glass in one hand, dangled a contract copy in the other, and said, "Mr. Fowwler, my son is an adult. He signed your contract without consulting me. However, there are discrepancies."

"Discrepancies?" Fine Print said innocently.

She held the glass close to the document. "Like you receiving twenty percent of his income and full control over his investments."

"You said two percent," the giant boomed.

Fine Print frowned thoughtfully. "Hmm, where could that zero have come from?"

"Simmer down, son. And what about this 'lifetime representation clause'?"

"You said two years!"

"Two years, a lifetime, hey, pro careers are short. One twisted knee and -- "

The giant jumped to his feet, a seismic event. We ran for it.

"You thief, come back here!" he howled.

"Son, stop. Wait."

If I survived and could make my peace with him, the giant would give us badly needed intensity. I ran harder than I had in 15 years, since I hung up my jock.

I shinnied down the beanstalk, yelling upward, "Pass this along to him, Fine Print. I'm offering five years, eighty million dollars. Seventeen-point-five mil signing bonus. Contract buyback option after three years. No-trade option if he wants it."

I hit the ground and ran to my shed for an axe, just in case the giant was sticking to his game plan. To my surprise, Fine Print Fowwler hadn't been right behind me. The giant was, carrying his mother piggyback.

"I liked what you said, the numbers in general, so we went on by Mr. Fowwler," she said. "Poor man was huffing and puffing like a locomotive. He needs a personal trainer."

The giant gently helped his mother down. "Mom's my new agent."

I didn't reply. That issue was between them and Fine Print.

"Let's go into the house and talk turkey, Jack," she said. "That signing money sounds a mite stingy."

"I'm flexible," I said.

"Bonus clauses?"

"A hundred thousand if he makes the Pro Bowl," I said. "A hundred grand more if we win ten games next year."

She flashed a yellow-toothed grin. "You're pathetic, Jack. You can't win or cover the spread. Eight games."

"Done."

"Endorsements?"

"I wouldn't worry. He's definitely unique."

"No roommates on the road. The boy needs space to stretch out."

"No problem," I said.

I looked up and saw Fine Print on the beanstalk, halfway between the clouds and the ground. He looked like a tree-hugger, inching downward, hanging on for dear life.

"Gimme that axe," the giant said, snatching it from me. "I can chop a lot faster than you can."

FAIRY GRANTS A RECORD 5 WISHES

Hugh Evans knows he's in deep doo-doo when he sees himself on the local evening news as Channel 6's Top Story. Not that he wasn't in a pickle earlier in the day when the cops came to his house. He'd spotted them getting out of their car and scrammed out the back door and through the alley.

Since he is a "white collar criminal", a SWAT team hadn't surrounded his place and crashed in. But if you believe the talking haircut standing in his driveway now doing a LIVE EYEWITNESS EXCLUSIVE, Hugh Evans is the worst monster to come down the pike since Bundy and Dahmer and the Enron sleazoids.

The reporter says, "Hugh Evans is a lawyer who vanished years ago. He was thought to be the victim of a criminal organization, but Channel Six has learned exclusively that he had resurfaced with a new identity and ran a Ponzi scam. Evans and his Ponzi scheme are thought to have decimated sixty-three senior citizens out of their life savings. The promise of a significantly increased return on their retirement nest eggs proved to be deceptive. Evans' house of cards collapsed. The allegations are particularly cruel because Evans' victims live on fixed incomes."

Evans looks at a photograph of himself that pops onto the screen. Thanks to plastic surgery, he sports a sincere gaze, graying hair, and a low-key, avuncular manner he enhances with a cardigan sweater.

The greedy geezers, they'd asked for it, Evans thinks as he mutes the ace reporter and gets up to answer the door. That would be room service and his dinner. He'd gone directly from home to this hotel and checked in under an alias. The desk staff was busy and hardly paid him a glance.

Evans figures to hole up here for a few days, then skip town after things cool off. He squints through the peephole and sees nothing. If they're pressed against the hallway walls, poised to storm him, what can he do? He's not about to jump from the 14th floor.

Evans grits his teeth and opens up. An extremely small man rolls in a food and drink cart. He's in forest-green tights and an old-fashioned hat with a feather in the brim. The waiter's such a shrimp, the peak of the feather is only chest-high to Evans.

Evans closes the door. "You're in a different uniform than the regular staff. Is this the start of, like, Medieval Motif Week? For a convention or something?"

The waiter uncorks Evans' wine and says, "I am a fairy."

Evans resumes his seat and humors him. "Fairy as in elf or leprechaun? Not the other, I trust. I don't swing that way."

"Correct, sire."

"Interesting," replies an amused Evans. This pipsqueak isn't young, perhaps his age or older, so he pitches him. "I suppose you've given retirement some thought. Unfortunately, people start planning much too late. However, thanks to a revolutionary new investment program I've developed, there's time to greatly improve your cash flow."

The fairy ignores his attempted flimflam. "May I pour your wine, sire, and grant you five wishes?"

"*Five* wishes?"

"Yes, five."

"I remember three wishes from the fable."

"Twas three for centuries, but we've liberalized. Skeptical clients invariably squander the first on a test wish and complain afterward. Our revised policy allows you to get it out of your system and begin on a level playing field, as it were."

"Isn't a fourth wish the next step? Why a fifth?"

"Market dynamics," says the fairy. "We're not the only organization providing the service. The competition is constantly raising the bar."

He sighs. "Who knows where the escalation will end?"

Evans gestures to the TV and Channel 6's continuing Top Story. "Okay, make this go away."

The television set vanishes.

Evans' shoes are untied. He literally jumps out of them. "Holy shit! You're for real."

"Obviously."

"Disappearing the TV set isn't what I meant."

"No problem."

The fairy snaps his fingers and the television reappears, still tuned to Channel 6. On his tiptoes, the fairy lifts a cover on the cart. "Mmm. The London broil is an excellent choice. Shall I dish you up?"

"No." Evans slumps in his chair, eyes wide. "My head's spinning. Let me try to make sense of this. I squandered two wishes making the TV go *poof* and rematerialize?"

The fairy replaces the lid. "Baby red potatoes and asparagus spears as a complement. Yum. Yes, but your traditional three wishes remain. I do approve of the new policy. It's customer-service oriented and less stressful for everyone involved. Again sire, wine?"

"Yeah," Evans says, snatching the glass from the midget and gulping it down. "As long as I'm being harassed by the law, I'll have no peace regardless how much money I have. Okay, let's make them announce that all charges are dropped."

The fairy claps his hands. "Done."

Channel 6 switches to the studio and a pair of cuties, one male, one female, with near-identical bulletproof hair. Evans unmutes.

"In a startling development, the District Attorney just announced he is dropping all fraud charges against Hugh Evans," says an anchor.

"Yes!" Evans cries.

"A substantial amount of the money was seized in Evans' offshore accounts, enough to satisfy the victims," her partner follows. "The restitution issue was key to persuading them to testify against Hugh Evans. Some victims were embarrassed and most just want to get on with their lives."

"My money," Evans says numbly. "My money. My money's gone?"

"You see, when we alter reality, corollary aspects also change. We have no control over associated and subsequent events."

"So if I use my next to last wish to ask for my money back, the charges would probably be reinstated?"

The fairy shrugs miniature shoulders. "I'm not privy to the workings of your overly-complex legal justice system, sire. We won't know unless we try, but you have drawn a logical supposition."

"Okay, Shorty. Let's do this. Let's go for a two-fer." Evans jabs a finger at the television. "I want to hear from that brain-dead duo that I'm getting my money back *and* that all fraud charges on behalf of the old farts are dismissed."

"Wishes four and five, sire."

"I can count, you twerp."

"Is that your final decision?"

"Go for it."

"In a further development," says an anchor, "we're advised that seizure of Evans' funds will be resisted by the offshore banking institutions. The process could take years. In the resulting confusion, the District Attorney's Office isn't hopeful that the charges will ever be reinstated."

Evans pumps a fist. "All right! I can clean out my accounts and hop a plane for Rio."

When the fairy doesn't reply, Evans turns. He's gone. Evans checks out of the hotel quickly. He starts for the airport and thinks, wait a second, I'm in the clear. Indefinitely. He heads home to pack his tropical clothes and spare toupee.

He's annoyed that his driveway is blocked by official cars. Not fuzzmobiles, but sedans with city plates. He walks in on civilians armed with briefcases and boxes and magnifying glasses.

"Who the hell are you?"

"Forensic technicians," says one, wide-eyed.

Evans laughs. "Searching for clues?"

"As a matter of fact, we are."

"You're trespassing. Get the hell out."

"It's him," says another technician.

Evans doesn't like the way they're looking at him and how one of the nerds is punching buttons on a cell phone. Evans backpedals, but they pursue and pummel him to the ground on the lawn. The technicians sit on Evans until reinforcements arrive.

The detective who snaps on the cuffs Mirandizes Evans and says, "That old saying about the criminal returning to the scene, I've never had it happen before in twenty-four years on the job."

Evans calmly replies, "Evidently you people don't follow the news. Those spurious charges against me were dropped."

"Yeah, we heard," said a detective.

"Well, get ready for the mother of all police brutality lawsuits, Sherlock."

"You must've had Channel Six on, Evans. They had to've been smoking locoweed when they announced you were home free on the charges. The newscasters swear it was on their copy, but nobody can find a trace of it now. They're peeing into bottles as we speak. You were hearing what you wanted to hear."

Evans groans as he is inserted into a squad car. No, he had heard what he *wished* to hear.

RUSSIAN GHOUL
RAISES THE DEAD

Vladimir Ilyich Larrionov was an unemployed Russian scientist. Moscow's Research Institute on Biological Sciences had let him go for lack of work. Then the Institute itself shrank to a skeleton staff that subsisted on donations. Larrionov was bemoaning this in a Veracruz bar to a California orthodontist who wished the guy would just shut up.

Dr. J. D. (Wally) Stockwall sipped his beer and said, "Downsizing. It happens."

Larrionov was not sipping his vodka. He was drinking it like water. "Of course I am lucky to be alive. Those crazy Cubans."

Stockwall was preoccupied. He'd had financial reverses of his own and couldn't afford this Mexico vacation. The only way he could conceal from his wife that they couldn't afford the trip was by taking it, although in a perverse way they could. Dr. Stockwall's malpractice insurance carrier had abruptly canceled him. Termination was instigated by an unfortunate incident that prompted an obscenely-slanted article in a professional journal entitled *Orthodontics and Gangrene. A Link?* Unbeknownst to Sally Jo Stockwall, they were traveling on this month's premium.

Their airplane to Cancun had blown an engine and made an emergency landing at Veracruz. A replacement plane wouldn't be in until the morning. Now Dr. Wally Stockwall was in this ratty bar – swinging saloon doors, drunken locals, soccer blaring on the TV – listening to a crazed Russki while Sally Jo pouted in the hotel room, pissed off that her husband had booked them on this cut-rate package.

"What Cubans?"

Larrionov said, "They misunderstand. They say I go to Cuba to assassinate their leaders. Not so. I go because I love them, these socialist giants. I go to be there for them when they die. I am lucky to escape and stow away on freighter to this city."

Larrionov was of indeterminate age. He had wild, jittery eyes and hair that looked as if it was styled by a finger in a light socket. The orthodontist had swooned at his teeth, rotted piers in a fetid mudflat. He'd written a mental estimate of $19,000, plus kickbacks from a periodontist and an oral surgeon.

"What were you planning to do them when they croaked?"

"Too late for Fidel. They cremate him like firewood. Immortalize them so they lie in state for all eternity. The revolutionary spirit will never be extinguished."

"You mean like Lenin's Tomb?"

"The maintenance of my namesake, Vladimir Ilich Lenin, and Uncle Ho, they are only remaining projects. That is why we were disbanded."

Stockwall snapped his fingers. "Wait a minute. You preserve dictators?

"Crudely expressed, but correct."

Stockwall's mind began churning. Imprudent investments had exacerbated his financial woes. His typical venture was as hopeless as an infomercial get-rich-quick hustle.

"So with the collapse of communism, your customer base is zilch?"

"I do not know this Zilch. Who is left of socialist giants, I ask you?"

The last of the old-school Commies, Stockwall thought.

"Easy, easy," he said. "This thing you do to the corpses, is it embalming or what?"

Larrionov drained his vodka and snorted. "Ordinary funeral embalming is child's play. We create masterpiece."

Stockwall signaled the bartender for another round and asked, "Have you ever considered the private sector?"

"Some colleagues desire to sell service. I say no. What we do is sacred."

Stockwall gave him a business card. "Like you, sir, I am a man of science."

Larrionov read: DR. J. W. (WALLY) STOCKWALL. GENTLE CARING ORTHODONTICS.

Balding and pear-shaped, Wally Stockwall was 37 years old. He owned a cramped clinic in a Van Nuys strip mall, sandwiched between dry cleaning and teriyaki. Soy sauce and dangerous solvents were imprinted in his nostrils.

He said, "I'm next door to Beverly Hills. I straighten the teeth of the stars. Please don't ask for names."

Larrionov drank his vodka. He did not ask for names.

"I'd like you to license me your process."

"No."

"How're you doing for money, comrade?"

Larrionov stared into his vodka. "I sleep in alley. I rely on generosity of strangers."

Stockwall slipped a 20-peso bill (roughly $1) under the Russian's coaster. "Always glad to help."

Larrionov nodded. "Am grateful."

"Comrade, do you know what the good life is?"

"Good life." Larrionov fluttered a bony hand. "Good life is for oligarch and Mafia and capitalist running dog."

"The good life is for you too. Ever been to Cancun?"

"No."

"Cancun is sun and fun, and you're invited as my guest. You'll have a blast."

"Why invite?"

"It's a chance for you to relax and rethink ideologies. The potential of what we're talking about here is unlimited."

"Is kind of you, but – "

Dr. Stockwall got up and slapped Larrionov on the back. "Outside the hotel next door. Nine a.m. You won't regret it."

~ ~ ~

Sally Jo Stockwall sat on the bed, TV remote in hand.

"Where've you been, Wally? You said you were going out for one drink."

Sally Jo Stockwall was a 35-year-old former dairy princess from Washington State. She had thick hips and a hardened baby face. Sally Jo had gone off to college to escape the farm and to snag a professional man. As her catch settled heavily beside her, a milking barn didn't seem like such a horrible place to be.

"I've been making us rich. That's all."

"A familiar tune."

Dr. Stockwall smiled. "Now, now. Let's not be grouchy."

Sally Jo shut off the television and sighed. "You aren't going to give me any peace until I hear your spiel, are you?"

When he was finished, she said, "Well, I have to admit, it's more promising than your last brainstorm, fully-computerized meat-cutting machinery."

"Automation to eliminate butchers and their outrageous union contracts," Wally reminded her.

"Too bad the software couldn't tell the difference between hogs and steers, bones and tenderloin."

Wally shook an imaginary salt cellar above his arm. "Go ahead, sweetums, rub it in the wound as deeply as you want. Feel free. I'll cut a deal with my buddy at the mortuary across the highway. He'll do the dirty work after hours, but he'll never know what's in the fluid."

"My Uncle George who had the strokes, he was done by a hack like your buddy," she said. "At the funeral, he looked like he'd been stolen from a wax museum."

"This process is at an entirely other level. The clients will be under my close supervision every step of the way."

"You have all the answers. Who'd be your clients?"

"Billionaires. Egomaniacal politicians. Anybody who yearns to be immortalized and can afford it. Don't you think a glass-topped casket would be a nice touch in a presidential library? We'll charge a half million, minimum. Plus scheduled maintenance. Franchises too. The sky's the limit."

"Show me the money," Sally Jo Stockwall said.

~ ~ ~

Larrionov appeared at 9 a.m. sharp. As the gaunt, shaggy Russian approached, Sally Jo Stockwall made a face and hissed at her husband, "What the hell is that?"

"I knew he'd be here. Commies have to eat too."

"Ick."

"Our golden goose, gumdrop. Make nice. Do you realize how long Lenin has been in Lenin's Tomb? In the photos, he looks like he's taking a cat nap."

"I'll stay upwind of Rasputin, thank you."

Their vintage turboprop wobbled into the air, climbed above the Gulf of Mexico, crossed the northern tip of the Yucatán Peninsula, and deposited them at Cancun International Airport. The Stockwalls and their companion took a taxi through a warren of streets to a seedy, walk-up hotel.

Larrionov and the Stockwalls checked into adjoining rooms. Sally Jo made doubly sure the connecting door was locked and frowned out a flyspecked window.

"Where the hell is my beach?"

Wally winked and said, "Cancun City is where the smart money stays at a fraction of the cost of the Cancun Hotel Zone, lovey pie. The impoverished natives employed at the posh resorts reside in this quaint burg. All we have to do is slip on our trunks, hop a bus, and we're there lickety-split. In Mexico, the beaches are public domain."

"*You're* there lickety-split," Sally Jo said, aiming and clicking the remote.

"C'mon, kiddo, it's an adventure into the unknown."

Oprah miraculously materialized in English.

"Let me know me what you discover, Captain Kirk."

~ ~ ~

Standing in the aisle, hanging on for dear life, Vladimir Ilich Larrionov and Dr. J.D. (Wally) Stockwall rode a crowded, speeding bus to a boulevard of high-rises. Wally could take or leave Cancun. Phantasmagoric from what he'd seen thus far, a blend of Disneyland, Waikiki and Taco Bell. More bikinis than in an Avalon-Funicello movie. Drunken American college kids and humidity that wouldn't quit.

They got off at a hotel shaped like a mock Maya pyramid. Stockwall picked it at random on the basis of garishness and size. Leading Larrionov through a chilled marble lobby, he pointed at the glass atrium,

228

watching the disoriented Russian gawk at bougainvillea dripping from walkway railings.

He said, "Is this paradise or is this paradise? The good life exponentially. The promised land is a trite way of stating it, but if you have the wherewithal, why not? As a man of science, you're entitled to appropriate compensation. Luxury is a natural component of your advanced education and expertise. This is a new age, Larrionov. It's acceptable to be rich, even in the former Soviet Union. Billionaire Russian plutocrats are a fact of life. Private property and wealth-building are here to stay. This is the twenty-first century, my friend."

Dr. Stockwall was attired in too-tight dark slacks and a too-too-tight tangerine golf shirt. Larrionov wore sandals, filthy argyle socks, red plaid trunks and a Hard Rock Café T-shirt. The orthodontist's capitalist gobbledygook swirled over his head with a couple of persistent flies.

They passed through to the patio, a pool that looked to Stockwall as large as Lake Michigan, and the beach. A turquoise sea lapped against sand as white as granulated sugar. Stockwall took off his loafers and white socks, and said, "Fun and sun. The quintessential good life."

"Never have big sun until Havana," Larrionov said, squinting upward. "In Mother Russia, if you want to see water, you saw hole in ice. Is too warm for me."

"Likewise. Shall we retire to a shaded table at the patio bar for a libation? My treat."

By the time the blistering, midday sun descended across the boulevard, Wally was out of cash. They were drinking on his plastic, vodka rocks for Larrionov while Dr. Stockwall nursed beer. Larrionov remained exasperatingly sober, but he was finally talking shop.

"Process is eternal. Vladimir Ilich is constant toil."

"Yes. Immorality certainly isn't easy. You alluded to scheduled maintenance."

"Must constantly monitor temperature and humidity. Must touch up twice a week by secret process. Every year or eighteen months, we study body and rub fluids on. We change suit of clothes as liquid seep and spot."

"Outstanding," Stockwall said, thumbs up. "We're essentially incorporating a mandatory service contract into every job. It's a license to print money."

He lifted his beer bottle in toast. "To a world-class biological science that cannot fall extinct. It would be an unspeakable tragedy to mankind."

"We do for love," Larrionov said, gulping his vodka.

"Yes, love." Wally framed his thumbs and forefingers. "A slogan comes to mind. 'Keeping the Dead Alive Since 1924'."

Larrionov sneered. "You ridicule Comrade Lenin's tragic death."

Stockwall threw up his hands. "You can't do for love if you've starved to death, Comrade."

Larrionov gazed into space.

Stockwall persuaded the Russian to join him for a walk on the beach. If Wally had to throw up, better there than here.

"A stroll clears your thought patterns," he said. "Allows for sharper analysis."

As they trudged in the sand, Wally upped the ante. "What do you think about relocating to America?"

"Me?"

"You."

"America?"

"I have important contacts who can resolve your visa and passport issues," he lied. "Face reality, Larrionov. You're basically a man without a country."

"America?"

"I guarantee you a home and hearth, not to mention freedom," he went on. "I have a funeral director associate. He'll provide us a professional venue. We'll pursue the estates of billionaires and politicians.

"We'll bid the jobs aggressively. We should be satisfied if the first assignments provide a modest profit. We'll be establishing ourselves. When we're in the chips, we'll immortalize your idols pro bono, okay? Your Cubans and that chubby little North Korean kook with the funny hair. Whomever."

"What is bid?"

"Bid means to compete monetarily to perform a professional service. Don't think for an instant your former colleagues won't jump on the bandwagon once we hang out our shingle. With us lowballing initially and you as chief scientist, they won't be able to touch us in regard to either price or quality."

"Monetary bid is not right."

"Please don't be offended when I say efficient business models are not a strength of your culture. Your gangster oil czars know that. I strongly recommend leaving that end to yours truly. To get us out of the starting blocks in a timely manner, I recommend we relay your formula and application procedures to my funeral director associate so he can evaluate the solution and purchase ingredients."

"No."

"You and your *nyet* attitude. I'm at my wit's end, Larrionov," he whined. "I'm being reasonab – "

Wally tripped over something at water's edge. The obstacle wore only swimming trunks and was spread-eagled flat on his face.

Wally got up and said, "Sorry, friend."

"No hear you."

"Passed out," Wally said in disgust. "These kids who come to Cancun to party can't hold their booze."

Larrionov knelt and rolled him over. "Is dead."

Wally gaped in horror at a fair-skinned man in his early 20s, average weight and height, mouth open, goggle-eyed. This was his first body. Dr. Wally Stockwall had never lost an orthodontic patient.

"Shouldn't he be bloated?"

"No drown," Larrionov said, probing him and sniffing. "Acute alcohol poisoning. In Moscow, in winter, people freeze solid on sidewalk."

Stockwall noticed an empty tequila bottle an arm's length from the corpse. "We have to notify somebody."

"Splendid condition," Larrionov said, holding Wally by a cuff.

The dictator preserver's eyes had had no definite color, but now they glowed banknote green.

Stockwall said, "What are you suggesting?"

"Dentist, did not like your greed before I have raw material. Raw material change everything. Has been *so* long."

"Larrionov, we aren't in Russia. Cancun is almost America. We can't."

"What is it in your nation you call a sample of what you sell? Large capitalistic consumer good?"

"A demo," Stockwall said.

"Demo?"

"Short for demonstrator. Like at a car dealership."

Larrionov hoisted the dead man's clammy wrist to his shoulder. "Hurry, take other arm. I brush sand off him."

"What on earth are you doing?"

"Demo," Larrionov said, raising his burden to its knees. "We have demo."

~ ~ ~

Larrionov and Stockwall walked their toe-dragging, head-lolling demo from the beach to the boulevard.

"Too much tequila," Wally said to passersby, who nodded knowingly. This was Cancun.

As the Russian held the corpse in an awkward embrace, arms dangling over his shoulders, Wally hailed a taxi.

"Too much tequila," he said, their prize wedged upright between them in the back seat.

"*Si*," the driver said. "*Muy mucho tequila.*"

In their hotel lobby, they shuffled by the desk. Wally grinned sickeningly and told the clerk, "Too much tequila."

"Excuse me, *Señor. Uno minuto.*"

Oh no, thought Wally. Oh no, oh no, oh no, oh no, oh no, oh no.

"The gentleman is an extra guest?"

"Um."

"Extra guests are to be paid for, *Señor.*"

"He'll be staying with Comrade -- Mr. Larrionov. Put it on my tab."

The clerk thumbed through his card file. "His name, please."

Name? A dead gringo. A gringo. Gringo. Greg. Greg the gringo.

"Greg," Wally said.

"Greg what, *Señor*?"

"Uh, Greg Gregg. Two g's on the second Greg. Gregg."

The clerk duly recorded the extra guest. On the landing, a perspiring and panting Wally Stockwall said, "Larrionov, should we be doing this? We need to be asking ourselves that question. At first blush, while creative and opportune, there is a substantial downside."

"Open door, dentist."

Wally fumbled with the lock, dropping the key twice. In Larrionov's room, they laid Greg on the floor.

"Please, Larrionov, we – "

"Go to room to wife. We begin tomorrow."

Wally couldn't get out of there quickly enough.

~ ~ ~

Dr. Wally Stockwall awoke in the morning to a hangover and Sally Jo's snoring. Appalled by what he and Larrionov had done, he lay there, eyes clenched, pleading to any deity Who cared to listen to transform yesterday evening into just a hideous dream.

No miracle was forthcoming. Suppressing a groan, Wally slipped out of bed and quietly dressed as he decided how to proceed. They'd wait until nightfall and dump Greg whence he came. Larrionov, the lunatic, Wally would ditch the rummy Bolshevik too and cut his losses. He realized he was not soaring on a fast track to a fortune, he was plummeting into poverty and jail.

He unlocked the connecting door and tiptoed through. The emaciated dictator preserver sat cross-legged on the floor, wearing only the red plaid shorts. He looked like a deranged monk.

"Brr," Wally said.

Larrionov gestured to the purring air conditioner in the window. "Powerhouse machine. Temperature like Mother Russia."

In bed, covered to the neck, was Greg Gregg the gringo. His eyes and mouth were closed. Blissfully, Wally thought.

"Larrionov, I've been thinking."

"Cannot sleep. I watch demo all night. Is young and fresh."

"What I've been thinking about is the laws we've violated. I understand that religious issues, the sanctity of life and so forth, are abstract and inconsequential to

234

a card-carrying communist. While the general concept of this demonstrator is fine, execution is dicey."

Larrionov gazed adoringly at Greg. "Can make him so we ship to America by United Service Parcel. Not worry."

"I can't stop worrying. You don't grasp the ramifications."

Larrionov thrust a sheet of paper at him. "List of things. Buy. Hurry."

Wally perked up. "The formula ingredients?"

"No. Generic, as you might say. Makeshift, not ideal. Chemical be sent from Russia later. We get, we purge demo and revitalize. Hurry, dentist. Go."

~ ~ ~

The shaken Dr. Stockwall set out to comply, abundantly aware that he should have his head examined. He stopped for a breakfast of eggs and toast and beer. After his third *cerveza*, Larrionov's position seemed less untenable. It behooved Wally to be open-minded in the gray areas. Greg was unidentified, possibly unloved, a wretchedly unhappy alcoholic, vacationing alone to his ultimate oblivion. The risk could be mitigated. It wasn't as if they'd be showing their demo at flea markets.

At last, this might be his shot.

Wally found what Larrionov needed. Fortunately the merchants took plastic and the clerks spoke rudimentary English. From a pharmacy, he bought chemicals, funnels, and tubing of various diameters. The only compound he recognized was formaldehyde. A supermarket provided paper towels, soap, rubber gloves, trash bags, buckets and vodka. Most alarming was his stop at a hardware store: industrial-duty needles, pry bars, twine, knives (boning, serrated and cleaver), and, Lord help him, a small saw.

When he returned, his feet were as cold as the dictator preserver's room. "I didn't like the way the druggist looked at me."

"Look, you say? Look? Not worry about look. I look at demo, his youth, his vigor. Cannot stop looking. Could be Vladimir Ilich in firebrand days."

Greg wasn't in the bed. "Where is he?"

"Bathtub. Ready to be immortal. Come see."

"No thanks."

"Your wife at door, ask for you. I say no see you."

"Good."

"Go to her. I finish."

~ ~ ~

Sally Jo Stockwall wondered out loud where the hell Wally had been. He said he'd taken a long, solitary stroll. "You were sleeping so soundly I didn't want to awaken you, lovey."

Despite him avoiding eye contact and smelling like a brewery, Sally Jo accepted his story. She even felt charitable toward Wally's stinky Russian golden goose. Someday, a Wally Stockwall scheme had to hit the jackpot. It was the law of averages. Why not pickled zillionaires?

The Stockwalls went to the Hotel Zone for lunch. They ordered chips, salsa, beer for him, and a frozen daiquiri for her.

Sally Jo asked pleasantly, "What's new with your mad-scientist friend?"

"I'm working on him. He hasn't entirely changed his mind, but he's weakening. I'm making definite headway."

"I knocked on the common door earlier and he came unglued."

"Larrionov has a lot on his plate, weighing the pros and cons. The profit motive is alien to him and his kind."

Sally Jo dipped a chip and said, "Well, I hope you settle this soon. We're not made of money."

Wally tried again to tally the number of crimes they had committed. Even if they got away with the offenses to date, how could they slip Greg through Customs like souvenir pottery?

Would Sally Jo stand by him if he were arrested? Would she agree to false alibis and perjure herself as a loving wife should?

Wally's hangover was competing with his declining morning buzz. He gulped his beer.

"Take it easy, Wally. You'll make yourself ill."

I already am ill, he wanted to scream. *I have never felt worse in my entire fucking life.*

"I'm okay, kiddo. Your concern is nonetheless appreciated."

"Something is wrong."

"Nothing, sugar pie," Wally said. "Nothing in the whole wide world."

~ ~ ~

At their Cancun City hotel, Sally Jo Stockwall took a nap. Two frozen daiquiris and she was drowsy. Poor girl, she couldn't handle any excitement. To a background of his wife's snoring, Wally slipped out and rapped lightly on Larrionov's hallway door, thinking that he had to put an end to the loathsome insanity posthaste.

The Russian admitted him to an odor that was part chemistry lab, part butcher shop. Wally slumped queasily against a wall.

"Do not worry, capitalist friend," Larrionov said, patting him on a shoulder. "Am done. Lovely, yes?"

Greg Gregg was, as before, under the bedding, as if counting sheep. Greg looked no different, but Wally knew better.

"Full garbage bags in bathtub," Larrionov said. "Go to sea tonight. Does Cancun have shark? Barracuda?"

Wally pitched to the toilet. He came out sniffling, dabbing his face with a washcloth, and said, "Comrade, we have issues. We have, essentially, basically, an unworkable business plan. Immoral if you're inclined to split hairs."

Larrionov passed him the half-empty vodka bottle. "Drink. Good for digestion. Make you at ease."

"No thank you. We have to end this, Larrionov. Terminate the project."

Larrionov addressed him with melancholy, rheumy eyes. "End? What of my masterpiece? My opal magnum."

"Your opal what?"

"What you call artistic masterpiece."

"Magnum opus."

"Yes. Magnum opus. Is what I say."

"Larrionov, this – creature isn't a symphony."

"Is superior to any music," Larrionov said.

"Regardless, it, he, has to go. I didn't think this out thoroughly. Mrs. Stockwall constantly chastises me vis-à-vis my investment strategies. I draw the big picture and falter on the details."

Greg Gregg the gringo sat upright and said, "Ahhhhhoooouuuu."

Wally yelped and crouched in a corner. Larrionov clapped his hands and cackled. He kissed Greg on the chin and rearranged him in a covered prone position.

"Vladimir Ilich and Uncle Ho do same," he said. "Vladimir Ilich have flailing arms. Like punching you. Remember Georgi Dimitrov?"

"No," the orthodontist whimpered.

"Was Prime Minister of Bulgarian People's Republic. When reactionaries pull down Berlin Wall, they take Comrade Georgi out of case and bury him in ground. Like rubbish."

Larrionov shook his head in disgust and laughed again. "They tell me that in old days, Comrade Georgi once jump out of case and dance a jig."

Wally gaped at him, horrified.

Larrionov slapped his knees, giggling. "Scientist and technician, they gasp like have heart attack. What I would give to be there."

"Spare me the anecdotes. Explain to me in layman's terms what just occurred."

Larrionov shrugged. "Difference in chemical purity, in concentration to what we use at Institute. Is spasm is all. Contraction of larynx and muscles. Tequila that kill him contribute. Formation of residual gases. Who can say? Is science, not black magic."

He wrenched Stockwall to his feet. "Come, come. Demo is anxious for us to buy him suit of clothes. Dark distinguished suit. Be presentable for America, the three of us, when we walk on airplane."

Dr. Stockwall trembled, chewing his nails.

Larrionov howled. "Is joke, dentist. Research Institute on Biological Studies humor."

~ ~ ~

Wally was desperate. It was impossible to reason with the demented Red. He agreed to go clothes shopping for the corpse and they settled on a time after dark to remove the bags of offal.

Wally spent the day pacing malls, racking his brain. He gradually devised a plan. Rather than cloaking Greg Gregg the gringo like a CEO, he selected casual wear. He'd noticed in his grisly shopping for Larrionov that powerful drugs requiring a prescription in the U.S. were sold over the counter. At a *farmacia*, he bought sedatives and a liter of vodka. He then rented a subcompact sedan.

At nightfall, Larrionov and Wally lugged two black plastic bags downstairs to the trunk of the rental car.

The Russian said, "Magnum opus not so heavy as when we go upstairs with him. Blood and bodily fluid wash down drain."

"Never mind the details."

Stockwall handed the laced vodka to the appreciative Russian and told him to enjoy.

The Cancun Hotel Zone was a narrow island shaped like a "7", linked to the mainland by short bridges, the Caribbean on one side, a lagoon on the other. Resort development ran virtually tip to tip. Only near the south end could Stockwall find a stretch of undisturbed land. Even in this slender break between hotels and condos, he could see construction cranes, silhouetted against the sky like praying mantises.

He parked as close to the beach as he could and popped the trunk. "I'll be the lookout. Don't take all night."

Larrionov was groggy from the vodka. Dragging the bags, furrowing the sand, the dictator preserver weaved and staggered to water's edge. He untied the bags. Instead of emptying the contents into the sea, he rubbed his eyes and curled up in the fetal position.

Damn, damn, damn, damn, Wally thought, backpedaling; I overmedicated. Ten more minutes of consciousness and the gore would be fish food.

To complicate things, joggers approached. An insane activity, day or night, he thought. Dr. Wally Stockwall did not run unless he was being chased. He went to the car before that happened.

Driving to the hotel, he figured to get rid of Greg and give Sally Jo the bad news that he'd been called home for an orthodontic emergency, that they had to catch the next flight out.

Wally brought the clothes he'd purchased for Greg into Larrionov's room. How he wished he could merely leave him, but both rooms were registered in his name. Prudence took precedent over squeamishness. He took a deep breath and threw off the bedding.

Sally Jo heard noises earlier in the stinky Russian's room, as she did now. She'd knocked, to no avail. She's had her fill of Wally disappearing to play silly games with his crackpot pal.

Sally Jo unlocked the connecting door, opening it to her husband bending over a young sleeping man, who was buck-naked except for a pair of shorts.

"Oh, my God!"

Wally spun around. "Lovey, it isn't what is seems."

"He's so young. Did you slip him a Mickey Finn?"

"Sal. Angel pie."

"You're out of your sicko closet, admit it."

Wally spread his arms. "Honeybunch."

"I just *knew*."

"There is a plausible explanation, my precious."

"Sicko child molester? Pervert!"

Sally Jo slammed the door so hard the knob fell off. Dr. Stockwall listened to drawers banging and suitcases tossed about. He waited for the sound of his spouse's footfalls in the corridor. Then he dressed Greg in the shorts, sandals, and an I ♥ CANCUN T-shirt. Stitches sealed an abdominal incision. Wally did not dwell on the particulars of the slice.

Their erstwhile demo was astonishingly light. Greg wasn't as loosey-goosey as yesterday either. Larrionov had rendered him stiff, yet pliable. He could be molded at the joints like a mannequin. They labored down the steps and Wally said to the clerk who didn't move his eyes from his comic book, "Too much tequila, too much tequila."

With Greg securely belted in, Wally started the car. He saw flashing lights and swung around the block. *Policía* cars squealed to a halt in front of the hotel. Out of the back of one came two cops and a handcuffed Larrionov. Presumably, the law had been summoned by the busybody joggers who took offense at the gore. Supporting the yawning Bolshevik, they (also presumably with his room key) entered the hotel.

Swell. Wally wondered where to go. Then he had a brilliant cerebral flash. Hide Greg in plain sight.

If Wally went to an isolated locale, it would be his luck to be nabbed disposing of the body, a gutted and embalmed one at that. In the hubbub of Cancun nightlife he would be leaving an acquaintance to savor his extreme intoxication alone.

Then off to the airport and home, to an uncertain future. Greg had been eviscerated in Larrionov's room, not the Stockwalls'. Wally was guardedly optimistic.

On the main boulevard, he parked in a public lot adjacent a shopping plaza. Darkness and decreased pedestrian traffic worked in his favor. Arm cinching the waist of his inebriated companion, Wally scuttled to a sidewalk bench. He informed potential witnesses with what was becoming a mantra, "Too much tequila, too much tequila."

They sat on the bench. Greg behaved admirably by staying vertical, although he leaned into Wally. This drew a raised eyebrow now and then, in a vein similar to Sally Jo's cruel accusation.

When Greg's true condition was revealed, his death could be blamed on violent drug dealers who had devised a more creative and less noisy method of eliminating an unhappy customer.

Loudly, Wally announced to Greg, "I'm going for coffee. A cup of java will perk you up. I'll be right back. Hang in there, guy."

"Marty!" screamed a young blonde woman in a flowered sundress.

The woman crossed the street, dodging traffic.

Fists raised, she cried euphorically at Greg Gregg the gringo, "Oh Marty, Marty, Marty, you sweet lovable drunk. When you didn't return from your swim, we thought you'd drowned. We have the police out looking for you, you twit."

Oh so carefully, Wally stood.

"Excuse me, sir. Are you with Marty?"

"No, no. We were sharing a bench. Ships passing in the night, as it were."

"Does he look normal to you?" the girl asked. "He's not responding to me and his eyes are weird."

Wally continued to retreat. "Sorry. I don't know what's normal for him. Frankly, he may have had too much tequila. Too much tequila."

Greg/Marty lifted his head as if baying at the moon.

"Ahhhhoooouuuu."

Dr. Stockwall stumbled to his car. Burning rubber as he accelerated away, he could still hear the girl's shrieks.

BUGSY'S GHOST TERRORIZES VEGAS

The airplane was a magic carpet to a weekend of sin, although Darla referred to the trip as research. It was a charter, not the newest in the commercial aviation fleet, a Boeing I think they made before they numbered them in three digits.

We boarded in mid-morning and many of our fellow passengers already had a nice glow. The couple in the seats ahead was pining for the good ol' days when you could light up anytime, anywhere, and enjoy a puff without being treated like a criminal. Amen.

The plane began to roll, making squeaking noises I'd never heard in a vehicle not pulled by livestock.

Darla squeezed the blood out of my hand and vice versa.

"Brick, are you sure this travel agent of yours is reputable?"

"Absolutely. Gets five stars from all his clients," I lied.

Luther was a bail bondsman I did skip traces for. He'd been run out of Las Vegas a few years back, for reasons unknown. When I zeroed in on an out-of-town deadbeat, he arranged the travel for us. The price was right.

As the vintage jet staggered into the air, I cocked my free thumb upward and said, "First cabin all the way."

I persuaded myself the plane wasn't gonna lose too many vital parts in midair and had me a siesta. I didn't unclench my eyes until the pilot announced our descent into Vegas.

I doubt if Darla noticed me fake-snoozing, on account of the unruly pile of notes on her tray. Darla Hogan teaches anthropology at a junior college and has more degrees than a thermometer. I, on the other hand, am an honor graduate of the Gumshoe Correspondence Institute of Private Detection. I assume I am. They didn't give out grades. When your check clears, you're in.

This scholarly project of hers was on why people gamble. She said she "wanted to pursue a different slant on an overworked topic and interact with the people during the gambling process", which meant to pester the hell out of people while they're deep into a losing streak. I told her I didn't think that was a very swell idea, but she ignored me.

I'm along as her research assistant. She has this notion of making a guinea pig out of me too, despite my telling her over and over again that when I plop my dough down, it isn't gambling, it's an investment.

"Brick, does the city look much different to you?"

Darla had never been to Las Vegas and my last visit was two decades ago, about the time the Mob was getting the bum's rush for good. I leaned across her and saw a sand-colored sprawl as flat as a poker chip.

"Same. Just a whole bunch bigger."

Then the wing dipped, hopefully not on its own volition. Below were a gigantic pyramid, a gingerbread castle, and the Manhattan skyline wrapped by a roller coaster.

"The Strip," I said. "It always changes."

"So I understand."

Darla had arranged our hotel, which turned out to be that humongous pyramid that was supposed to be Egyptian if the Egyptians had built them out of black glass. Nine Boeing 747's would fit in the atrium of this thing. I knew this because our placemats told us so.

"This end of the Strip used to be blacktop and sagebrush," I said as we had a snack and a drink while housekeeping finished cleaning our room. "Did you see all those construction cranes out there? They've taken the wrecking ball to billion-buck monster hotel-casinos and replacing them with billion-buck monster hotel-casino-theme parks. Next time we're here, the Strip will go halfway to Guadalajara. A bummer. It's not the real Vegas anymore."

"Bricklin Bates," she said, patting my arm. "Relax. You have to accept that your romantic image of Las Vegas as a gangster–controlled Sodom and Gomorrah is obsolete."

On the sidewalk, I'd seen geezers in walkers and rug rats in strollers. Disneyland with an edge. I nodded heavily. She was right. Maybe I am hung up on the darker aspects of life, but that's how we'd met. Darla had been stalked by her ex-boyfriend. Her restraining order wasn't worth the paper it was written on.

She'd wisely let her fingers walk on by my competition advertised under sissy categories like Investigators and Security Advisors, and stopped at Private Eye. She called the only firm listed: mine.

The creepoid was my age – the mortal side of 45 – and still lived with his mother. I stuck to him like glue, hoping he'd stub his toe legally and we could have him thrown in the slammer. He stayed just beyond the 100-foot restriction, but with a car full of high-powered optical gear, he was basically in her face.

The guy was Looney Tunes. Someday he'd come off his spool. Then he'd be a model prisoner on death row.

I'd flipped big time for Darla and was determined that nothing of the kind would happen. Darla returned my feelings, which made me crazy to protect her. Maybe as crazy as her beau from hell.

At least that's what he must've thought one fine night. I tiptoed to his car and yanked the son of a bitch out through the window by whatever body parts of him I could grab onto. We had a productive conversation I didn't share with Darla and I'm taking the Fifth with you likewise.

Last we heard, he lives three time zones away with a maiden aunt who he participates in quilting bees with. He's eligible to try out for the Vienna Boys Choir too.

"The transformation of Las Vegas as a family destination makes my study exceptionally intriguing, Brick. Nationwide, the gambling industry is booming. State lotteries, Indian casinos, bingo, online betting. Yet this city remains the core of gambling in America. Gambling and Las Vegas are synonymous."

Darla's a tiny woman 10 years my junior. Closer to 20 years younger if she ever finds out my bona fide age. She's got the world's biggest hair covering that big brain of hers, and great big round owl's glasses.

"We could go see if our room's ready," I said, definitely changing the subject.

Darla has the sweetest leer. She read my dirty mind and played a little kneesie. "Brick, they said an hour."

"Close enough," I said, signaling for the check. "They gave us the key card. They can work around us."

"Filthy old man. We have twenty minutes to go. We'll go for a short walk first, okay?"

We compromised on short short and went out into a warm afternoon. Two weeks before Christmas, the desert sun was low, as harsh as a flashlight. The sidewalk was gridlocked with families who should've been home, shopping and stringing lights.

I started complaining to Darla about how they walked side by side, no matter how damn many of them there were, when an old black Ford coupe bounded up from the curb, scattering man, woman and child alike. I smothered her in my arms and we did a fast low-down waltz up against a wall.

The Ford, a '46 or '47, kept coming. I got a good look at the driver as he fired an automatic pistol through the open passenger window. He was wearing a double-breasted suit, a fedora and a sneer. There was a fake Christmas tree set in a pond at the hotel next door with ornaments the size of cantaloupes. A couple of them exploded. He hopped the curb and swerved on two wheels in the opposite direction.

"Jesus," I said as we came out of our crouch. "He's a dead ringer for Bugsy Siegel."

"Warren Beatty?"

People were dusting themselves off, looking around, laughing. They thought it was a publicity stunt in a town full of stunts. They must not know what a muzzle flash is, must not've seen those globes blow up. "Nah. I don't mean the movie. C'mon."

Our tin can of a rental car was at the entrance, still not valet-parked, keys in the ignition. We hopped in and I stood on the gas pedal. We fishtailed into traffic, in hot pursuit.

"Brick, it can't be Bugsy Siegel," Darla said, trying to hang on and buckle up at the same time. "It was probably a promotion. Reckless, yes, but – "

"With live ammo? No way. Our boy was playing for keeps."

"He's been dead for ages."

"Since June of 'forty-seven. He was rubbed out in the living room of Virginia Hill's La-La Land mansion."

"My closet academic," she said, eyes widening. "My hero *and* my historian. I had no idea"

"Not hardly. Cops and robbers are my niche. Like it or not, and the present Vegas honchos would rather forget he existed, Bugsy is the father of Vegas as we know it. See him?"

"I lost him too. He may have turned two streets ahead."

"Yeah," I said, smiling. "He had to've."

"How do you know?"

"Cuz of the color on that hotel there, kiddo. Flamingo."

~ ~ ~

The Flamingo Hotel was now the Flamingo Las Vegas Hotel and Casino, a far cry from Bugsy's heyday (I explained to Darla as we parked and went inside). In the mid-1940s, the East Coast Mob had put Benjamin (Bugsy) Siegel in charge their L.A. interests. Alert to the fact that gambling was legal in Nevada, Bugsy took a liking to this dusty, sleepy little town and had a greedy vision of anything goes.

To build the original Flamingo, he hustled $1 million out of his bosses, Meyer Lansky and Lucky Luciano. You have to remember, back then this was a few miles out of town, in the middle of nowhere. Thanks to Bugsy's sloppy management and his sticky fingers, the final tab came to $6 million.

"A cost overrun to make a Pentagon procurement officer blush," Darla said.

"Worse yet, opening night, December 26, 1946, was a big flop. The weather was crummy, cold and rainy, the turnout worse. Siegel shut the joint down and reopened in the spring. Though it began showing a small profit, Bugsy was not forgiven for the monetary discrepancies."

"The ultimate in hostile takeovers," Darla said as we entered the hotel. "Brick, what are you going to do if we find him here?"

Damn good question. "I'm sure you're right that it was a promotion. Maybe they had small powder charges in those ornaments. Hollywood-type outfits control this town. To satisfy my curiosity is why we're playing my hunch."

We wandered into a gift shop. They had plenty of knickknacks like coffee cups for sale. Nothing referring to Mr. Benjamin Siegel in sight. I told the clerk that I was interested in a keychain of picturing Bugsy spraying lead. She just looked at me.

Darla dragged me out into the casino. It had the old-timey ambience I fondly remembered of the town. Smoke hanging against low-ceilings. One-way glass over the tables to spot cheaters. Cards flipping over on green felt. Roulette wheels spinning. Forests of slot machines going chinka-ding-chinka-ding-chinka-ding around the clock.

"Him," I said, pointing at an island cocktail bar named Bugsy's Bar. "The guy in the shades, stogie, porkpie hat and the Hawaiian shirt covered with a herd of parrots."

"He made a quick change if it is. What do you recognize?" Darla said.

"His attitude."

We took seats beside him. I said, "Lousy aim, Bugsy. You didn't even wing anybody."

He turned to me slowly and exhaled smoke in my face. "Don't call me Bugsy, pal."

I actually enjoyed the nicotine cloud. Darla'd gotten me off cigarettes, but like they say, you can take the boy away from the unfiltered Camel (or did I have that backasswards?). But how he said it, cold mean eyes shooting laser beams through the dark lenses, is why my arms became a mountain range of goose bumps.

"Sorry, Mr. Siegel. Or can I call you Ben? Benny?"

He blew a perfect smoke ring. "Suit yourself. I go by Ben the Deuce. Nice job bird-dogging me."

"Thanks. It's what I do."

"You the heat?"

"Private. On special assignment. Nothing to concern you, Ben."

"Good. You'll live longer."

The Deuce, I thought. I knew that Siegel had kids by a wife back east before he took up hot and heavy with Virginia Hill, but I hadn't heard of any following in the old man's footsteps. I kept that thought to myself and ordered us a round.

"Mr. Bugsy or whoever you really are," Darla said, leaning forward from the other side of me. "You're an excellent actor. You're wonderfully convincing. What's the purpose of the publicity?"

He stared at the backbar and shook his head, muttering, "Dames."

"Easy," I muttered to Darla.

"The hotel," he said. "They didn't retain nothing except the color here and there."

"Times change," I said, humoring him.

"We'll see," he snarled. "We'll see whose town this is."

"Talk to me about the Deuce situation," I said.

"What's to talk about?"

"You tell me, Bugmeister."

"I was born in Europe and bounced around. Forget what it says on my birth certificate and driver's license. I know who I am."

I've heard of actors drenching themselves in their parts. This was ridiculous, but I played along. "Good luck."

"Luck's for suckers," he said, flashing a smile that lowered the room temperature 10 degrees. He tossed some money on the bar for our next round and left.

"Like you said, he's damn good," I told Darla. "Almost real. Did you catch what he said about Europe?

Virginia Hill, his main squeeze, shuttled cash Bugsy had skimmed from construction costs to deposit there. She happened to be in Europe when he was whacked. Coincidence, huh? Allegedly she was tipped by the Mob to scram out of town before the hit went down. You don't suppose she's his mommy?"

"You don't believe that man, do you?"

"Uh, no," I said. "The actual Bugsy was born and semi-raised in Brooklyn. You?"

"No," she said, tapping a spot on the bar where our car key had been. "However, acting might not be his only profession."

~ ~ ~

After we reported the rental car stolen and hoofed 2 miles to the big, black pyramid. We tried to check in and were informed that there was a glitch and they'd be done with our room momentarily.

Okay, fine, that gave us a few minutes for business before heading upstairs for an afternoon of debauchery. Darla whipped out a notebook and scanned for a research victim. I double-checked a wad of sports clippings and suggested we take care of investing my investment.

As we walked to the hotel's sports book, I said, "These people you're gonna interview on the slots, the blackjack and dice tables, I agree they're gamblers with monkeys on their back. Me, it's a one shot deal."

Darla took my hand and sighed. "An investment."

"There you go. I bet one ball game. The game that jumps off the page at me as handicapped *wrongo*."

"Yes, Brick. You're clairvoyant."

"Don't be a wisenheimer. Knute Rockne or somebody once said, it's not whether you win or lose, it's how you do against the point spread. You can take it a step farther and I have for today's pick. You can bet the over-under. They give you a number and you decide if the teams combined are gonna score more or less points than that.

"Well, lemme tell you, whoever set an over-under on tomorrow's Bills-Patriots game of twenty-nine is demented. Considering their passing games, no way could those two teams rack up less than twenty-nine points."

"If you say so, Brick."

I did say so, to the sports book clerk, shelling out enough dough to blanch the color out of Darla's cheeks. We reconnoitered the slot machines. They were pretty much everywhere.

Darla sidled up to an old lady. A cigarette dangled from her leathery lips. She was feeding her Social Security check into it in such a rhythm you could tap your toe to the sad tune. She told Darla where to stick her study, several locations on the human body I am not gonna repeat to you.

Up to our room we went.

"Denial and hostility, two impediments to recovery," Darla said in the elevator, writing in her notebook.

"If you say so."

At the door, I patted my pockets for the key card. We heard noise and knocked. The maid would let us in.

Except the maid didn't answer. A well-stacked blonde in a mini-mini skirt with a lot of hard miles etched in her face did. She was with a colleague of the brunette persuasion who was wearing even less. Behind them was a room service tray, food and buckets of bubbly piled high. Ben the Deuce sat on the bed – our bed – yelling into the phone.

"Whadduya mean, my name don't cut no ice no more and, hell no, I'm not kidding. Hello. Hello."

Darla gave the girls the evil eye. They took the hint and skedaddled. Ben shouted several choice profanities and slam-dunked the receiver.

"They'll find out who I am," he added.

"What the hell are you doing?" I demanded with an intimidating snarl.

Ben the Deuce had made another quick change. He wore pleated slacks and a shiny, expensive dress shirt. He appeared to be unarmed.

Affording me nary a glance, he began to dial. "I need me a base of operations."

"Wanna be a jerk, okay fine. We'll holler for hotel security."

"Go ahead. I just put 'em on my payroll."

"Brick, get him out our room," Darla said through clenched teeth.

Providing you swallowed his story, here was a joker descended from a guy who'd broken the Ten Commandments and done the Seven Deadly Sins before he was voting age. To be on the safe side, I wrapped a paw around the handiest weapon.

"You heard the lady, Deucemeister," I yelled.

He finished dialing, paying me no attention whatsoever. I shook up my weapon and released my thumb. off flew the cork. French champagne geysered all over him.

"Hey, goddamnit," he shouted, flying off the bed. "The shirt's pure silk. Cost five hundred smackers."

"My compliments to the silkworms."

I continued shaking and firing, but was running low on ammo. Darla cut loose with a fresh bottle and blasted him out into the hall.

We locked the door and decided what to do next: why we came upstairs in the first place. Afterward, we dug into the chow, which hadn't been touched by Ben and his painted ladies. We were running low on the fizzy stuff, but we had enough for a light buzz that led to other things and eventually a nap.

We woke up after dark, how it's ideally done in Vegas. To fully appreciate this town you gotta adapt to the circadian rhythms of a vampire.

"Do you think he'll be back?" Darla asked.

"Nah. He'd've ventilated the front door by now."

"How comforting. The man is obviously insane. Delusional and violent."

Anywhere else on the planet, yeah, he'd be a few bricks shy of a load. But Vegas, where a hotel up the Strip blows off a homemade volcano on schedule and another has pirate skirmishes in a pond right off the sidewalk.

Could be real, though, Bugsy's ghost. I couldn't rule it out, not in this burg.

"Well, he is different."

"Different. You have a gift for understatement. Shouldn't we be reporting him?"

"Live and let live. They'll nab him in our poached rental car sooner or later."

We went down to the casino and spent the night mostly people-watching. Darla interacted with folks during the gambling process. Results were definitely mixed. The winners wouldn't let her go. She was their good luck charm, their four-leaf clover. The losers accused her of being a jinx, the casino's shill.

I hung out in the sports book, keeping an eye on my investment. Waitresses in frilly skirts and net stockings brought you free drinks while you watched ball games on about 14 different screens. If this wasn't Heaven, it was in the same neighborhood.

The over-under on my New England-Buffalo game had fallen to 27½. I couldn't believe it; over-unders seldom went south of 35.

I removed my emergency stash from the secret compartment in my wallet and my other emergency stash from my sock. It was like when Microsoft went public. You'd have to be crazy to hold off buying the IPO.

"They're so irrational," Darla said, sitting down with me, discouraged. "I'll never be able to compile any kind of solid data."

"Ever gambled, Darla?"

"Once, I bought a one dollar lottery ticket at a convenience store. It didn't do anything for me."

"Living on the edge," I said, earning a bony elbow to the spare tire.

~ ~ ~

Mid-morning, I phoned the desk to make sure Ben the Deuce's room service charges had been removed from our bill. I'd been prepared to do battle, but was informed sweetly that a Mr. Segal or Seagull had paid them and, furthermore, we had an unlimited room service account, compliments of Mr. Sego.

"He's bribing us to not snitch," Darla said.

"Works for me."

I'd planned to have breakfast ordered up anyhow, to be covered by my football investment profit. We ate and watched the news. The big national story was on a blizzard blasting the eastern seaboard. A clip showed a guy in Portland, Maine hunting for his car in a snow bank. Poor slobs, I thought.

Local news led off with happy news yuk-yuk. Sightings had been reported of the most notorious mobster in the city's past.

"Who shall go unnamed, no matter how much you bug me for his name," said the anchor.

"Is this in the context of UFO and Elvis sightings?" asked the co-anchor. "A ghost story for the ages?"

"Could be, could be. He's an unholy terror. In the space of twenty-four hours, he shot up a Christmas tree, created scenes in five casinos, and attempted telephone shakedowns of prominent hotel-casino executives. Whoever he is, he's soaring at interplanetary velocity."

"Is there a festival or some such going on?"

"You know where we are. There's always some such going on."

I shut it off.

"He's escalating," Darla said.

"Not our problem," I said. "Besides, a profile as high as his, they'll throw a net over him by the end of the day."

She was skeptical, but our flight out was this evening and we had mucho to do. I had a ball game to enjoy, then rake in my winnings. Darla made a beeline for a craps table, where a couple of yokels on a hot streak were talking to the dice like they were their pet poodles.

I nestled into a chair directly in front of the screen that carried my game and ordered a complimentary cold one. Something was bad, bad wrong with that picture. Namely, the snow that was the genuine article, not bad reception. And that contraption they had on the field that looked like the Zambonis they use on hockey rinks.

They were plowing the center of the field so they could see the yard lines. Players landed flat on their butts oftener than they didn't. Nobody could move the ball. It ended 6-zip with those 6 measly points coming off the toe of some scrawny Brazilian
place-kicker.

"Dice players are great believers in fate," Darla told me. "They live by a karmic philosophy based on statistical streakiness and flow and momentum. Of course they don't articulate it like that."

"No, I don't imagine they do," I mumbled through gritted teeth.

"Speaking of momentum? Isn't that the word football announcers use incessantly? By the way, how did your game go?"

"Peachy keen. Poked in the eyeball by the fickle finger of meteorological fate."

"Oh no."

I gave her my last quarter. "Drop this in a slot. Make it a clean sweep. There's a saying in these here parts that you're only the temporary custodian of the casino's moola."

"Brick, I don't gamble – oh very well, stop rolling your eyes."

Darla plunked the quarter into the nearest one-armed bandit and yanked the electronic lever. Spools spun round and round, and stopped on three pieces of the same flavor of cocktail fruit. Then the machine went berserk, howling and chinka-dinging and flashing its lights like there was a five-alarm fire.

As the counter racked up numbers. Darla's eyes grew bigger than her eyeglasses. If it's been pre-electronic-timey, you'd need a gallon can to catch all the quarters.

I planted a slobbery kiss on her flushed cheek and said, "Kiddo, you made up for that low-pressure front that clobbered Buffalo. And then some."

She gave me this goofy-scary look I'd never ever seen before, did an about face and started feeding the winnings into the bandit. I said, "What the hell you think you're doing?"

"Acting on the premise that this device is electronically – what is the correct term? – compliant."

"Loose," I said.

"Yes, loose," she said breathlessly.

Darla pulled the lever like a pro. It'd gone as tight as Scrooge, but that just made her play faster. I had a few choice words on the evils of gambling, but held them to myself, on account of I didn't care to have "investment" bounced back in my face.

I felt a solid round object against my spine. It could be only one thing.

"Ben the Deuce, I presume."

"Turn around slow and do what I say," he snarled.

He was decked out in candy colored slacks and pullover. He could be 10,000 other guys in town. He'd rendered himself invisible.

"Nice disguise, Benny. Hide in plain sight."

"Shaddup and c'mon. We're gonna talk."

"You're the boss. You got the gat."

I pried Darla from the bandit. Ben and the bulge in his pocket steered us outside.

"I got a proposition for youse two," he said. "The old crowd is gone. Moe, Gus, Icepick Willie, they're all gone."

"Memory Lane," I said.

"I need a new front organization and you're perfect. You both got moxie and the dame here got brains."

"Thanks, I think," I said.

"See, who's running Vegas these days is these here – entertainment conglomerations."

The Deuce spit those last two words out like he'd stepped on something.

"What I gotta have to move in on these clowns is a legit front," he went on. "I supply the muscle and the dough. You do what I tell you. They see you, they don't see me and the boys. You smile, be nice, sign papers. I do the rest. Before you know it, the town's mine again."

"What boys, Mr. Deuce?" Darla said. "As you stated, all your psychopathic comrades are in the distant past."

Ben shuddered. "Sister, you don't wanna know, except that they speak Russian and are meaner than snakes. You start first thing tomorrow morning. I got a deal cooking to buy minority stock in a couple of casinos. Then I move my boys in."

"Thanks, but no thanks," I said.

"Yes," Darla said. "We sincerely do appreciate you kind, um, proposition. However – "

"I ain't asking, lady, I'm telling."

I shifted between him and Darla, shaking my head, calling his bluff. If he was an actor on some flaky promotion, this should be the end of it. He'd walk away. If he was either a nut case or who he said he was, Bugsy's psycho genes surging through him, we had us a problem.

The Deuce's kisser wrinkled like a beet and turned red as a prune. The gun he slipped out of his pocket looked the size of a cannon.

We had us a problem, but I maintained my cool.

My game plan was to wade in with knuckle sandwiches and hope for the best.

Darla stepped around me. "Mr. Bugsy Deuce, will you please settle down for a moment and listen to me?"

Bugsy replaced the shooting iron. "Spit it out, sister, and make it fast."

"I am not your sister, thank goodness. Please swivel your head and observe your surroundings. No, this is not a trick. My companion won't hit you over your head while you're not looking."

Speak for yourself, I thought.

Ben did as he was told and said, "I'm seeing crowds of suckers and chumps. So what?"

"Are you conceptualizing the demographic mix?"

Darla and her big words. Bugsy looked at me. We looked at her.

"Those Las Vegas visitors you see are from nine to ninety. Nine months, that is, the ones in the strollers. Families far outnumber the carousers and lowlifes you evidently romanticize as potential customers."

"Yeah," I said, catching on. "Check the wheels too. Minivans and SUV's chock full of crumb crunchers, Gramma along too to babysit while Mom and Dad do something daring like attending a show headlining singers they'd thought died twenty years ago. I'll lay odds that not one in a hundred of those vehicles are stolen."

"Yeah?" Ben said to me, his face drooping.

I shrugged.

"The shops, cafes and entertainment, Mr. Deuce," Darla said, sweeping an arm. "Haven't you noticed that three-story-high soda bottle?"

"They do everything big," I said.

He squinted. "Sody pop?"

"The store next door is devoted entirely to chocolates."

"Chocolates?"

"Yuppie coffee everywhere you look," I said. "You're craving a double tall decaffeinated vanilla latte, no *problema*."

"Increasingly, live entertainment is geared to kids too," Darla said. "Gamblers I attempted to interview cut their sessions short because of family activities. The powers that be bank on children cajoling their parents into future family bonding excursions."

"Chocolate, brats, coffee?" Ben said, choking on a sob.

"Hey, in a lotta respects it's the same as the Mob's Vegas," I said, beginning to feel sorry for him. "The chorus girls are alive and well, and the bosses won't object if you're determined to lose your shirt. I saw ads for pawn shops where you can hock your car, even your RV."

"Yeah?" Ben said, perkier. "What's an RV?"

"Brick, you're not exactly helpful."

"Oops, sorry."

"Lady, I'm afraid you opened my eyes. My city, my dream, it's ruint forever."

"I'm sorry, Mr. Bugsy. I'm afraid that Las Vegas is hopeless in terms of your warped ideal."

"Wholesomeness run amok," I said.

"I'm going home to Brooklyn. It can't of changed this much."

"You be the judge," Darla said.

In the time it took to give each other a quick glance of relief, Ben bugged out, pun intended. Darla suggested we find another compliant slot machine and put our windfall to work. I didn't like this addiction she was developing, so I made a counter-suggestion, a place she's always been a sucker for: a library.

There wasn't anything for me to do there, but Darla was happy as a clam compiling her research notes.

In the taxi to the airport, she said, "That was an excellent library. I found a wealth of material on the life and times of Bugsy Siegel. Virginia Hill may have had children, but none by Siegel."

"Sure?"

"Positive."

"Who was our Ben the Deuce?"

"Whomever you desire him to be."

Our plane was delayed. Naturally the airport was crawling with slots. We'd've had a hassle slipping so many quarters through the metal detector anyhow, so I gave in to Darla. To teach her a lesson. On the evils of gambling.

Assisted her, as a matter of fact. We were getting some small payoffs that slowed the process and we didn't have all night. As we pulled handles side by side, we gazed into each other's eyes.

We saw reflections of flow, of momentum.

Darla cranked faster.

I cranked even faster than she cranked.

● ● ●

ABOUT THE AUTHOR

A prolific author, Gary Alexander has written a score of novels and more than 150 short stories. One story appeared in *Best American Mystery Stories 2010*, another in *Ice Cold*, a Mystery Writers of America anthology. Alexander is a nonsmoking, nondrinking vegetarian. He does, however, abuse caffeine and chocolate.

The New
Atlantian Library

New AtlantianLibrary.com
or AbsolutelyAmazingEbooks.com
or AA-eBooks.com

www.ingramcontent.com/pod-product-compliance
Lightning Source LLC
Chambersburg PA
CBHW070447030726
47503CB00004B/934